THE PRIVATE LIFE OF
ELIZABETH, EMPRESS OF AUSTRIA

THE PRIVATE LIFE OF
ELIZABETH
EMPRESS OF AUSTRIA

by

BARBARA CARTLAND

FREDERICK MULLER

First published in 1959 by Frederick Muller Ltd.
London NW2 6LE

Printed and bound in Great Britain by
REDWOOD BURN LIMITED
Trowbridge & Esher

CONTENTS

ILLUSTRATIONS

ONE

1837-1853

ALL over Munich the bells of the churches were ringing on Christmas Eve, 1837. The city was already showing signs of becoming the most beautiful in Europe, for the year had marked another stage in the tremendous constructional operations carried out by King Ludwig I.

It was his ambition to make his capital the centre of the Arts for the civilised world. But in mid-winter, Munich, the second highest capital in Europe, can be bitterly cold. And the eve of Christmas had brought hard frosts and lowering grey clouds which betokened a heavy snowstorm.

Maximilian Joseph and his wife, Ludovica, the Duke and Duchess in Bavaria (*Herzog in Bayern*, a special title), had arrived in the city from their country residence of Possenhofen. Their visit was partly because of the weather, but chiefly on account of the child that was expected. The Duchess was at this time twenty-nine years of age, and this was to be her third confinement.

She was a handsome woman, very conscious of the fact that she was the daughter of a King, Maximilian I of Bavaria and of his second wife, Caroline of Baden. She and her sisters were known as the "six unhappy sisters" because their father's choice of husbands had brought them little but misery.

It was, in fact, only the consciousness of her social position that enabled Ludovica to endure her marriage. She had gone to the altar weeping and, as she had anticipated, she had every reason to be unhappy. First, because of the constant infidelities of her husband, and secondly, on account of his almost complete disregard for the responsibilities of his position—the latter undoubtedly being a more serious sin in her eyes than the infringement of his marriage vows.

Both husband and wife in the manner of the dynasties of Europe were related by blood. They were members of the house of Wittelsbach, which, apart from a reputation extending over seven centuries for usually wise and tolerant government, also had a formidable record of eccentricity which at times became insanity.

The continuous inter-breeding which had occurred over the whole period of the family's pre-eminence was taking its toll. In the course of a hundred years thirty members of the family had behaved so strangely that even their long suffering relatives and servants were forced to admit that they were mad and in need of restraint.

This mental instability, when it had not reached the border line, invariably made them delightful and attractive persons. They were usually easy going, amiable and always there was that quality so unusual among the kings and princelings of Central Europe of being more interested in beauty than power.

Maximilian Joseph, like his wife, showed no signs of insanity, although his father, Pius Augustus, had for most of his life suffered from what was euphemistically described as an "overclouding of the intellect".

Among the people of Bavaria he was known as "The good Duke Max", a description engendered not by his virtues but by his predilection for the more plebeian joys of life and his willingness to take part in carousals and adventures with the most lowly of his people. In Britain the description for him would have undoubtedly been "good old Max", which possibly conveys a better insight into his character.

His marriage, like all marriages in the Wittelsbach family, had been purely one of political and social convenience. In fact both Duke Max and his bride, Ludovica, had been reared to regard holy matrimony as purely a means of strengthening the position of the family and for the continuance of it by the production of children.

Duke Max duly cohabited with his wife at reasonable intervals and was usually on hand on such social occasions as made his presence essential. But he loathed the strict and rigid atmosphere of Court life.

It was with the utmost difficulty that he could be persuaded to put on a soldier's uniform or to review any of the regiments of which he was the Commander. He had not the slightest interest in affairs of State, and as there were not many that really affected him, his advisers soon gave up even observing the formality of letting him know of the political events in Bavaria.

At the same time the Duke was a real patriot, for he loved his country deeply. For days on end he would roam around the mountains, feasting his eyes on the scenery and, unlike many of his relatives, having no desire to build huge castles. He was content with Possenhofen, his own old moated castle with its high towers flanking the four corners and its pointed roof. Everyone loved "Possi" as they called it, although the place was badly in need of repair.

Fond of his home as he might be, the Duke was continually leaving it. He liked nothing better than to sit all evening at a table in some remote mountain inn or even spend the night in a goatherd's hut. Within a year or two of his marriage these daily excursions were extended into weeks and even month-long disappearances.

He went shabbily dressed in the costume of the Bavarian highlanders—short green trimmed jacket, soiled buckskin shorts, bright green woollen hose and hob-nailed boots. And he usually travelled without a servant in attendance.

He was, however, always careful to take a considerable sum of money with him, and naturally the story of the Duke who liked to play lavish host to his people spread far and wide.

He was always sure of a welcome in the villages which, at that time, were still virtually completely cut off from the rest of the world, and in the inns and beer houses which could be found among the slums of Munich which King Ludwig had so far left intact.

The welcome that Duke Max received in these places was

in fact so complete that a long retinue of generously endowed illegitimate children were the souvenirs of his journeyings.

Some of the more attractive young women whom he seduced were actually invited to take jobs on the estate at Possenhofen, with the result that numerous progeny, bearing on their faces the unmistakable mark of their paternity, were to be seen romping around the farms and the stables of the ducal estates.

The Duchess made no public protest although she had some sharp things to say to her husband in private. The situation was especially bitter as the Duke made no secret of his preference for his bastards, and was obviously bored and uninterested in his legitimate and carefully regimented son and daughter.

He could, however, avoid listening to his wife's reproaches on this and other domestic matters because there were two distinct households in the castle—the Duchess's on one floor. his own on another.

This Christmas Eve, as it happened, the Duke was with his wife in Munich, not because he had any particular desire to be present when his third child was born, but because the cold at Possenhofen was almost unbearable. But that was no reason, he thought, for him to stay with her and listen either to her unceasing complaints and reproaches or her groans when the labour pains began.

He was anxious to share the boisterous joys of the common people at Christmas time, and had brought with him for this very purpose his zither.

He had the previous summer become an enthusiast for this musical instrument. The son of a Viennese innkeeper, named Johann Petzmacher, had been given the high-sounding title of "Director of Chamber Music", in order that he could be paid a lavish income and travel around the country-side with his ducal pupil.

There were whispered rumours in Court circles that this friendship marked an ominous development in the Duke's emotional life. But in reality it was merely a means to satisfy his new craze to become an expert zither player.

The Duke's success as an exponent of the art was not unnaturally enhanced by the fact that of all the zither players who went from inn to inn, he alone handed out money instead of asking for it. Even so he became an expert, he undertook a musical tour through Germany, and in later years when making an expedition in Asia and Africa he played sitting on top of one of the pyramids of Cheops.

The baby was born at forty-three minutes past ten. When the Duke arrived back in the early hours of the morning he was feeling sentimental, perhaps because of the beer he had drunk, perhaps because it was a season of goodwill, and he insisted on seeing the child. She was crying, but when the nurse put her in his arms she promptly fell asleep.

The Duke had seen many babies, in fact too many of them had been a trouble to him one way or another. But this baby seemed different, why he did not know. He stared down at the tiny face with its closed eyes and he had a strange feeling that this child would mean more to him than any other he had bred.

"The little Christmas Princess has been born with a tooth in her mouth, your Grace," the nurse said proudly.

"Like Napoleon!" the Duke murmured absent-mindedly; he was still staring at the child.

He chose her names—Elizabeth Amalie Eugenie—but almost from the first he called her "Sisi". He made a habit of visiting the nursery whenever he was home and the child soon learnt to look for him, holding out her arms in greeting whenever he appeared.

The affection between them was strengthened by Ludovica's lack of interest in Elizabeth as she grew from infancy to childhood. This new daughter, she discovered, was a tomboy —mischievous, emotional and disobedient. She was quite unlike her elder sister, Hélène, who, four years older, was a grave-faced little girl who even at the age of seven took life very seriously.

Ludovica had been somewhat annoyed that her third child was a girl, and when Elizabeth was seen to have all her father's character and almost none of her mother's the antipathy increased. There was no question of neglect but Ludovica was content to leave Elizabeth's upbringing almost wholly to the nurses, and to concentrate on Hélène, who apparently was more intelligent, more amenable and more likely to become a graceful member of the Wittelsbach line.

Elizabeth did not mind. She was able to run more or less wild, and she could do exactly as she liked with her governess, who adored her. The woman never reported to her mistress that her pupil simply refused to do her lessons and that, for hours when she was supposed to be in the nursery classroom, she was in fact romping with the workers' children on the estate, some of whom were, of course, her half-brothers and sisters.

By the time Elizabeth was eight her father was constantly taking her on brief excursions in the vicinity of Possenhofen. He announced that he would personally see to the child's tuition in deportment. This enabled him to demand his daughter's company for at least a couple of hours on any day he wished.

The deportment consisted chiefly of hard physical exercise. He walked little Elizabeth off her feet and in summertime when she complained that she was tired he advised her to strip off her clothes and bathe in the lake. Soon she was swimming like a fish—a rare attainment in those days for a girl in her position.

He also taught her to ride, not in the usual stilted manner of ladies taking the air on a safe and sleepy old mare, but on skittish ponies accustomed to clambering sure-footed over the rocky ground and galloping full out on the flat.

The Duke was a great lover of horseflesh. During wintertime when the family moved to Munich, he amused himself by giving performances in his riding school. This was a polite name for what was in fact a private circus.

He had an uncanny influence over horses, teaching them

such complicated tricks that other horsemen were amazed at his success. He imparted to Elizabeth his secret, which was that demonstrative affection plus a strict discipline could make the most high spirited stallions amenable. In fact, they would obey his intricate and often fantastic orders without difficulty, and he would entertain his guests with mounted quadrilles, pantomimes on horseback, and hunting scenes.

Munich was scandalised by reports that the Duke was often to be seen standing in the centre of the circus ring shouting orders to his horses and cracking his whip, while his daughter, her auburn hair flying out behind her, rode round and round, sometimes even bareback.

The Duke never had the slightest compunction in permitting Elizabeth to ride thoroughbreds which were only half broken-in. She naturally had some falls, but he always told her to remount immediately despite the frantic and frightened protests of her governess. This poor woman hung around the "riding school", as fearful of the consequences of the Duchess discovering what was going on as of a serious accident to her charge.

Ludovica did, of course, know what was happening. But she preferred to leave things as they were. There were five more children now, and another expected. The wayward Elizabeth was best left to her own bizarre devices. Obviously "she was her father's daughter" and the time must soon come when the Duke tired of the girl's companionship. . . .

But Maximilian did not tire of "Sisi" as he had tired of every woman he had ever known. Their closeness grew as the tomboy child become a lovely adolescent girl.

Elizabeth at this time began to be dispirited by the emotions of adolescence. Sometimes when she was laughing and gay with the sheer joy of living, tears would fill her dark eyes.

She had vague longings she did not understand, wild impulses and ecstacies, all of which she tried to put into words in a little manuscript book.* In this secret diary she also

* This little book is now in the possession of the Empress's grand-daughter, H.I.H. the Countess Waldburg-Zeil.

wrote poems, usually inscribed in red ink and illustrated with little sketches.

Once she thought herself in love with a young man called Richard she had only seen once or twice, but, as she confessed in a poem, his brown eyes haunted her.

Later Richard died after an illness and Elizabeth wrote another poem entitled "A IHN" (To Him) which began:

> "Once more the die has fallen
> And Richard is no more."

However, she consoled herself with her horses—galloping wildly across the countryside alone, but unafraid.

One of the happiest days of Elizabeth's girlhood came when her father took her, after first abjuring her to secrecy, to the bell-ringing carnival at Mittenwald. They had to get there by "Nonsense Day", which fell on the Thursday preceding Lent. The celebration was really an excuse for somewhat riotous behaviour before the severe austerity of the fast began.

The cobblers were entitled to catch any girl in the streets and take her into their shops, lift her skirts and measure her for a pair of shoes. As soon as she was released, the coopers, whose normal task it was to make the barrels for the town's Bavarian beer, would grab her and take her into the carpentry sheds where, amidst a lot of horseplay, they would pretend to measure her for a skirt.

As a reward for taking part in these ceremonies each girl was given a mask and a sort of shawl with numerous bells attached to it.

The Duke Max, whose easy attitude to morals was well-known, took an enormous risk in encouraging his daughter to participate in these revels. But she came to no harm. Life to Elizabeth was a fairy tale, it had a lovely unreality which showed in her face and created a kind of protective aura about her which people instinctively recognised and respected.

The Duke was already a legend among the people, Elizabeth was rapidly becoming one. Tales of her beauty and her sweetness were repeated by peasant to peasant, from village to village.

Yet had Elizabeth but known it, this idyllic period of her life was drawing to a close. She, who knew little or nothing of history, was oblivious of the fact that historical events had marched alongside her throughout her life. In the vast Empire, whose borders were almost within sight of her home, Fate was about to reach out and shape her destiny.

The man the gods had chosen for her partner in their wayward games was of her own generation, a relative, but personally unknown to her. His name was Franz Joseph.

On October 1st, 1848, Franz Joseph had been proclaimed Emperor of Austria. It was the year of revolutions throughout Europe. The Hapsburg monarchy tottered, and the expectation of all the revolutionaries was that it would collapse.

That it did not do so was largely due to the activities of the Archduchess Sophie, sister-in-law of the Emperor Ferdinand and a sister of Ludovica. When the Emperor abdicated, it was Sophie's son, Franz Joseph, who was proclaimed Emperor. He was called "the People's Emperor" because he was regarded by the milder revolutionaries as someone to be shaped into an Austrian Napoleon.

He was a conscientious and serious young man who throughout his boyhood had been carefully protected from grasping any implications of modern political thought. He was trained to believe that the dynastic power of the Hapsburgs existed at the express wish of God, and that it was his duty to see that the Divine wish was fulfilled.

The bigotry and obstinacy of mind which his education and upbringing had given him did in fact stand him in good stead. Always close at hand was his ambitious and ruthless mother, determined not only that her son should be the means of evading imminent disaster for the crown, but that he should strengthen its position.

For two years she dragooned and disciplined him in the difficult routine of being more than a figurehead of the

Empire, and it was with a sense of horror that she realised in early 1851 that Franz Joseph was no longer a boy but a man.

Disquieting stories came to her ears of the admiration he felt for first one of her ladies-in-waiting and then for another. It would have been all very well, the Archduchess thought, if he had merely indulged in flirtations with them, or had amused himself with brief love affairs with wives of some minor courtiers. But her serious minded young son apparently imagined himself to be deeply in love with almost any personable young woman with whom he came in contact.

The discreet and penetrating enquiries which she put in hand confirmed that he conducted himself in a most honourable manner in his meetings with the ladies, but at the same time made no effort to disguise the strength of his passion for them. One of these was the coquettish Countess Elissa Ugarte of whom the Archduchess strongly disapproved.

She had herself chosen the female in whose arms the young Emperor had been introduced to the "necessities" of love. This ceremony was regarded as a matter of the utmost importance in all the Royal families.

When the Emperor was eighteen, his mother picked out a buxom and voluptuous blonde from the Kremsier district. A hardy, energetic race of peasants of mixed Slav and Germanic blood inhabited the Kremsier. The women had supplied the best wet nurses to the nobility for many generations.

A variety of *initiatrices* during Franz Joseph's youth were all of the same type. He was to show a marked preference for this Rubens mould all his life.

The ruthless character of the Archduchess Sophie, frustrated for years while she was just the wife of her pathetic and supine husband, was unleashed for a display of unsurpassed ambition when her adored Franzi was hurriedly thrust on the throne. Only too aware that her son had inherited much of her husband's traits and far too few of her own she pledged her life to driving him.

He should, she swore, achieve the power which she, with her hard unfeminine character, yearned to attain for herself. Vicariously she intended to enjoy all that the Imperial rank could bring to the Emperor.

It was she who dreamed of a seemly love affair, an engagement approved by the Imperial Government, and a wedding that would enthral and enthuse the aristocracy and the common people alike. The romantic dreams that she contrived—a queer mixture of accidental joy and carefully ordered formality—were hers alone. She confided nothing of them to her son, for they lacked one figure. . . .

The lovely, clever and yet meek young wife at her son's side was but a vague and ethereal shadow. When Sophie's mind conjured up some name so that the face took shape and the figure form, her ambitious dreams promptly ended. The girl was unsuitable!

Perhaps she was of too lowly a caste; or she showed dangerous tendencies towards independence of thought; she might be pretty but characterless, or have character but no beauty. One after the other, the possible brides for Franz Joseph were reviewed in the Archduchess's mind and discarded.

Alarmed that all her careful schemes would be brought to naught if Franz Joseph should assert his independence—for he had officially been declared to be of age as soon as he had assumed the Imperial Crown—the Archduchess devoted herself to the problem of finding him a wife at the earliest possible moment.

Hard and overbearing, disliked by the few families whom she regarded as her social equals, and feared by all those who were her inferiors, the Archduchess had hardly anyone in whom she could confide. Indeed, the only person to whom she could safely unburden her soul was her sister, Ludovica.

She summoned the Duchess to Vienna, and the latter, quite as ambitious for her eldest daughter as Sophie was for her son, instantly suggested that Hélène would make a suitable match.

Socially, this was perfectly true, the marriage would

strengthen the alliance between the Houses of Wittelsbach and Hapsburg. The genetic problems of consanguinity had rarely worried either family. The two women talked over the matter for many hours in the Archduchess's private apartment. Sophie even admitted to Ludovica that her son was showing regrettable traces of independence of thought and action, which might make a blatantly arranged union impossible to complete.

"But you say that Franz is very susceptible," Ludovica observed. "I can assure you that Hélène is now an extremely lovely girl; surely all that we have to do would be to throw them together?"

The Archduchess agreed that this was a possible solution and the two women planned that the Lenten Carnival period should be particularly brilliant that year.

Balls and receptions were arranged for every night during the week before Ash Wednesday. Hélène was told that she would be going to stay in Vienna with her mother. And it was then explained to her that the object of the visit was that she should catch the eye of the Emperor.

Unfortunately, Nené, as Hélène was called in her family circle, objected violently.

"I hate Vienna and Viennese people," she said. "And I don't like what I have heard about Franz Joseph."

Ludovica, who had never envisaged the possibility of a girlish revolt when listening to her sister's complaints about the obstinacy of her son, stormed out of the room in a fury. She was so upset that she determined to speak to her husband about it, unwilling as she was ever to consult him about family matters.

She found the Duke after some hours of search, fishing by the lakeside. He listened without emotion to her long description of her visit to Vienna and even longer list of complaints about her daughter's obstinacy. Then he rose from the bank on which he had been sitting, and collected his rod.

"You have been making such a noise that it is no use trying to fish here any more," he grumbled. "I am going round to the other side of the lake, and I would ask you not to follow me. As regards Nené, I suppose you haven't noticed that young Thurn and Taxis has been seeing quite a lot of her, riding over whenever he thinks Nené might be by herself? I should think he'd make her a far better husband than that fellow in Vienna."

Ludovica was too angry and surprised to answer. She hated to admit that she was quite unaware that her daughter had been seeing Prince Thurn and Taxis and she also wondered how much her husband had been encouraging them.

She returned to the house and her lonely apartments on the first floor, determined, in spite of this disquieting information, to take Hélène to Vienna and arrange a match with the Emperor. It would be a brilliant marriage. Unfortunately the proposed bride was not only reluctant but adamant.

Ludovica did everything in her power to persuade Hélène to change her mind. The girl actually threatened to enter a convent if the marriage was forced upon her.

For once, Duke Maximilian gave up his wanderings and stayed around the castle in order to defend his eldest daughter. He took a perverted delight in encouraging her to thwart every proposal her mother made. The weeks passed and it seemed that nothing could be done. Then at the suggestion of the Archduchess Sophie, guile was decided upon.

It was normal for the Imperial Court to move in the hot weather to Ischl. Sophie wrote that she would insist on the Emperor arranging this for August. In due course the Duchess Ludovica received an invitation to the Imperial Court at its holiday residence which was, to all intents and purposes, a summons.

Even the Duke Max had to admit that there was no possibility of his wife refusing it. But, and here was the snag, he didn't wish to go himself. He loathed, he said, the "smug, bumptious Sophie." Poor Ludovica was in despair; first Hélène, now Max.

"You have got to accompany me," she raged. "And behave properly."

The Duke, realising that ultimately he would have to go, capitulated on one condition.

"I'll come if Sisi can come with me," he bargained. "It will be an abysmally dull proceeding but she'll cheer me up —she always does."

"Very well!"

These two words changed the course of history.

Ludovica was at her wits end but she battled for her side of the bargain. If Elizabeth accompanied them would the Duke wear proper clothes and leave his zither behind?

Duke Max sighed but agreed.

There was no doubt that Elizabeth kept him in a good temper on the long journey to Ischl. She wrote to a friend in her pretty German handwriting relating how elegant "Mama and Nené looked" and adding—

"But how solemn! As if they were going to a funeral. Poppie and I enjoyed it and acted as if we were going to a circus. It was useless to cheer up those old dummies. They looked as if they had just eaten sour pickles—and they acted as if they had the tummy ache from them."

Unfortunately the long drive was too much for the Duke's good resolutions. Before they arrived at Ischl he announced that he preferred the freedom of living incognito, and that he intended to leave the cavalcade, taking Sisi with him.

They put up at the "Golden Cross" Hotel, which was close to the Imperial residence, the Archduke signing the visitor's book as "Max Phantasus, Author, of Munich, and his daughter, Elizabeth Phantasus."

Shortly afterwards the Duchess Ludovica and Hélène joined them. The Duchess, while fully aware all Austrian society knew of the hostility which existed between her husband and herself, did not intend to parade the fact by residing at a different establishment. Nevertheless she gave her full name and the two parties lived quite separately in different parts of the hotel.

Ludovica was not particularly upset by her husband's unpredictable behaviour. She had other important matters

to occupy her mind. It had been agreed with her sister,
Sophie, that on the following afternoon she should bring
Hélène to the Archduchess's boudoir for a cup of coffee and
a *"torte"* at about four o'clock.

Franz Joseph was expected to arrive from Vienna earlier
and he would, without warning, find himself in the presence
of his future fiancée when he came to pay his respects to his
mother.

Great care was taken to see that the Emperor's staff heard
nothing of this arrangement, but Ludovica had not thought
it necessary to tell Hélène to keep the matter to herself.

That night Hélène crept into Elizabeth's bedroom on the
other side of the hotel and, in tones verging on panic, told
her what was afoot.

"I can't do it Sisi—I can't marry him. Oh, God, what am
I to do?" she cried.

Elizabeth was full of sympathy.

"Don't worry Nené" she said soothingly. "I'll spoil their
plans. I'll come along at exactly four o'clock, I'll tell Aunt
Sophie I've called to see her and she can't do anything but
ask me to stay. Then if Franz Joseph does arrive he certainly
won't be able to talk about marriage!"

TWO

1853-1854

THE husband proposed for Hélène should have been desirable in the eyes of any girl, irrespective of his exalted position. Franz Joseph was handsome, slender and broad-shouldered. His eyes were of a startling, magnetic blue, wide apart and set off by a broad, intelligent forehead. His complexion was fresh, boyishly tanned and glowing with health. He had reddish brown hair and he wore a small silky moustache.

It was not unnatural that ladies were delighted when he evinced any interest in them, even if their own rank or married state made anything but a clandestine affair impossible.

Early in his youth Franz Joseph had discovered how attractive he was to the opposite sex and the ease of his conquests had inevitably engendered a certain amount of cynical contempt for women. He could not envisage a rebuff because he had never experienced one.

Certainly Hélène's qualms about the marriage which was to be arranged for her must have been unique. Her repulsion was however not a personal dislike of Franz Joseph but because she was already in love. Neither she, nor anyone else, could be expected to suspect the blessings of her escape.

Few women of any age could at that time see any fault in the glittering, seemingly immaculate vision who was His Imperial, Royal and Apostolic Majesty Franz Joseph I.

The trouble with Franz Joseph was that as a human being he was submerged in the traditions of his family. That in time he became a great Emperor was due more to the experience that came with the years of his very long life, than from any natural heritage. The Hapsburgs had political power

thrust upon them, and neither by temperament nor tradition
were they fitted for it.

The House of Hapsburg began its fantastic career when
the Archdukes of Austria held the beautiful but agriculturally
worthless lands on the borders of the Holy Roman Empire.
They kept themselves apart from political intrigue to such an
extent that, in the fifteenth century, a Hapsburg was elected
Emperor, chiefly because he was regarded as quite harmless.

The heads of the family were always landlords, rather
than rulers, and their pre-occupation was entirely with the
possession of land. The fact that people lived on it was
an inconvenient burden. The considerations of race, trade
routes, natural resources, and urban developments, never
entered their heads until the realisation of the existence of
these facets of civilisation made them rather unwilling
participants in their control and growth.

Their pride in their possessions created a dynasty in which
marriage was utilised simply to increase the acres in Hapsburg inheritance. In their turn, these advantageous marriages
produced progeny among whom the estates had to be divided
and once again, there had to be marriages in order to amalga-
mate them.

Slowly, over the centuries, the Hapsburgs gained owner-
ship and a feudal control over territories scattered around
Central Europe which were so vast that they fell naturally
into place as the territories of an Empire. Their great contri-
bution to the development of modern civilisation in Europe,
although it was not intentional, was to prevent, until the
present day, the domination of Europe by any military
power.

Simply because of the fidelity of the peoples over whom
the Hapsburgs ruled, aggressive nations like the Russians
and the Turks; power-greedy men like Gustavus Adolphus
of Sweden and Napoleon, and the princelings and statesmen
of the North German countries were prevented from turning
Europe into a single and invincible entity.

With the emergence of powerful and highly organised

European nations at the turn of the eighteenth and nine-teenth centuries, the Land of the House of Hapsburg—as the family still called their vast Empire—stretching from Lombardy in the West and to Transylvania in the East, and from Dalmatia in the South to Bohemia in the North was an anachronism.

The young Emperor was quite untrained in the diplomatic thrust and parry, with a scarcely concealed sabre rattling in the background, which was the recipe for nineteenth century government.

All his education had been directed to stress to him the importance of maintaining the tradition of the Hapsburgs. This was to keep the power which came from the possession of land within the family, and to follow a policy aimed at preserving a way of life which had changed only in the lavishness of its ritual and the strictness of its convention during five centuries.

There is no one more bigoted than a young person who has, after early misgivings, been converted to an outlook which is more appropriate in the minds of grey-beards. Therefore Franz Joseph, who was now to be forced into a traditional marriage of family convenience, was more a symbol of tradition than a potential lover.

Prodded by his mother he agreed to go to Ischl in August, a few days before the celebrations of his birthday, which was on the eighteenth. The Archduchess had not talked much of Hélène for some time and he had no inkling that this was anything more than a brief holiday, at a resort which was normally used by the Imperial family in the summertime when Vienna became too hot.

On August 16th he arrived, his mother having gone ahead some days before. As the royal coach rolled down the Traun Valley, the Emperor saw a young girl running madly to catch a kid which had wandered away from its dam among a flock of goats browsing on the stubble of a recently cut hayfield.

The little animal was gambolling this way and that and

was within a few yards of the road. The girl was obviously afraid that it would be run over by the procession of coaches.

Franz Joseph motioned to his adjutant to tell the driver to rein in his team, and the heavy coach rumbled almost to a stop just as the girl caught the protesting kid and lifted it up in her arms. Then she turned and smiled. As she did so she saw for the first time the Imperial insignia and promptly dropped to a curtsy, her long, auburn hair falling around her face as she did so.

"A pretty girl, that!" Franz Joseph exclaimed.

"The peasants of the Salskammergut are noted for their beauty, Sire," his adjutant replied.

"That was no peasant girl," retorted the Emperor. "Didn't you note the quality of her dress or that she was not barefoot?"

The adjutant murmured that this did indeed seem somewhat incongruous in a goatherd.

An hour later, as he was sitting in his mother's apartments, the Emperor saw the little goat girl again.

She was wearing a fresh, white dress with a blue sash and her long flowing hair had been tied back with a ribbon. In her hand she held a posy of wild flowers for her aunt. Elizabeth was duly carrying out her promise to her sister.

She entered the room without the formality of being announced, and seemingly as oblivious of her aunt's frown of reproof as she was unaffected by the sight of the Emperor. His appearance was, of course, perfectly well known to her from portraits in her home.

"God greet you, cousin," she said pleasantly as she crossed to her aunt and kissed her on the cheek.

"Who are you?" demanded Franz Joseph, startled into an apparent discourtesy in his curiosity.

He took in every detail of the exquisite oval shaped face which was turned towards him as if in surprise at the sharpness of his tone.

Two scimitar-shaped eyebrows were winged over almond shaped dark eyes, half veiled by long lashes. She had a small, straight sensitive nose, a soft alluringly curved mouth and a firm cleft chin. A long shapely neck gave her an inimitable air of breeding, and her slender body moved with the grace of a goddess.

She was the loveliest creature Franz Joseph had ever seen and her voice as she answered him was so sweet and musical that it almost compelled him to listen to her.

"I'm your cousin Elizabeth of Bavaria."

Dark eyes met blue eyes. Something magnetic passed between them. The Archduchess, Ludovica and Hélène were all forgotten, so for a moment was the Hapsburg dynasty.

Franz Joseph was barely polite to his aunt and apparently deaf to his mother's rather pointed comments. He hardly glanced at Hélène and talked only to Elizabeth.

Things were clearly getting out of hand. It took Ludovica some minutes to realise, much to her surprise, that she had more than one marriageable daughter. Sophie, on the other hand, was furious, she disliked her schemes being altered by a hairsbreadth.

Anyway, she found Elizabeth's whole attitude quite reprehensible. She was, she thought, fortunately, too young to have the reprehensible moral outlook of her disgustingly unconventional father, but she seemed to have inherited his feckless and wanton disregard for the conventions.

Over and over again that night Sophie recreated in her mind that moment when the girl had entered the room. She saw the light of mischief in her dark challenging eyes, she saw the sudden glow of interest which had altered her son's rather stiff expression at the sight of her. Sophie dared not imagine the consequences should that flicker of interest be fanned into real love with all its consequences to herself. She shivered at the very thought.

Meantime, the general plans of the Court could not be altered. The brief meeting between Franz Joseph and Hélène of the afternoon was to be the introduction for a closer acquaintance during a dinner given by Duke Max and his wife at their hotel that evening.

It was to be a semi-formal occasion, unscheduled in the Court Circular, as the Emperor had retired to private life for the duration of his holiday, but etiquette prevented Elizabeth being present as she was still officially scheduled as a child.

The meal was a very stilted affair. Hélène, who realised with relief that the Emperor was not interested in her, said virtually nothing, and Franz Joseph made no attempt to talk and only replied briefly when courtesy demanded it. Duke Max was quiet until he had drunk rather too much, when his remarks became boisterous and hearty, producing a wan smile from the Emperor, angry looks of warning from Ludovica and a basilisk stare of contempt from the Archduchess.

It was not until the meal was ending that Franz Joseph bestirred himself.

"I would ask a favour of my delightful host," he began. "Surely it's the custom in Bavaria, as in my country, for children to come down to meet the guests over dessert? I should much like to renew my acquaintance with my cousin Elizabeth."

There was complete silence for a moment. Everyone realised what this seemingly innocent remark really meant. No one regarded Elizabeth as a child in fact, even if she was one by social standards.

The Duke darted an ill-concealed grin of conspiratorial triumph in Hélène's direction and gave a servant the order.

Elizabeth must have expected something of the sort, for she arrived neatly dressed, with her hair carefully brushed and be-ribboned. She played the little girl rôle insinuated by her presence amiably and well.

After curtsying to the Emperor and the Archduchess she crossed to her father's side and nestled against him. He put his arm affectionately around her until a chair was brought. Then he peeled a peach which Elizabeth ate daintily, her occupation with the fruit adroitly preventing the need for conversation.

Franz Joseph remained silent too after the first smile of greeting. He sat watching her, toying with the stem of his wine glass and making no attempt to conceal his interest.

Finally, when the women rose to leave the men alone, the Emperor turned to his mother and said that he felt tired and would also like to take his leave.

"Tomorrow is a busy day," he went on. "You are giving a ball, aren't you, Mother? It must be the most delightful occasion with some of the gaiety of Vienna transplanted to Ischl. No one must leave until after midnight. Will you find that too exhausting, cousin?" he added, speaking directly to Elizabeth.

Conscious of a sudden stiffening among those at the dinner table, he added hastily to Hélène:

"And you, cousin Hélène! Will you be ready to dance until dawn?"

Both girls replied enthusiastically that they could dance for ever if necessary. It was impossible under the circumstances for the Archduchess Sophie to point out that no invitation had been extended to Elizabeth, or that it was incorrect for a girl who had not made her debut to be presented at a Court Ball. For once in her life she had to admit to herself that she was beaten. She knew beyond all doubt that her son had already chosen his wife.

Early next morning the Archduchess was hardly out of bed before Franz Joseph rushed into her room and said excitedly:

"Do you know Sisi is enchanting?"

"Sisi!" replied the Archduchess stiffly. "But she is only a child."

"I dare say, but look at her hair, her eyes, her charm, her figure! She is delicious!"

"Slowly," the Archduchess said firmly. "You know nothing about her yet. We must examine her more closely. You have plenty of time. There is no hurry! Nobody expects you to become engaged at once."

"No! No! It is better not to take too long over such

things,"* Franz Joseph cried, and he rushed away in the hope of seeing Elizabeth.

At luncheon, which was a big, formal meal, the Emperor never took his eyes off his young cousin, who was sitting at the far end of the table. The Prince of Hesse, who did not know what was going on, said to the Archduchess Sophie jokingly:

"So far Sisi has eaten nothing but some soup and salad. She must be fasting for some reason or another."

Elizabeth blushed deeply and looked so lovely as she did so that Franz Joseph spent the afternoon with his mother talking of no one else.

The Archduchess realised angrily that nothing she could say would change his mind. And at the ball that night when Elizabeth appeared, wearing a pink and white muslin dress with a small diamond arrow in her hair, the other guests became aware that something romantic and sensational was happening.

The Emperor danced the cotillon with his little cousin. What was more, in addition to the usual flowers, he gave her all the bouquets he should have presented to the other ladies with whom he danced.

When Elizabeth later was asked if this surprised her, she replied: "No, it only embarrassed me!"

But at the end of the evening the Emperor's deliberate action in taking her hand and leading her to the waiting carriage showed everyone that an official announcement was imminent.

Next morning Franz Joseph was at the "Golden Cross" hotel by nine o'clock asking for a private interview with the Duke and Duchess. After they had greeted him, he made a formal proposal for the hand of Elizabeth.

Ludovica, while convinced in her heart that this was an insult to Hélène, could not help but be pleased. Mother-in-law to the Emperor was a position which every woman of her generation in the Kingdom would envy.

* This conversation is based on a letter from the Archduchess Sophie to her sister, The Queen of Saxony.

The Duke was obviously upset and the words of acceptance were forced stiffly to his lips. Franz Joseph's exalted position did not impress him. If he must part with his beloved Sisi, he wished to part with her to a man. To him Franz Joseph was just a tinpot soldier who had turned Austria into a military state. In addition, from the talk among his own friends he had always heard that the young Emperor was "an inconsiderate, unimaginative ass."

More than this, Franz Joseph had reigned five years and during that time, before he was twenty-four years old he had signed two thousand death warrants.

But there was no question of the Duke doing anything but give his formal consent. He had also to agree to the Emperor's request that Elizabeth should be told immediately of his proposal, although she was not to be forced to reply at once.

The Emperor left and Elizabeth was summoned to the room and the Duchess told her what had transpired.

"How could I not love him?" she exclaimed. "But how can he think of me? I am so young and unimportant. I would do anything to make the Emperor happy, but will it be a success?"

Already the thought of her future rank alarmed her and later that day she said to her governess:

"I am already fond of the Emperor—if only he were not an Emperor!"

After Ludovica's talk with Elizabeth, during which the girl wept a great deal and said very little, she wrote a note to the Archduchess telling her of Elizabeth's consent to the marriage.

It was not yet seven o'clock the next morning when Sophie sent on the note to Franz Joseph. He was radiant with delight and went first to see his mother and then before eight o'clock was at the hotel.

He met the Duchess, thanked her and unceremoniously rushed away to find Elizabeth. She was already up and came to the door when he knocked. For one moment the two young people looked at each other, then Franz Joseph clasped Elizabeth in his arms and kissed her passionately.

As was the custom of the Court, High Mass was celebrated daily at eleven o'clock. Franz Joseph insisted that Elizabeth and her parents should attend in order that the Church's blessing could be given to their betrothal.

The Emperor waited on the steps at the chapel door. The Archduchess was beside him. They watched for the carriage bringing Elizabeth and her parents. As Elizabeth walked towards them the Archduchess hesitated and then took a step backwards.

Elizabeth stood still, bewildered as she met her first problem of public ritual. Then she saw her aunt's hand motioning her to stand at the Emperor's side. Elizabeth obeyed, very sweet and attractive in her shyness, and the small procession moved into the chapel, the Archduchess taking second place.

All Ischl had heard what had happened at the ball on the previous night. Now even the doubters knew the stories must be true. Franz Joseph led Elizabeth to the steps of the altar and said to the priest:

"Reverend Father, this is my future consort. Give us your blessing!"

But six days were to pass before the world could be informed. Genealogists had to probe into the antecedents of Elizabeth; priests be consulted on religious questions; lawyers delve into the intricate and dangerous factors of consanguinity; politicians and diplomats discuss the nationalistic factors involved.

Finally on August 24th, 1853, the *Wiener Zeitung*, mouthpiece of the Hapsburg dynasty and of the Imperial Government, published the formal announcement:

"HIS IMPERIAL ROYAL AND APOSTOLIC MAJESTY OUR MOST GRACIOUS SOVEREIGN AND EMPEROR, FRANZ JOSEPH I, HAS DURING HIS STAY AT ISCHL, AFTER RECEIVING THE FULL CONSENT OF HIS MAJESTY, KING MAXIMILIAN II OF BAVARIA, AS WELL AS OF THE DUCAL PARENTS OF THE BRIDE,

BECOME ENGAGED TO THE PRINCESS ELIZABETH AMALIE EUGENIE, DUCHESS OF BAVARIA, DAUGHTER OF THEIR HIGHNESSES DUKE MAXIMILIAN JOSEPH AND THE DUCHESS LUDOVICA, NÉE ROYAL PRINCESS OF BAVARIA. MAY THE BLESSING OF ALMIGHTY GOD REST UPON THIS AUSPICIOUS EVENT, SO FRAUGHT WITH JOY AND GLADNESS FOR OUR AUGUST IMPERIAL HOUSE AND LAND."

The Viennese were delighted. The romantic story of "love-at-first-sight" between the Emperor and the lovely sixteen-year-old girl from Bavaria was something which appealed to their sentimental natures. Stories of Elizabeth's charm, her beauty and her simple home life were the sole topic of conversation in the markets and beer gardens. Her likeness was soon to be found in every hut and home in the whole Empire.

Elizabeth with her parents stayed a month at Ischl and a lady of the Court wrote to her son—"Happiness shone on the faces of the youthful pair, the weather was bewitching and life seemed to lie before them as one long summer's day."

It was, however, inevitable that Elizabeth should gradually become aware that she was marrying not merely the man she loved but the despotic figurehead. The knowledge intimidated even her carefree spirit.

She was also aware that the Archduchess was casting critical glances at her and was already beginning to find fault. In fact Sophie told Ludovica that Elizabeth should take more care of her teeth. It had been her first criticism to Franz Joseph.

"You are right!" she said the day after he had proposed to Elizabeth. "She is very pretty, but she has yellow teeth."

Franz Joseph stored this in the back of his mind and a month later he wrote ecstatically to his mother about his fiancée and reported rather tartly that her teeth were now perfectly white.

But this was only one of the Archduchess's complaints; she was not pleased at the engagement and Elizabeth could not help but be conscious of it every time she met her cold, hostile eyes.

At a dance held soon after Elizabeth's betrothal Freiherr von Weckbecker, the adjutant to the Emperor, tried to be kind to the young Princess who had looked dismayed during the long, elaborate presentations. He knew what a strain it was to be constantly stared at by the crowds and surrounded by the elderly men and women of the Court whose critical eyes indicated that they regarded stilted manners and a knowledge of protocol far more important than charm.

He walked with Elizabeth to the terrace which afforded some relief from the stifling heat of the August evening.

"You enjoy dancing?" he asked gently.

"The dances of my own country—yes," she replied, recalling the joyous prancings outside country inns while her father played his zither and the young men and girls of the village romped together.

"But the formality of these balls," she went on, blushing at the admission, "frightens me a little. I don't know how I shall get through it all without the assistance of a dancing master."

Dancing masters, ladies deeply versed in Court etiquette, teachers of deportment, language tutors, and a dozen other experts were soon to assist Elizabeth to attain the manners and decorum of an Empress.

Obedient to the demands of her sister, Ludovica immediately engaged experts to transform her daughter from a "wild rose of Bavaria" into an effete, hot-house flower to grace the Viennese Court. For a month, while the Emperor remained at Ischl, lessons could only be given for part of the day.

But Franz Joseph had once more to assume "the yoke" of Sovereignty. He was really sad at settling down again to his affairs in Vienna and wrote to his mother:

"It was hard and depressing to take a leap from the

earthly paradise of Ischl to this writing table existence and masses of papers with all my cares and troubles."

Elizabeth and her family returned to the family residence at Munich. It was more convenient than Possenhofen now that winter was approaching and she was also to be removed from the temptations of her liking for open air life. In fact regimentation began in earnest.

The girl was appalled by it all. Only the visits of Franz Joseph, which he made at least once a month, revived the thrill of romance and made life endurable. Because she loved him she determined that she would learn as quickly as possible all that was required of her. In that way she realised she could soon be with the adorable, though sometimes mystifyingly remote, young man who had captured her heart.

Franz Joseph was also madly in love. After a brief visit to Munich, followed by a few days at Possenhofen, he wrote to his mother, "I love Sisi more every day, and feel surer than ever that no other woman could suit me as well as she does."

The date of the wedding of Elizabeth to Franz Joseph was fixed for the following April. The young Emperor had been anxious for the ceremony to take place during the Christmas period, but the Archduchess was horrified at the thought of a gauche young girl becoming a Royal Consort without training.

She inveigled the priests and statesmen to make any sort of excuse to Franz Joseph, so that he would gain the impression that it was quite impossible to complete the preparations for the marriage in a shorter period.

This meant that the young couple only had a few brief unsatisfactory moments together when Franz Joseph could get to Munich or Possenhofen. It was, however, during these visits that the Emperor became aware that his fiancée had a will of her own. His accounts of her to his mother grew a little cooler but he still found Elizabeth adorable and loaded her with presents.

The Prussian Minister had watched the Emperor with a

critical eye. He noticed that the Duke Max and his future son-in-law did not get on well and not only his gaiety and lightheartedness was suspect, but also Elizabeth's.

"Eye-witnesses assure me," he wrote home, "that during his stay here the monarch closely observed every footstep and movement of his fiancée and that the very decided will, which is a leading trait in the young Princess's character, did not escape his penetrating eye. It appears that in this connection some significant hints were dropped, and since the Emperor's departure people feel a rather more serious atmosphere prevails in the ducal castle."

Relationships between the two sisters were somewhat strained when the Archduchess Sophie informed Ludovica that it was her responsibility, as the mother of the future Empress, to make up for lost time and to try to inculcate some education into her wayward daughter.

The result was that, despite the protests of the Duke, Elizabeth had to endure long hours of tuition in deportment, Court etiquette, and as an afterthought, some scholastic training.

This strict discipline, almost cruel in its intensity, nearly banished the natural feelings of excitement and expectancy which the Emperor's proposal had aroused in Elizabeth's heart. Besides which, the combination of long hours of work and the lack of fresh air to which she had been accustomed, made her feel ill.

The approach of her birthday and Christmas gave her some respite. For a few days she managed to play truant with her father. He tip-toed to her room late one night and told her now that the snow had fallen, he had planned a sleigh ride into the Tyrolean mountains.

Elizabeth retrieved her zither from a cupboard, where she had hidden it, and early one morning, before the rest of the household was up, she met the Duke in the stable yard, helped the groom to saddle the horses, and they were both miles away before it was properly light.

Breakfast was at a mountain inn where Duke Max was

well known and was served by a pretty young girl of the same age as Elizabeth, and looking remarkably like her. Then the sleighs were brought round, and for the rest of that day and most of the next Elizabeth enjoyed for the last time the carefree life that she loved.

The two itinerant musicians even managed to find an inn where, so far as they could discover, their identity was unknown. The Christmas festivities were already beginning, and that night Elizabeth played her zither to such effect that the dancers made a collection of money for her.

"It was the only time in my life that I ever earned money," she used to recall many years afterwards.

When the two wanderers rather shamefacedly returned to Munich, Ludovica with difficulty observed the spirit of the season, and there were no recriminations.

A servant in the livery of the Hapsburgs had arrived shortly before their return with a gift of some jewellery from the Emperor to his fiancée.

Elizabeth hardly looked at the jewels but was childishly overjoyed by the message which accompanied them written in Franz Joseph's own hand.

He had inscribed: "A Christmas gift to a Christmas child."

Franz Joseph had another Christmas present for Elizabeth. This was a parrot from the menagerie at Schönbrunn. Elizabeth was thrilled with the bird. On Christmas Day she complained of the cold, and on January 16th a special Imperial courier arrived with a magnificent fur cloak for her. But in a tiny lace-edged note she wrote to her former governess she could only talk of the attractions of the parrot.

The Duke was also a recipient of a package from Vienna. It enclosed a formidable mass of documents sent by the Imperial Cabinet and outlining the wedding day procedure. He took the papers to his own apartments and read through them with growing consternation and alarm at the results of his efforts to rescue his daughter, Hélène, from a marital union which she had not desired.

He saw now that a vast political machine was taking over

the tom-boy daughter he loved so much but—ever a realist
—he accepted that he could do little or nothing to alter
things.

The formal arrangements drawn up by the Emperor's
advisers seemed to insinuate that the teenage girl would be
little more than a puppet in a romantic spectacle designed
to eradicate from the memory of the people the disturbing
political events of a few years before.

"Her Royal Highness, the Bride," he read, "on her way
down the River Danube from Straubing, will be privately
welcomed by the Emperor as she reaches Austrian soil at
Linz and will be conducted by His Majesty to accommodation
prepared for her, where she will remain overnight. The State
welcome will take place at Nussdorf the following day.
Thence His Majesty, the Emperor, will personally escort the
Royal bride to Schönbrunn. On all stages of the journey a
Court Chamberlain will be in attendance to describe the
beauties and historic importance of the places on the Royal
Route."

The point of the last sentence was not lost on any of the
household. Right up to the actual marriage ceremony efforts
were to be made to educate the uncouth little foreigner in
details of Austrian history, of which the authorities seemed
to be in no doubt that she was ignorant.

The Duke then started to read another document, but
laid it aside with a snort of disgust before he ordered a
servant to take it to the Duchess. It was a precise and detailed
schedule of the items and financial stipulations for the
marriage settlement, the date line for completion of which
was given as March 4th.

The hand of the Archduchess was clearly to be seen in
this document, which went to tremendous trouble to ensure
that the bride came equipped with everything that she
would need for her new position.

It enumerated clothing, footwear, toilet accessories and
other personal items down to the last possible detail. Elizabeth
was, for example, to bring 17 dresses for formal occasions,

4 high-necked silk dresses, 6 dressing gowns, 19 thin summer dresses pink, violet, corn coloured and forget-me-not blue, and 4 ball dresses. She was also to have 168 chemises— no more, no less—five dozen pantalettes and her stockings were to be 84 pairs in wool of stated colour and 84 of Italian silk.

Proof was to be sent that the bride's father would hand to his daughter 50,000 gulden, on or before March 4th, whereupon the Emperor in his turn would bestow twice that amount on his bride.

The Duke had not read that paragraph and his wife had to have one of her rare interviews with him to see that he complied. Fortunately he was a man with a vast income and very simple tastes, and while he himself had not the faintest idea whether he could afford it, he agreed to ask his Household Comptroller to look into the matter adding:

"These Austrians strike a hard bargain. They get a gift of my loveliest daughter and expect me to pay for their privilege. I can't think this is justice, considering the resources of the Hapsburgs are twice as large as mine."

The 50,000 gulden which Elizabeth had to bring with her, while admittedly a considerable sum, was available without undue strain on the family resources. To the infinite relief of Ludovica, by March 4th all documents had been signed, all items of the trousseau inspected and approved, and an acknowledgment that the marriage settlement was completed received from Vienna.

For his part, the Emperor, besides the 100,000 gulden, promised a *Morgengade* of 12,000 ducats. This was for the ancient custom of *Sachsenspiegel* which was a gift a bridegroom gave to his wife the morning after their wedding night, in compensation for the loss of her virginity.

On Easter Sunday, April 16th, a gala concert took place at the Royal Court of Munich. The members of the diplomatic corps wished to pay their respects to the Emperor's future wife before her departure. Elizabeth wore a rich *parure* of diamonds and her new Orders for the first time. She looked exquisitely beautiful but very serious.

"The young Princess," wrote the Prussian Minister, "in spite of the brilliant and exalted position which awaits her at the side of her august bridegroom, seems to be deeply affected at saying goodbye to her old home and exalted family circle, and the expression in which this could be read cast a slight shadow over the most Serene Princess's face, radiant with all her youthful grace and beauty."

Elizabeth started on her marriage journey on April 20th. She was dressed in a dark green travelling costume and wore on her wonderful hair a small toque with a hunter's feather at one side. The Duchess had arranged for a carriage with six horses to take her from the family residence to Straubing on the Danube.

Ludovica's idea was to make the occasion a triumphal procession from the start, but Elizabeth was crying bitterly as she entered the carriage and the occasion was anything but a triumph.

She had never realised until this moment what it would mean to say goodbye to her home and all those she loved—to the gardens, to the lovely Lake of Starnberg, to the distant snow-clad Alps, to her dogs and horses, to her village cronies and the children with whom she had always played, and to Possi itself!

The carriage with Elizabeth and her parents, and the procession of wagons carrying the servants and her trousseau, in seventeen large trunks and eight smaller ones, proceeded to Straubing where they were all transferred to a small steamer. This took them down the Danube as far as Passau, on the frontier of the Empire, where a deputation came on board to welcome Elizabeth. They then proceeded to Linz.

They arrived at dusk and the bells in the twin towers of the old cathedral rang out a welcome.

There were also crowds of people and a riot of flags, the Austrian red and white, the Hapsburg black and yellow, flew from every house. There was a delegation of townsmen. The "Hymn of the Hapsburgs" was played with the crashing of cymbals and rolling of drums and the cannons thundered a salute.

Franz Joseph was waiting to welcome Elizabeth. He looked extremely handsome in a resplendent uniform but seemed over-conscious of the fact that this was a public occasion. He stood stiffly at attention as Elizabeth, in a white lace mantle, stepped ashore from the little steamer. He bowed ceremoniously over her out-stretched hand, and merely brushed the back of her hand with his lips.

There was no smile on his face, but Elizabeth gained some comfort from the fact that his eyes were sparkling with admiration. She turned and smiled at the spectators, then taking out her handkerchief waved it in response to their cheers. She captured every heart at that moment, by her beauty and her spontaneous gesture.

It was already almost twilight as Franz Joseph escorted her to an open carriage to drive with her to a house in the lovely old Hauptplatz, which had been made ready for the guests.

Large crowds shouted "Long live the Emperor's bride," as the carriage drove the short distance. Immense quantities of spring flowers had been brought into the city, and they festooned the streets. At the entrance to the ancient section of Linz, a triumphal arch completely covered in sprigs of fruit blossom bade Elizabeth welcome. In the gathering gloom, the flames of bonfires leaped skywards from the crown of every hill.

Elizabeth made a few attempts at conversation with Franz Joseph but got no reply. The young Emperor seemed completely occupied with watching the actions of his subjects and acknowledging the cheers.

She gave an involuntary shudder. The spring evening was turning cold, but it was from a sense of lonely desolation that she gathered her cloak closely around her.

When the carriage pulled up at the house, Franz Joseph jumped out and then lightly took Elizabeth's hand as she alighted. In an effort to overcome the barrier which seemed

to exist between them, she said that she hoped he would
come in for a few moments. In a rather shocked tone Franz
Joseph exclaimed that this was quite impossible. His visit to
Linz had been rather unconventional and had taken place
despite the somewhat violent protests of his mother.

The official programme provided that he should welcome
her to his Empire outside Vienna, and for that reason it
would be necessary for him to travel right through the night
in order to reach his capital and then set out to meet her in
full procession. Elizabeth murmured that she understood and
tipped her face for a kiss of farewell. There was none.

The Duchess hurried her to the house and after a meal
sent her straight to bed.

"Tomorrow will be an even busier day," she said warn-
ingly.

The next morning the rising sun of a really beautiful
spring day glittered on the waters of the Danube and the
bells of the city churches once again began to ring out. For
once in her life Elizabeth had not risen from her bed the
moment she had awakened. Subconsciously she dreaded
the day's activities and strove to delay them by feigning
sleep.

Ludovica, informed by a frantic servant that the girl
appeared to be still fast asleep, burst into the room and shook
her almost angrily. With uncharacteristic solemnness Elizabeth obeyed, allowed herself to be dressed, and without any
breakfast set off for the steamer which had been brought up
to the quayside during the night, and went aboard.

The vessel had thousands of roses, grown in the South East
of the Empire and rushed to Linz by relays of coaches timed
to arrive during the night, tied to the rails, the mast and
every projection.

They were already wilting and by the time the journey
was over, most of them were blackened by the soot from the
steamer's funnel.

The cabins had been draped in purple velvet, and the
heavy and funereal atmosphere that the hangings imparted

to the airless accommodation gave Elizabeth a feeling of physical nausea. She insisted on remaining on deck.

This delighted the citizens of Linz, and as the boat chugged down the river, moving swiftly on the current, swollen by the spring thaws, Elizabeth heard the awe-inspiring sound of cheers from many thousands upon thousands of throats.

A journey of more than one hundred miles lay ahead. Silvery bells pealed from every little chapel they passed but soon there were long stretches of open country with no sign of a house or even a castle. They passed the monastery at Melk, deep bedded in the cherry orchards, the vineyards of the Wachau, and the winding channels of the Donaustruden. It was all so lovely that suddenly the Duke, forgetting his misery at the thought of losing his beloved Sisi, tossed his hat in the air and asked Johann Petzmecher for a tune.

"Give us something gay, Johann! This is a wedding not a funeral!"

Ludovica protested but no one listened. Soon Elizabeth was dancing and singing the songs of the Bavarian highlanders. Then she and her father called for beer! They were thirsty and the sailors must also be given beer to celebrate.

"Supposing people should hear of this!" the Duchess cried in agony, but the Duke only laughed.

Actually the story that the Bavarian bride of the Emperor had behaved like a peasant on her way to become Empress of the stiffest and most formal Court in Europe was whispered around Vienna. But it never reached the newspapers. Franz Joseph controlled the Press.

The brilliance of the morning was overshadowed by grey clouds and it began to rain. Still Elizabeth refused to go below and the official guide for the journey, appointed by the Emperor, got soaked to the skin as he recounted the historical importance of the places they passed. Elizabeth hardly heard what he said. She was drinking in the beauty of the countryside.

It was dawning on her that this country was now hers, and she began to dream of wandering among the crags and precipitous hills which bordered this lovely river. Almost gaily she allowed her mother to supervise her change of dress in readiness for the ceremonies when they reached Vienna.

Long before the church spires and roof tops of the capital came in view she could see the puffs of smoke from cannon around the walls and later she heard the dull boom of their salute.

A stiff breeze had got up and the clouds were breaking. There had been some trouble with the engines of the steamer and it was considerably behind schedule. Hundreds of the notability had been waiting impatiently and uncomfortably at the quayside since shortly after midday.

Members of the Government, the Church, and the leading families of Austria had a large marquee in which to sit. Foreign ambassadors, members of the municipal council of Vienna, and the other large towns of the Empire had been jammed in rows on two open platforms for upwards of four hours.

Elizabeth stood beside her mother, dressed in rose pink silk with a white lace mantle. She was so overcome by the number of beautiful uniforms and the pomp of purple carpets, the myriads of flags and the enormous crowds being held back by troops in the background, that she could hardly stop her legs from shaking.

Worst of all, there seemed to be no sign of Franz Joseph. Perhaps he, too, was suffering from a similar attack of nerves, for until the last moment he had hung about at the rear of the marquee.

Then the natural exuberance of a young man in love overcame the scruples drummed into him by his mother and her advisers. He horrified the old guard, and delighted the ordinary people, by literally running down the quay, and, before the garlanded gangway had been fixed in position, he grabbed the rails of the ship, knocking the wilted roses out of the way, and vaulted on to the deck.

Gone was the remote and cold formality of the previous evening at Linz. He called out one word "Sisi!"

Elizabeth was as nonplussed by this approach as she had been disappointed by his earlier coldness. She stood like a statue as he put his arms around her and kissed her roundly on the mouth. She neither responded nor repulsed him. Her sense of relief and happiness were too deep for her to react immediately.

But as he turned away and with infinite gentleness took her arm, she felt a warm glow of love and tenderness and she let her body lean close to his.

Forgotten in a moment were all those carefully repeated exercises on the correct form of a stately progress, with her arm bent well away from her body, and the deferential lowering of her head. She was unaffectedly laughing while tears ran down her cheeks during the short walk to a carriage drawn by the magnificent greys from the Imperial stables at Lippiza.

The Archduchess Sophie glowered at the scene, an Ludovica was almost trembling with fright at the thought of the reprimand her sister would bestow on her before the day was over. But the two leading characters in the pageant were oblivious of criticism.

Franz Joseph had his arm round Elizabeth and she was looking up into his face with adoration. It was obvious that with difficulty they remembered to acknowledge the cheers of the crowd.

"*Hoch Elizabeth!*" the people cried. "*Hapsburg, Wittelsbach hoch!*"

The entrance of Elizabeth into her future capital was a resounding success. While on that day at least, the Emperor was loved with a genuineness he had never known and was not to know for another sixty years.

THREE

1854

THE procession reached the Schönbrunn Palace an hour later, the journey through the streets of Vienna being slow because of innumerable stops as civic dignitaries, officers of various regiments, groups of Government officials, and representatives of the City's trading companies were presented to Elizabeth.

She rather enjoyed it all despite the heavy formalities of the words of welcome and the critical eyes of those who approached her. Now that Franz Joseph had become a human being once more everything seemed endurable.

At last the coach turned through the main gates and passed between the bronze eagles which Napoleon had set up there as his emblem of victory while he lived at the Palace, and which had been, strangely enough, left by the Hapsburgs when once again they took possession of their home.

The ostentatious wealth of the Schönbrunn was something tangible in which the young Emperor could feel a pride. Despite crowds of people who had managed to obtain permission to enter the grounds of the castle, and the hundred-and-one presentations Elizabeth was supposed to have made to her, he insisted on showing her some of the sights of his spectacular home.

Elizabeth became quieter and quieter as he hurried her from one vast room to another, followed by a horde or courtiers and members of the Royal entourage. To the young girl the place seemed more like a museum than a home, as indeed it was, and at her age she had little taste for art or beauty that was not a part of nature.

The Schönbrunn had been completed nearly a hundred years before, on the site of a very ancient palace which had

been built in the fourteenth century. This had been replaced
by a second palace after the first had been destroyed by fire,
and in its turn was razed to the ground by the Turks in 1683.

Elizabeth was taken to see the apartments which Napoleon
had used and in which the great French General's unfortunate son, the Duke of Reichstadt, had lived virtually a
prisoner, and died because he no longer had the will to live.

The Emperor than hurried her on to look at some of the
adjoining buildings, including the beautiful little rococo
theatre where Marie Antoinette had danced and sung as a
young girl in the rôle of a shepherdess in a pastoral comedy.

From a window Elizabeth had a glimpse of another
building which she was told was the Court menagerie.

"But I want to see that at once," she exclaimed. "Please,
Franz, may we visit the animals—you can show me the rest
of the Palace tomorrow."

This expression of interest, the first that she had shown
since they had entered the palace, broughta questioning look
from the Emperor. His demeanour changed immediately to
a cold imperiousness and he told Elizabeth brusquely that
there was no further time for sightseeing.

"We must make an appearance on the balcony," he said.
"The crowds are waiting to see you."

This was called "*Represantationspflicht*"—the duty of keeping
up a fine front—and was part of the exhausting Royal métier
that Elizabeth was to find would rule her life from dawn to
sunset.

Franz Joseph led her to the balcony overlooking the main
portals. Thousands of people had gathered outside the gates
and were calling for their future Empress. Suddenly there
was a hush. A delicate, lovely figure appeared on the balcony
holding on to the arm of their young Emperor. There was a
gasp, then roar upon roar of raised voices.

"*Hoch! Hoch!*" they yelled. "*Hoch Elizabeth!*"

Elizabeth looked pale and tired as time after time she gave
a stiff little bow. She still had not learned the trick of putting
on a smile to order, and there were many in that crowd who

thought that the beautiful young Princess was cold and unresponsive.

But standing in the background, Ludovica, usually imperceptive, saw that Elizabeth was almost at the end of her tether. She asked the plump and perspiring Master of Ceremonies whether the time had not come for the bride of tomorrow to retire.

The dignitary heartily agreed, for it was no part of the plan that the Emperor should be seen for long in the company of his future wife on the eve of his wedding.

He approached Franz Joseph and in an undertone murmured that it was time for the Princess to be taken under the care of her mother. In that Court, where ritual was master, the Emperor knew he had to obey. After a dozen or more presentations, once again there came that cold and formal kiss on a hand very lightly held and from lips that had no warmth in them.

Elizabeth felt her mother take her arm and she was led away. Once in the privacy of the apartments allotted to them, physical and emotional exhaustion overcame her, and she undressed and went to bed, refusing all food except for a glass of milk.

She fell asleep immediately, to be disturbed later by nightmare dreams in which she was running down interminable corridors, flanked by long lines of portraits of domineering men and women, in pursuit of Franz Joseph whose figure always seemed to be drawing farther and farther away.

The next morning there was no time to ask her how she felt, for she was by now merely a cog in the mechanism of an Imperial marriage. By ancient custom a bride of a Hapsburg, together with all the female relatives of both herself and the groom, had to undergo religious instruction and spiritual cleansing in an involved ritual called the Christian Doctrine.

This took up almost all the morning and had to be undertaken while fasting. The clothes worn at this service were virtually those of women doing penance and Elizabeth, although she never had a very profound religious sense, was considerably disturbed both mentally and spiritually as the evil of human sin was stressed to her.

In the afternoon, after a simple meal and a very brief rest, Elizabeth was taken to her mother's apartments, where Ludovica helped Elizabeth read the nineteen-page lithographed programme of the wedding ceremony. After which the excited ladies-in-waiting dressed her.

She wore a white satin dress embroidered in gold and silver and adorned with myrtle blossom and over it a gold embroidered mantle with a train. In her glorious hair, over a veil of Brussels lace, she wore a tiara of diamonds and opals, the gift of the Archduchess which she had worn at her own wedding, and entwined with it a wreath of myrtle and orange blossom.

Round her neck she wore a necklace of diamonds and at her breast a bunch of fresh white roses. The sight of the perfect blooms gave Elizabeth more pleasure than any of the jewellery she wore. They made her think of the loving words her father had spoken to her the night before she left Possenhofen.

"You will always be the Rose of Bavaria," he said.

As the church clocks of Vienna struck five, there was a formal knocking on the door of Ludovica's suite by the Master of Ceremonies. Resplendent and carrying his wand of office, he announced that it was time for the procession to the church to start.

He said this in a loud and singsong voice, and then immediately, in a hissing whisper, enquired of Ludovica whether the bride had perused the instructions for the ceremonial which had been furnished to her under the title of "Most humble Reminders."

The Duchess replied that her daughter had done so, which was not in fact quite true. Elizabeth had wearily thrown them aside and her mother had read some of them aloud, hoping that what she had said was being taken in.

Outside, the state coach, as ornate and beautiful as Cinderella's glass carriage, was waiting. The spokes of the

wheels were of pure gold and Rubens had decorated the
doors. Black velvet covered the interior making a perfect
frame for Elizabeth's fragile beauty.

It was drawn by eight white horses, and each one was
held by a groom in mediaeval Spanish costume, a symbol of
the Hapsburg's family's connection with Spain. Very slowly
the cavalcade moved forward along roads decorated with
orange blossom and spring flowers. The crowds were
tremendous.

The first stop was a new bridge which connected the outlying parts of the city with the ancient section within the
ramparts. By the Emperor's command the construction of it
had been pushed ahead day and night so that today it could
be used for the first time.

The coach stopped at the approach of the bridge and the
Burgomaster of Vienna, through the window of the coach,
asked permission to name the bridge "Elizabeth Bridge".

The young bride was genuinely charmed with the idea,
which was one of the things which had been kept secret from
her, and in her youthful innocence, she almost believed that
this was a special omen of good fortune.

Ignoring all those "Most humble Reminders" about
decorum and sitting still, she leaned out of the window and
admired the new bridge. It was decorated with statues and
immense quantities of shrubs and flowers, the scent of which
filled the air.

"My bridge!" she exclaimed excitedly.

The sight of the solid stonework and the pillars standing
so serenely in the fast rushing Danube gave her a sense of
reality and endurance for her new life which none of the
ceremonial or even the religious instruction had brought to
her. She could not know that the bridge was indeed a symbol
of her future. It was destroyed a few months before she met
her tragic death.

The coach began to move again and on the other side of
the bridge, the councillors of the city of Vienna stood awaiting to welcome her. One stepped forward with a tiny piece

of bread as a symbol of the city's official welcome to their future Empress, and as an acknowledgment that she would be its first citizen, coming next to the Emperor himself.

The moment she dipped the bread in the salt and placed it in her mouth an officer standing on the bridge waved a banner and instantly all around the ramparts the cannon, which had been firing salutes of welcome ever since the coach had started on its way, sank into silence. Then the church bells ceased, except for those of the Augustine Church where the wedding ceremony was to take place.

As the coach approached the church, young girls strewed roses on the roadway and Elizabeth saw Franz Joseph in the uniform of a General with the wide sash of the Golden Fleece across his breast.

He stood staring straight ahead with his hand at the salute, neither smiling nor moving. And with a sinking of her heart Elizabeth saw that cold impersonal look on his face which she was so quickly learning to recognise.

Ludovica's hand restrained Elizabeth from moving when the coach stopped. The girl had little desire to do so and indeed would have been glad if the earth had opened up and swallowed her. With increasing nervousness, she watched the enormous procession form into place.

First came choir boys and then Prince Archbishop Rauscher, an old man who had been Franz Joseph's tutor, and behind him, seventy Archbishops and Bishops in their gold-embroidered and jewel-encrusted vestments. As soon as they had disappeared through the doors of the church, the secular section of the procession began to move forward— the heralds, pages, Court functionaries and Privy Councillors. Next, Archdukes of the Empire and lesser members of the House of Hapsburg.

The Emperor, still at the salute and still staring straight ahead, turned and followed his relatives and Ministers, leaving a gap of a few yards so that he walked in solitary majesty.

Elizabeth watched him move slowly up the steps to the

door. Then, at an impatient nudge from her mother, she
alighted from the coach, and remembering what she had
been told about a slow and dignified walk, moved towards
the Archduchess Sophie, who had now taken the place
where her son had been standing.

Her prospective mother-in-law took Elizabeth by the right
hand and her own mother walked on her left. A conglomer-
ation of ladies of the Court formed up behind and the bride,
aged sixteen years and four months, passed through the
doors.

When she stepped down from the coach, her mother had
adjusted the veil of Brussels lace which covered her face.
Even though ten thousand candles burned within the interior
of the church, the gloom was such that she could hardly see
where she was going.

There was a pause while Bishops sprinkled her with Holy
water and her ladies-in-waiting formed up on either side to
hold her train, which till then had been gathered close to
her by a couple of pages. Suddenly she felt a stronger, firmer
grip on her right arm, and turning her head a fraction
she saw that Franz Joseph had taken his place beside
her.

Music filled the air and the bridal couple moved slowly
forward. Ahead in front of the High Altar was a *pre dieu*
covered in white velvet under a canopy of white and gold.
The couple knelt down and the music ceased, to give them
a few moments, silence for private prayer.

They rose and the Princearch Bishop of Vienna took one
hand of each of them and clasped them together. In a dream
Elizabeth felt someone hand her a ring and in a dream she
felt her fingers take it, move towards to Franz Joseph, and
place it on his finger.

A voice spoke the formidable list of names and titles of the
man she was to marry:

"Emperor of Austria—Apostolic King of Hungary—King
of Bohemia, Dalmatia, Croatia, and Slovenia—King of
Jerusalem—Duke of Lorraine—Duke of Modena, Parma,

Piacenza and Guastalla—Hereditary Count of Hapsburg and Kyburg in Switzerland—Count of Hohenembs—and Grand Voyvode of Serbia."

Elizabeth did not hear her husband's pledge to her, nor feel him put the ring on her finger. Only vaguely came the soft, kindly voice of the old Archbishop:

"Now you are united in lifelong loyalty and faith, one to the other, an example to all people. You, exalted Princess, will find in your husband a friend who has joined himself to you by indissoluble ties; he will feel your joys and sorrows as his own, and you may open your heart to him, relying in all faith on his steadfast devotion amid all the events of this changeable earthly life; he will be at your side with never failing sympathy, he will prove your protector and your strength, your joy and your hope, your pride and your honour."

The words ceased and the music began again. Drowning it all came the thunder of cannon and the crash of bells which shook the fabric of the church. Elizabeth turned at a whispered instruction and placed her hand on the stiff and unyielding arm of her husband.

She emerged from the gloom of the church, her face now unveiled, and gasped thankfully at the fresh air of a lovely spring evening.

The huge crowd, being beaten back by the troops, were almost out of control. She caught some of their enthusiasm and smiled for the first time since she had crossed her own bridge. For the moment, she was a bride full of hope and happiness for the future and unafraid of the fact that she was now an Empress sharing in the rule over nearly forty million people, and Consort of one of the most important Kings on earth.

With reason did some of the members of the House of Hapsburg, crowding behind the Royal couple on the steps of the church, say to one another "She is not only the youngest but certainly the most lovely Empress who has ever graced our Dynasty."

The journey back to the Schönbrunn was marred only by the continued remoteness of Franz Joseph, who seemed to be completely occupied with behaving in the correct regal manner in acknowledging the cheers of his people. They parted as soon as they were inside the palace. Elizabeth was rushed away by her mother in order to get ready for the wedding banquet which took place almost immediately.

On entering the banqueting room, she felt a sense of elation in the changed attitude of the people around her. No longer was there any of the thinly disguised contempt for her youth and lack of knowledge of Court etiquette. A religious ceremony had now made her a Hapsburg and the second most important one in the world. She was secretly a little amused when her mother, and even her terrifying aunt, curtsied to her.

Under the stimulant of wine and good food eaten off gold plate, Franz Joseph became much more human. True, his conversation consisted largely of telling her of the importance of various people at the table with details of their relationship to him. But there was an increasing warmth in his eyes, and he was attentive to her.

Elizabeth unaffectedly began to enjoy herself. It was all like a wonderful play in which she was playing the leading rôle. The beauty and excitement almost overwhelmed her, and she was conscious all the time of Franz Joseph. The look in his blue eyes when they rested on her mouth was almost a kiss.

Yet by half-past nine when the party ended she was very tired. As Franz Joseph escorted her to the Royal apartments she thought how exhausted she felt and how the heavy coronet of diamonds had given her a headache.

Her ladies-in-waiting undressed her.

"I'm so weary," she said. "I shall sleep well tonight!" She smiled but the lady-in-waiting to whom she had spoken looked anxious.

"I'm afraid it's been a long day, Your Majesty."

"You look frightened," Elizabeth accused her. "And so

did my father when I kissed him goodnight! What is the matter?"

The lady-in-waiting murmured something unintelligible. Outside she and the other ladies agreed miserably that "the child was too young and obviously completely innocent."

In the Hapsburg archives the Court Chamberlain recorded—"Their youthful Majesties retired to their inner apartments at half-past nine of the clock."

FOUR

1854-1855

IF the etiquette of the Austrian Court had permitted the Emperor and his bride to be regarded as human beings for just a few days the mutual love of the young people would have been allowed to grow naturally. It might well have enabled them to withstand the rigours of their official lives in the years to come.

Unfortunately a honeymoon, which was regarded as normal for the most poverty-stricken peasants, was not the privilege of their Emperor and Empress.

It is true that a token gesture was made to human emotions by arranging that the bridal couple should spend a few days at the summer residence of Laxenburg Castle, but this was in no sense a private holiday. The Lady of the Chambers, Countess Eszterhazy-Liechtenstein, and a couple of dozen ladies-in-waiting attended the bride. The Emperor had an even larger retinue; they were, however, all on his personal staff and as there was no one concerned with the Government, it was thought that this was a sufficient gesture to indicate he was relieved of his State duties.

Worse still, the Archduchess accompanied the couple, and she insisted on having breakfast with them every morning. This meal took place in the privacy of the bridal suite under conditions which Sophie considered informal but which, in fact, necessitated the presence of a dozen members of the Court and as many servants.

The morning after her wedding Elizabeth, white faced and exhausted, had lain in bed after Franz Joseph had left her. She did not think of breakfast, she wanted nothing except to be left alone.

In the breakfast room the Archduchess scanned the table. Beside the Emperor's chair someone was missing!

"Where is Elizabeth?" she enquired.

"Naturally I am having breakfast sent to her room," Franz Joseph replied.

"Naturally?" the Archduchess raised astonished eyebrows and her voice was sharp. What was the meaning of this? Was Elizabeth planning to introduce a new custom? She had never heard of such a thing! Barring illness, the Royal family ate their meals at the same table or not at all!*

Franz Joseph rose uncomfortably to his feet. Twenty minutes later, very pale with dark lines under her eyes, but composed, Elizabeth entered the breakfast room.

She soon saw that she was not expected to contribute to the conversation at this, or any other meal. Although etiquette demanded that any conversation should be started in order of precedence, and no one of lower rank could initiate the mildest topic with a person of superior rank— which made Elizabeth second only to the Emperor himself— her mother-in-law was rude enough to pretend not to hear such attempts as Elizabeth made to be pleasant.

After her first day as a wife, and after a mild protest to her husband had resulted only in a rather horrified reproof, she sat in silence.

But it was spring, the grounds of the castle were beautiful in their new foliage, she was young, in love, and there were horses in the stables!

Although the Emperor spent this travesty of a honeymoon in one or other of the uniforms of the regiments of which he was Colonel-in-Chief and could not therefore relax sufficiently even to stroll arm in arm with Elizabeth around the grounds, she simply went off by herself. She would order a horse to be saddled and once on its back would gallop until the animal was exhausted.

But there was no real escape. A horrified lady-in-waiting saw her help one of the grooms to brush her horse down after she had been riding. As was almost inevitable she

* This episode was recorded by the Countess Marie Festetics and was related to her by the Empress.

trotted straight to the Archduchess and reported the matter.

Sophie rebuked Elizabeth as if she was speaking to a delinquent child.

In the privacy of their own suite, when at long last Elizabeth and Franz Joseph could get away from the boring entertainments which took place in one of the salons of the Castle each evening, the bride and bridegroom spoiled their short hours of privacy by futile arguments about etiquette. If either had been a little more tolerant they would have admitted that they were both wrong and found a compromise.

Franz Joseph was already submerged in an ocean of ritualistic behaviour which ill became a young man who wished to demonstrate his love for his bride. Elizabeth, thanks to the years of unconventional behaviour by the father whom she adored above any other being on earth, should have realized that her new position must be approached with dignity.

Because Franz Joseph was wildly attracted to Elizabeth and she wanted above all things to be loved, they made up their quarrels, but the anodyne of passion merely stifled their incompatibility for a few hours. It did nothing to destroy it.

Perhaps if they had been able to remain in one another's company longer, they would have come to an understanding. But Franz Joseph was so dominated by his mother, and by his own rather fearful sense of tradition, that he was quite incapable of deciding anything for himself.

Already in his heart he knew that he had broken written and unwritten laws in that sudden and uncharacteristic insistence that he would marry Elizabeth. What was more, he was already accepting these disputes as proof that he had been wrong to follow his inclination instead of obeying his mind.

Quite willingly he sank back into the comfortable rôle of a ruler ruled by those around him. Three days after his marriage, when his mother said at luncheon that she had been into Vienna and was appalled by the sight of his desk at the Schönbrunn, he murmured that he had himself been conscious of the way in which he was neglecting his State duties. By mid-afternoon he was back at work.

The smallest action of the Central or of the local governments of his Empire had to be endorsed by the Imperial signature, and hundreds of documents awaited his attention. He had no idea what he signed and hardly wanted to know, accepting without question a murmured explanation as one or other of his Ministers placed paper after paper in front of him and withdrew it as soon as it had been initialled.

With the Emperor out of the way the Archduchess redoubled her efforts to discipline her daughter-in-law. She regarded it as her duty to make her son's wife into a good Empress. But she was harsh, tactless and unsympathetic.

She was incapable of understanding her niece's childlike nature, and exaggerated her innocent passion for horses, dogs, birds and nature into a crime. Elizabeth, on the other hand, was very sensitive. Once people had hurt her, she never trusted them again. In fact they became enemies in her eyes.

What was more galling than being constantly rebuked was the curtailment of her liberty. Elizabeth could not take a step without two or three ladies-in-waiting in attendance. No grooms were allowed to lead the horses from their boxes. Walks around the grounds were discreetly controlled by the ladies-in-waiting to a slow meander along the terraces immediately surrounding the house.

It was understandable that Elizabeth was so restricted that she felt desperate. She was a prisoner, a caged bird. To comfort herself she wrote a poem:

> "O that I had not left the way
> That would to freedom me have led!
> O that I had not gone astray
> On vanity's broad path instead!

Now in a prison cell I wake
The hands are bound that once were free
The longing grows that naught can slake
And freedom! Thou has turned from me!

I waken from a vision rich
Wherein my spirit captive lay,
And vainly curse the hour in which
Freedom! I gambled thee away."

Elizabeth had to keep this poem locked up. It was a strange pathetic cry from a bride of only two weeks and something she would have found hard to explain to her mother-in-law.

More pressing than this sense of being trapped was the natural one of sheer loneliness. Her mother had been sent back to Bavaria as soon as the wedding was over. There was no one around her that she had known for more than a week with the exception of the Archduchess. Bewildered as Elizabeth was about the seeming coldness of her husband, at the same time she pinned all her hopes on him as the only possible companion.

One evening she insisted, despite the indirect reproofs of her ladies-in-waiting, that she would not dress for dinner until she had greeted her husband as he returned from his work in Vienna. She walked up and down on the lawn bordering the main drive-way from the gate for more than an hour.

When his coach with its out-riders rumbled to a stop and Franz Joseph alighted, she ran across the grass and threw herself into his arms, putting her arms around his neck and kissing him passionately on the mouth. He smiled at her, murmured a greeting and gently disentangled her clasped fingers from his neck.

Franz Joseph was not entirely insensitive. He recognised the hunger to give and receive affection which had impelled his wife to embrace him. For this reason he made no protest about it, nor did he prevent her from slipping her arm through his and clinging close to him, as they walked towards the house.

But his eyes were not those of an adoring husband looking down on the face of his beloved. His glance was only for the rows of windows and towards the doors where the flunkeys stood like statues. He visualised the gossip that must already be beginning within the palace.

Within minutes of the couple reaching their private apartments and going each into their dressing rooms to prepare for the evening banquet, there was the formal and rhythmic knocking on the door of Elizabeth's boudoir from the staff of the Master of the Household. Hardly had Elizabeth's servant opened the door than the Archduchess Sophie walked in, her face dark with anger.

"I have come," she began, so far forgetting herself in her fury that she did not wait until the maidservants had scurried out of earshot, "to correct your Majesty on a point of behaviour. Your Majesty is putting herself in an impossible situation, and worse still injuring the reputation of the Emperor himself, by such a display of uncontrolled vulgarity as was seen by the domestics and the members of the Court a few minutes ago. More reserve must be shown."

The final sentence contained the first direct order which the Archduchess had dared to speak to her daughter-in-law. Technically, as she well knew, she was herself infringing the rules of etiquette. But such was her anger that she had decided that open warfare was the only possible policy.

In this moment mutual dislike by both women degenerated into mutual hatred. The Archduchess believed that she had intimidated the girl, because Elizabeth's eyes filled with tears, but they were tears of anger and resentment. Completely unversed in the wiles of Court and family intrigue, Elizabeth had no real idea of how to combat the viciousness of her austere and ambitious aunt, but she had an unbreakable courage.

For a full minute the two women glared at one another, silent and motionless. Finally the Archduchess turned and stalked majestically from the room.

Although she was shaking with nerves after the scene that

had taken place, Elizabeth motioned to the maid to come forward and dress her for the evening. At dinner and during the boring concert which followed she was very quiet but her head was held high.

Back in the private suite she sent a message to her husband in his dressing room that she intended to sleep alone that night. Womanlike, she half hoped that he would burst into her room unannounced. But the conventional Franz Joseph merely sent his adjutant in person to convey his compliments, to trust that there was no suggestion of any indisposition of health and to express his wishes that she would have a good night's rest.

"I desire you to thank his Imperial Majesty," Elizabeth answered, catching perhaps for the first time nuance of tone and phrasing which could be so useful in the formal message. "I ask you further to give his Imperial Majesty my assurances that I am perfectly well and hope that he too has an undisturbed night."

For some weeks afterwards Elizabeth was left almost entirely to her own devices at Laxenburg, seeing her husband only at breakfast and dinner when invariably there were persons on either side of the Royal couple who demanded attention and prevented any intimacy of conversation between husband and wife.

Once or twice Franz Joseph came to her bedroom and was for an hour or so the adoring and tongue-tied young man who was all Elizabeth imagined a lover ought to be. While she had by no means accepted defeat in defending her own personality, she was already developing a fatalistic attitude towards her husband, knowing that any attempt to change his attitude was virtually futile.

Simply to get out of the way of the Archduchess by day she spent more and more time in the Franzenburg, that strange building, half museum and half palace, which Franz Joseph's grandfather had built on a tiny island in the middle of the lake which lay beyond the Laxenburg Castle.

The place was crammed with a hotch-potch of works of art.

These had been virtually looted by the old Emperor during his travels round his domains, by the simple method of praising whatever took his fancy so extravagantly that his host had to take the hint and demand the honour of presenting it to him.

There were complete sections of monasteries, churches and castles taken down piece by piece and then reconstructed in the Franzenburg. The place was desolate and quiet, most of the objects of art—the pictures, the furniture, the altars and statues—covered with the dust of years.

Elizabeth wandered round the place for hours, and then, in order to revel in the contrast, would roam around the overgrown gardens which stretched between the building and the edge of the lake. The inevitable lady-in-waiting who accompanied her on these expeditions would in the evening make her way, dusty and dishevelled, and utterly fatigued, to the apartment of the Archduchess and report the Empress's strange activities.

Sophie listened in silence. She was quite content that her son's wife should remain out of the way on the island all day where visitors would not note her strange behaviour. But everything she heard merely strengthened her intentions to break the spirit of this little "upstart Bavarian" and turn her into a seemly puppet on the throne beside her son.

Soon the time came when even the semblance of the honeymoon came to an end and the Royal couple returned officially to Vienna. On the first evening there was a State Banquet. Significantly the Archduchess Sophie decided at the last moment not to have a list of "Most humble Reminders" sent to her daughter-in-law so that she would know how to conduct herself at this function. Recognising that her adversary was a young woman of considerable spirit she hoped to win by allowing embarrassment to be her ally.

The thought of attending a magnificent Banquet in company with her husband, even though it would obviously be a heavy and formal affair, rather attracted Elizabeth.

It was to her mind a party which meant gaiety and excitement, and this Elizabeth, after the lonely miserable time at Laxenburg, wanted as a stimulant to her flagging spirit. She knew that she was completely untrained in her rôle as Empress, but being highly intelligent she was ready to learn by discreetly watching others.

Unfortunately for her she was not aware that no one could do anything on such a formal occasion until she had done it first. Consequently, when the Master of Ceremonies came to escort the Royal couple to the banqueting room and Elizabeth appeared on her husband's arm, moving to the two vacant places at the table, she was almost frightened by a hundred pairs of staring eyes that were fixed on her.

Her husband stood motionless and so did she. Everyone else did the same. There wasn't a movement nor a sound. As well as she could without moving, Elizabeth looked round the room, wondering how long this was going on.

The whole business seemed to her ridiculous, and after a couple of minutes she threw discretion to the winds and sat down. Thus by good fortune she did what she was supposed to do, for no one in that room from the Emperor himself to the most insignificant Baroness from some outlying estate of the Emperor's dominions could have possibly sat until the Empress—the first lady of the Empire—did so first.

Her troubles were not yet over. Everyone was now seated but there was still silence. Elizabeth turned to her husband and whispered to him the enquiry as to when the meal would begin.

"Now that you have spoken the food can be brought in," he replied.

The few whispered words between the Royal couple were noted by every guest in the room and they too began conversing. Simultaneously menservants appeared with the first course, and Elizabeth, who was hungry, looked at her plate with expectant pleasure. She began to remove the gloves which reached beyond her elbows. Nothing she could have done would have caused more of a sensation!

A few words from the Archduchess sitting on the other side of the Emperor sent a footman rushing to the place where the Mistress of the Robes sat. Blushing with embarrassment, the lady came over, bent down over Elizabeth and whispered urgently:

"Your Imperial Majesty has deemed it appropriate to remove her gloves. It is unfortunate that etiquette forbids it, Your Majesty."

Elizabeth's temper rose. Attempting to make her retort a whisper she said, clearly enough for anyone along the table to hear in the embarrassed silence:

"That is ridiculous! No reasonable person wears gloves at meal times."

Thereupon she took up her knife and fork and began eating the fish set before her. She was hardly aware that for a full minute no one else in the room had moved. She had put the guests in an impossible position. As Empress, whatever she did was correct and had to be imitated, but to imitate her with regard to removing gloves would be an unpardonable breach of good manners.

Every activity at the Banquet was in fact controlled by the Master of Ceremonies, who stood a little to the side and behind the chair of the Emperor, and by a series of almost undetectable signals told the rest of the company, who were not in view of the Royal couple, what was going on and what they should do. He was in a quandary, just as much as the guests. He took refuge from the problem by giving no sign whatsoever.

The Archduchess, taking precedence after Elizabeth, had to make the decision between turning the meal into a terrible fiasco which would reflect on the dignity of the throne or of admitting by her actions the rectitude of Elizabeth's behaviour. Her face was grey with rage as she too slowly removed her gloves and began to eat.

The Master of Ceremonies gave an imperceptible nod with downcast eyes and every lady in the room removed her gloves and took up her knife and fork.

The Emperor himself, never a brave man at times of crisis, had pretended to be oblivious of the whole thing, neither supporting his wife nor reprimanding her. But a few moments later even he had to do something about his embarrassingly unconventional Consort.

A footman approached in company with the Royal vintner.

"Would your Majesty deign to take Imperial Tokay or Claret?" he asked.

Elizabeth, who was now really enjoying her meal, looked at the bottles on the vintner's tray and said brightly:

"I think I will take a glass of beer."

The iron self-discipline of the servants could scarcely withstand this remarkable reply. They darted looks of consternation at one another, but made no move to meet with the Royal request. It was extremely doubtful if they could have done so, for except for the more lowly servants who were housed in outlying parts of the palace, beer simply did not exist.

Franz Joseph tried diplomacy.

"I know beer is the national drink of your native Bavaria," he said not unkindly, "but I am afraid that at State Banquets in my capital it is *de rigeur* that only wines are served."

"But I don't like wine," Elizabeth protested. "And I really would prefer beer."

"We will see about it next time," the Emperor murmured placatingly, motioning to the vintner to pour Elizabeth a glass of Tokay. The hubbub of conversation began again and the rest of the meal passed without incident.

The Archduchess did not intend to go to bed without reproving her daughter-in-law for the frightful errors of bad taste that she had committed. Elizabeth was perfectly aware of what was coming, for she noticed that her husband had mumbled something about a few urgent affairs of State that demanded his attention, and had escaped so that there was no possibility of his being dragged into the argument.

The Archduchess came alone. She told Elizabeth to dismiss her maids and then demanded an explanation about the gloves and the beer. Elizabeth answered angrily that she had no explanation to give beyond that of common sense and personal taste.

"*Mein Gott!* Do you think you can eat like a Bavarian peasant? Are you trying to disgrace the Emperor, the Court, the House of Hapsburg? You have shocked everyone—even the Country will be disgusted by you."

Elizabeth accepted the challenge.

"You forget, Aunt," she began, deliberately omitting all titles of courtesy and treating her enemy simply as a relative in her own family, "that you yourself are infringing the dignity of the throne by speaking in this insolent manner to your Empress. As for the idea of gloves during meals! Why, the custom must have been initiated by an Empress with ugly or diseased hands!"

Sophie dared not remain any longer in the room. She was in such a temper that she felt that if she was there a moment longer she would so far forget herself as to slap her daughter-in-law across the face. That, she admitted to herself, would indeed be an unforgivable infringement of etiquette.

The incidents at the banquet were the first of a long series of unpremeditated breaks with convention on the part of the young Empress. Deliberately adopting an imperious attitude which was in reality quite foreign to her nature, she blithely pursued a policy based on the premise which had to be adopted in the Court of: "I am the Empress; I can do no wrong."

As soon as some lady in-waiting announced in shocked tones that what her mistress was doing was a departure from the rules of etiquette, Elizabeth replied in the most regal tones that she could muster:

"From this moment onwards the departure from the rule becomes the rule."

Sometimes she upset the servants by her behaviour. There was the time, for example, when she had been at the Schön-brunn for a month, when she decided that she would like to take a bath.

After an hour or two of hectic preparation she was conducted to a distant part of the palace, close to the kitchens,
where a somewhat battered tub had been filled with hot
water. She refused to bathe in this room, which was little
better than a dungeon, and demanded that a bath should be
available in some room nearer to her own suite. This was
provided, but carrying the hot water to it gave the staff a
considerable amount of work which they disliked.

When the Archduchess heard of this she coined a phrase
which dogged Elizabeth for some time to come. "Our equipment," she said in her most acid tones, "is not good enough
for the eccentric Empress."

The eccentric Empress—the phrase travelled through the
Hofburg corridors. What did it mean? It was a word often
used in reference to the Wittelsbachs. Was Elizabeth ill—
or mad?

Elizabeth felt a web of gossip closing in on her. On entering
a room unexpectedly she could hear the guilty hush that fell
upon her entourage. She felt herself watched, spied upon,
whispered about. She became timid, shrinking from contact
with those about her.

Before she was twenty years old she had retreated into a
shell that no one seemed able to pierce.

On another occasion she broke with the tradition that an
Empress must only wear a pair of boots or shoes once. Among
the details of the lives of previous Empresses which were
kept in the Hapsburg archives were those for their rules for
footwear. It was shown that many an Empress in the past
had been provided with six or seven thousand pairs of shoes
during her reign.

As every pair of shoes or boots was hand-made by the
most expert craftsmen in Vienna they were extremely
valuable and a lucrative source of extra income for the
maids who purloined them the moment the footwear were
removed.

For a time, Elizabeth had not noticed in her general joy
at the lavishness of her trousseau that even though she might

change her riding boots used in the morning for some walking shoes during her stroll round the park in the afternoon and then into some satin shoes for an evening function, that these never appeared again.

At her home in Possenhofen she had often run around the grounds bare-foot in the summer-time. In the winter she had worn comfortable boots of soft leather, and during her long walks with her father in the mountains, heavy but well made peasants boots designed for flexibility and comfort.

The result was that her feet were slim and muscular, but soon they became tender through the constant wearing of new fashionable but tight footwear. One morning, when easing her leg into a pair of riding boots, she exclaimed rather petulantly:

"I know the others got wet yesterday but they should be dry by now. I will wear those instead of these new ones."

"But they are no longer available, your Imperial Majesty," replied her maid. "They were given away yesterday evening, according to the rules of the household."

Elizabeth immediately gave the order that henceforth none of her shoes or boots must ever be given away without her express permission.

Orders for new footwear soon had to be cancelled because the cupboards were getting crammed with boots and shoes. The royal cobblers were annoyed, but not so much indeed as the servants who had obtained more money from the sales of the Royal footwear than they did in wages.

Once Elizabeth actually crept out of the palace, in company with a protesting maidservant and wandered around Vienna. She was unrecognised by the crowds, but the servant was dismissed by the irate Archduchess when the escapade was discovered.

Events like these made Elizabeth unpopular with the palace staff, for as is usually the case the servants were greater sticklers for tradition and more fervid haters of change than their employers. But among the middle classes of Vienna the gossip which spread about the young Empress's modern and unconventional outlook increased the popularity which had begun when the citizens of the capital had first seen the Emperor's bride.

The high regard which the tradesmen, immigrants and radicals had for the Empress was soon noted by the Viennese Police whose job it was to keep a careful watch on the political climate of the city. These pro-Elizabethans were the very people whose attitude was infinitely more dangerous to the stability of the throne than any potential uprising of the working people of the towns or the peasants in the country.

The fact that the Empress Elizabeth was popular with the commoners would automatically have made her unpopular with the Austrian aristocracy, even if they had not already followed the Archduchess's lead. Almost inevitably political factions emerged which were to affect the destiny of Austria and her dominions for a century to come.

On the one side were the people who looked forward to a new age and believed that in due time the Empress would be a useful tool with which to attain it. On the other were the entrenched forces of the landed aristocracy behind the Archduchess, and through her influence, the Emperor.

Most dangerous of all to Elizabeth's future happiness was the fact that the tremendously powerful Church was wholeheartedly on the side of Sophie.

In the final analysis Austria was governed by the Church as a relic of the days when it had been, in fact as well as in name, the Holy Roman Empire. The priests of the Church gave their views to the Archduchess and she in her turn told them to the Emperor.

If there were times when Franz Joseph as a very young man queried any of the decisions of his Ministers, it was when they seemed to clash with those which his mother had told him were of divine origin.

He was genuinely devout, very conscious of the fact that one part of his nature was unstable and prone to wickedness. With the result that his anxiety to placate an avenging God when he could be an instrument of good on behalf of his people was a very powerful motive for his actions. Because of this innate piety he probably disliked his wife's irreligious attitude far more than her social lapses.

Elizabeth as a completely happy young girl had passed unscathed through that period of adolescence when, because of repressions and frustrations, preoccupation with religious observance so often coincides with sexual development. But the Duke, who practised a private form of agnosticism while observing the minimum of formal religious duties, had a dislike of the priest-politician.

Elizabeth had formed her opinions on his and she also disliked the drawn out and ostentatious ceremonies of the Church. This was not to say that she was in any way impious, but she regarded religion as an entirely personal and private matter.

In Vienna at the time there was however no tolerance about such religious attitudes. Because her absence from innumerable church services, which were to all intents and purposes State functions, was very noticeable, she aroused a sense of suspicion and even horror among persons who would otherwise have condoned or forgiven her other peccadilloes.

Slowly and remorselessly the Archduchess Sophie engineered the erection of invisible barriers around the Empress which were designed, if not to break her down, at least to cordon her off from friendships which could become dangerous.

Everywhere the Emperor received hints given in terms hardly removed from deep condolence on his misfortune in marrying such a girl. Soon the attitude which had caused him to write to a relative: "I am as much in love as a lieutenant and as happy as a Greek god," changed to a rather pathetic impatience of his wife's quixotic temperament.

On occasions he referred to her with a rueful smile as "his troublesome child". To her face he was even more severe.

When he was informed one evening that Elizabeth had again gone out into the streets of Vienna, causing such crowds to collect that the Police had to make a charge to disperse them and keep the common people at a respectful distance from their Empress, he said bitterly:

"You seem to be under the delusion that you're still tramping around your Bavarian mountains. Have you forgotten that you are Empress of Austria and what is due to your position?"

Elizabeth's eyes were full of pain as she answered: "But it was only a day or two ago that you thought that it is my duty to show myself to the people as frequently as possible."

"Yes, Yes!" replied Franz Joseph wearily. "That was when I was trying to persuade you to come to High Mass with me."

But "the troublesome child" was fulfilling one of her duties. Elizabeth was pregnant.

FIVE

1855

THE child Elizabeth was to bear had been conceived in June during one of those brief moments of happiness when mutual passion turned an Emperor and his Consort into a man and woman.

Elizabeth's mind was so carefree and immature that for the first few weeks she had been unaware that she was to have a child. Afterwards, when she was sure of what was happening, she kept the news to herself in case her daily life should be still further restricted.

She did not know that the Archduchess, her eagle eye missing nothing, already suspected the truth and had written to the Emperor saying:

"I do not think Sisi ought to spend so much time with her parrots, for if a woman is always looking at animals, especially during the early months, the children are apt to resemble them. She had far better look in her looking-glass or at you. *That* would have my entire approval."

After a couple of months Elizabeth's natural desire to share the good news with Franz Joseph made her tell him at a moment when he was being kind and loving. He was obviously pleased and was about to make some affectionate remark when Elizabeth added, "Please do not tell Madame Mère!"

Immediately the by now familiar barriers of misunderstanding arose. With a look of mystified consternation Franz Joseph said:

"But the child is not just ours. It belongs to the Empire. My mother and my Government must be informed immediately."

Elizabeth had given her husband the news one bright cold morning while she was preparing to go for a gallop.

She went just the same, refusing to go with her husband to the apartments of "Madame Mère", as the Archduchess Sophie was now called.

Franz Joseph discovered that he was unaccountably tongue-tied in giving his mother the news. For half an hour he spoke of trivialities and by the time he finally voiced the good tidings Elizabeth was returning towards the Palace.

By sheer illfortune she had spurred her horse to a gallop for the last hundred yards or so just as her husband and mother-in-law looked out of the window.

Madame Mère glared with cold disdain at the slim young figure of her daughter-in-law, her cheeks pink from the exercise in the frosty air, and her body moving rhythmically to the horse's movements.

She turned to her son and said frigidly: "Let us hope that she will make amends for her behaviour by giving you a son. That is, of course, if she does not achieve her seeming wish to give herself an abortion."

Uncomfortably Franz Joseph left his mother's apartments and hurried down to speak to Elizabeth. Angry reprimands leapt to his lips as she ran towards him, her eyes full of happiness and love. At first she listened calmly to what her husband had to say but she frankly did not understand the reason for his alarm and rightly suspected that he, a man, was merely repeating what he had heard from his mother.

Angrily she told him that on her journeys with her father she had known all sorts of women while they were expecting babies. She had seen them working in the fields and going about their normal duties one day and caressing their babies on the next.

"But they are little more than animals!" Franz Joseph retorted. "I cannot imagine that as the Consort of an Emperor you would wish to behave like some illiterate peasant woman—even if she were a Bavarian!"

Elizabeth was getting a little tired of the growing frequency of aspersions about her lowly birth. What was worse, the ceaseless veneration of rank and ancestry she saw and heard every hour of her waking life was having its effect. She was becoming very conscious of her inferiority of breeding in comparison with the exalted Hapsburgs.

With an effort she kept back the angry words in reply to her husband's cheap taunt. She took refuge in the traditionally feminine excuse of having a headache and retired to her room. When, an hour later, a lady-in-waiting approached her where she lay on the couch to announce that the Archduchess wished to converse with her, again the headache was given as an excuse.

In fact there was no headache. Elizabeth felt perfectly well. She was the type of young woman whose body and mind blossomed in pregnancy and right into the New Year she continued to insist on at least one daily ride, or, if the weather was too bad, to enjoy a walk of one or two miles.

These physical activities of hers aroused a lot of scandal, for by this time it had been officially announced that the Empress was in "a delicate state of health and would be attending no public functions."

At that period all women who could afford it virtually retired to their beds for the eight months of their pregnancy. The sight of the expectant Empress riding a fiery and tempermental mount, as was seen by the public when she reached the outskirts of the park, caused misgivings and horror even among those who had hitherto been her allies.

It was a wise and kindly doctor who eventually took her in hand. He was a Jew, and only his consummate skill had given him the privilege of being a Royal physician. He knew that he had much to lose and nothing to gain by complete frankness. As a physician he wanted to do the best for his patient, but he was well aware that the birth of an aristocratic baby was twenty times more dangerous than the birth of a child in a Viennese ghetto.

Boldly, and despite the presence of two ladies-in-waiting as chaperones during his examination of Elizabeth, he said to her:

"The child you are to bear will prove beyond all possibility of criticism that you are capable of fulfilling your destiny as Empress, Your Imperial Majesty. For my colleagues and myself this responsibility is also a very great one. Should we make an error I hardly like to think what might happen to us. It would certainly be counted as treachery against the throne. We shall, of course, exert all our skill, principally for your sake, but also to obviate that criticism which many in Vienna would be only too glad to make. You, your Imperial Majesty, also know how harsh and unjust criticism can often be. Let us try together to see that there shall be no justification for criticism."

Elizabeth understood what he meant. Meekly she asked for his instructions and from that day onwards she followed them meticulously until the birth of the child in the early hours of March 5th, 1855.

As soon as the arrival of the baby was imminent Elizabeth, together with most of the Court had moved to Laxenburg. From March 1st a large crowd consisting of members of the Hapsburg family, Court officials, priests, were hovering around the Imperial suite.

There were also various nonentities who because of the tradition-ridden conventions of the Empire were supposed to be present at the birth so as to ensure that there was no possibility whatever of a substitution for the child.

Custom had been slightly relaxed so that only immediate relatives of the mother and her medical attendants were actually in the room at the time of birth.

The Bishops remained behind a screen. They had brought their holy water with them so that the child could be baptized if there was any risk of a still-birth within minutes of its emergence into the world. What was more, with the help of a somewhat frightening device, they could even baptize it while it was still in the mother's womb.

A system of mirrors and a door slightly ajar permitted others who insisted on their rights to view the actual birth to see for themselves.

Elizabeth, with her slim young body and tiny pelvis, had

a hard time in giving birth to her first-born. She was not frightened because it was not in her nature to feel physical fear. She hated the tearing waves of pain and would have gladly sought relief in the natural outlet of screaming aloud at them. But through the mist that seemed to envelop her in that badly-lit chamber, with the heavy curtains closely drawn, she saw watching her the piercing, dark-coloured eyes in the white, set face of the Archduchess Sophie.

Once or twice she groped with her hands where she thought her husband might be, and, finding nothing, moved her head to look for him. But he had not been able to bear the sight of his wife in pain and was slumped on a chair in the ante-chamber.

At last came the final burst of agony and slowly, very slowly, peace and lethargy stole across her. Only dimly did she hear the cry of her child. When she opened her eyes once again the mist was gone and so was that hard, demanding face of her mother-in-law. The Archduchess Sophie was already talking to her son.

"It's a girl—unfortunately," she said sourly, and beckoning to her ladies-in-waiting stalked from the room.

Among all the rest of the people in the ante-chamber the whisper went round from mouth to mouth: "It's only a girl."

Franz Joseph went into the lying-in chamber and gently embraced his wife.

"You have seen the baby?" Elizabeth whispered through dry lips.

"Yes," he replied. "It's a little girl."

Somehow, although he had not intended it, the description of the baby's sex sounded like a reprimand. The contempt of the Archduchess had spread like a plague into the minds of every person hovering around the Imperial suite. It affected the midwives who now took over from the doctors. It even tainted the calming, comforting words of the aged priest who knelt by Elizabeth's bedside to lead her in prayers of gratitude for God's mercy and blessing.

The baby was very weakly. She was christened Sophie after the Archduchess. Elizabeth was not even consulted. The insistence that Elizabeth had somehow sinned in producing a daughter had a serious psychological effect on her and she was for a time within an ace of suffering from melancholia.

She made a confession to her old nurse whom her mother had sent from Possenhofen that before she became pregnant she had implicitly believed that her marriage would be annulled because of her sterility. "Just as Napoleon annulled his marriage," she said, "in his anxiety to produce an heir!"

Her nurse comforted her, praised her baby and told her to rejoice that she was a mother. But Elizabeth was little more than a child herself and the idea that she had failed Franz Joseph by not giving him a son brought on a definite mental upset which only a real love and understanding on his part could have prevented.

The millstone around the necks of all the members of the House of Wittelsbach was the fear of madness. For generations every child had grown up with first-hand knowledge of some eccentric uncle, or some half-crazed aunt, even if they had been lucky enough to escape the tragedy of seeing insane parents.

Dark stories of ancestors chained and manacled, whose deaths were a merciful ending to a travesty of life, were the folklore of the nursery in the mansions and castles of the Wittelsbachs. With the added terror that they were true stories.

Those members who were tainted were in no position to care. The completely sane, of whom Elizabeth was one, worried perpetually about their awful inheritance and thus were inclined to accentuate the slightest symptom of morbidity or depression.

Elizabeth had been feverish after the birth of her child. The post-puerpereal upset was so usual that little notice was taken of it by her doctors, and, being a healthy young girl, she quickly threw off the physical symptoms. As is usual, the mental injuries remained far longer and the depression she felt was aggravated by the coldness of Franz Joseph.

The baby was whisked away to a wing of the palace and put in charge of a corps of wet nurses selected more for their purity of morals and appropriate ancestry than for their physical health.

Elizabeth had dared to suggest that some young mothers from her father's estates should be engaged for the task of feeding the little Princess. But her mother-in-law's sneering comments on the Bavarians in general and the morals of the women on the Possenhofen estate in particular, had shocked her as much as if she had been hit across the face. In any event the request was categorically rejected.

For ten days Elizabeth never saw the child. The excuse was made first that her own fever might be contagious, and when that had disappeared, that the baby was so weakly that the slightest upset to the quiet and careful regimen would have a harmful effect.

When the formal christening took place and the mother had to hold the child for a few moments, Elizabeth was appalled at the sight of the tiny face beneath the veil of lace. The skin was so transparent that there was a blue tinge to the cheeks. The eyes opened momentarily but seemed to see nothing. In fact the child was barely hanging on to life, but to Elizabeth the supine, listless appearance made her think that the baby was an imbecile.

She fought continuously to see her baby after that—but all in vain.

"Give her the child," the Archduchess said to her son, "when she cannot even discipline herself? Never!"

The young Empress of Austria even suffered the indignity of having the door of her child's nursery slammed in her face by a menial who said gloatingly that he did so by the express order of the Archduchess.

There came a brief respite from Elizabeth's unhappiness with the arrival of summer. Even Sophie had to agree that

Vienna was no place for a weakly child, and the usual
journey to Ischl was arranged.

There Elizabeth was able to see her baby occasionally and
to satisfy herself that while the child was physically weakly
there was nothing wrong with her brain. The baby's blue
eyes were bright and intelligent. Her pathetic crying was at
least vigorous, and the movements of her little hands, as for
the first time the mother felt the tiny fingers grasp her thumb,
were firm and perfectly co-ordinated.

The country air, coupled with Elizabeth's own return to
health and the easier atmosphere of a Court relaxing on
holiday, revived her resolution to be a good wife.

Once or twice Elizabeth's father had talked to her of the
happiness and comfort a woman can bring to a man. He
had done so in order to excuse himself in his daughter's eyes
for his infidelities, unspoken about between the two but, as
each was perfectly aware, well known. His words had shown
Elizabeth something of her father's yearning for love, and
she had understood, even if she said nothing.

Slightly shocked as she had been by her father's affairs
with common young women, she had noted her mother's
indifference to him, and contrasted it with the love-light she
had sometimes seen in a woman's eyes when she and her
father had arrived at some mountain village.

Elizabeth had early in life learned that there could be
more happiness in a poverty-stricken farmhouse than in a
palace. Brought up in considerable luxury, it had mystified
her until adolescence brought some realisation of the gulf
between wordly and emotional joys. Deep within herself she
would give to her husband all that her father found among
his lights o' love.

When she thought of her life with Franz Joseph before she
married him, she planned that when they were together she
would banish from his mind all the worries and burdens of
his official life. She had imagined that she would watch from
the background the Emperor carrying out his work in the
full panoply of State, but when the pomp could be set aside

she would be able to put her arms round him and lead him
into a secret world of their own.

Yet Franz Joseph could not understand and did not want
to enter the secret world which was so much a part of
Elizabeth's life. The yearnings of the half-child half-woman,
which were based on something spiritual and fairy-like, were
completely behind his comprehension.

Yet in moments of passion, she surrendered to him not
only her body but her heart and soul and imagined, in her
innocence, that he did the same. She was at those times filled
with joy because she knew that she made him happy. It was
not her fault that he preferred to throw aside these priceless
gifts through a misguided sense of his destiny.

Now, at Ischl, for a few days, while his mother had
returned to Vienna for some political intrigue, Franz Joseph
became a pleasant, easy-going young man and her lover.
He was quite happy to tramp along the lakeside and up into
the mountains with Elizabeth. The hovering adjutant and
servants were told to keep their distance, and the Royal
couple even tried a childish trick of escaping from their
'gaolers' by running pell-mell when boulders or trees had
offered hiding places.

Elizabeth was sometimes physically exhausted by this
untoward activity so soon after the birth of her baby, but
she thrived because it was a return to her old active life, and
there was the spur of a laughing, happy husband to help her.

Fervently she prayed during that brief holiday that her
cup of happiness might be filled even more by another child
conceived in the love of that second honeymoon. It was, of
course, impossible so soon after the birth of Sophie, but
the barriers of misunderstanding remained down long enough
for Elizabeth to get her wish before the year was ended.

There were no more happy days together when the Court
returned to Vienna, but sometimes in the evenings in place
of the more usual cold stilted Emperor, Franz Joseph came
to her with a boyish, pleading look that she quickly learned
to recognise. Then she would sit at his feet reading poetry

to him until he sighed in relaxed happiness and his hand would stroke her long, silky hair.

When she was able to tell him, in the late autumn, that she was again pregnant he was genuinely delighted and full of pride. Rather to her consternation, however, he began to treat her as something fragile and weak.

"It is very soon after little Sophie," he said one evening. "You must take great care of yourself. I was talking to my doctors today and told them our news. They say that every consideration must be shown to you in your delicate state."

Elizabeth soon learned that "every consideration" included her husband regarding her as an invalid. His warm affection changed to cold courtesy, and as quickly to virtual indifference.

There was also a new misery which Elizabeth had never imagined could happen. While she was expecting his second child Franz Joseph was unfaithful to her. He had, from his youth, been highly susceptible to women's flattery, but during the first year of their married life he had disciplined himself to fidelity.

With Elizabeth's pregnancy making their sporadic physical relationship impossible, he had returned to the flirtations and *affaires* in which he had indulged as a bachelor.

He was careful to select married women whose husbands would not dare complain and who would themselves not be likely to get any foolish ideas about any open recognition of their rôle as the mistress of an Emperor. But the gossiping and prurient-minded ladies-in-waiting took good care to let Elizabeth overhear what was happening.

Her reaction was one of disgust rather than anger. With her completely open mind, unencumbered by prejudice, she might in all honesty have accepted the victory of a young, pretty and unattached woman in the rivalry for her husband's love. She would have admitted that through no fault of her own she was failing her husband and would have comforted herself that after the birth of her baby she could resume the battle. Being very conscious of her beauty she would have few doubts about the outcome, even though, as she had to admit herself, she was very ignorant in love-making.

The realisation that her husband preferred women who were, to her at the age of nineteen, well into middle age, physically unattractive and married, aroused a feeling of revulsion. It made her feel befouled that Franz Joseph should leave her for such women.

As soon as she was able, after the birth of her daughter, Elizabeth went to all the balls and receptions that she could, not, as her critics suggested, in order to spoil the chance of her husband continuing his flirtations during these functions, but to take measure of her rivals.

She was so greatly disturbed by what she saw that for the first time in her life she used to cry herself to sleep night after night. She saw only too well that the two or three women having affairs with her husband had an alluring sophistication with which she could not compete. She noted the artifice they used to hide their age.

But she overheard too some of their risqué and suggestive conversation, which obviously delighted all the menfolk who crowded around them. If this was what Franz Joseph liked and wanted, then she had lost him for ever!

A sense of desolation and defeat lasted with Elizabeth for many weeks, aggravated by her natural physical weakness after the birth of her child and by the frustrations caused through the deliberate hostility of her mother-in-law. But gradually, because she was young and her mirror told her she was beautiful, her courage returned. By the autumn she had made up her mind to make one last valiant attempt to make her marriage a reality.

She would get Franz Joseph away from the artificialities of the Viennese Court. She would take him to the lakes and mountains, the woods and fields which were her spiritual home and there, with his mistresses out of sight, she would win him back with her own simple but deep love. She was not a little surprised when, having put this suggestion to her husband, she found that he was agreeably disposed towards it.

The truth was, that having persuaded three ladies of the Court to bestow their favours on him simultaneously, his love life was becoming embarrassingly complex. There had already been some shrill arguments in public which, with difficulty, the Court officials had quietened before the Archduchess Sophie heard them.

Worse still, as some of the bolder Ministers dared to inform their Emperor, the rivalry of the three women and the fury of their cuckold husbands had given rise to dozens of bawdy stories. These were not merely the tittering amusement of the Palace and the great families of Vienna, but also the subject of boisterous, contemptuous laughter in the common taverns of the capital.

SIX

1856-1860

WHILE Elizabeth was wondering how to get her husband to herself, the Emperor was advised by his Ministers that it was time that a formal visit was made to some of his dominions.

Franz Joseph welcomed the idea, not only because it would solve his private problems but also because, after a twelve day tour in Carinthia and Styria, he was infatuated with his wife again. All her life Elizabeth had the power to arouse her husband's passionate and adoring love for her whenever she could get him alone.

On their return to Vienna, Franz Joseph had even been brave enough to oppose his mother's wishes as regards the children, and entreated her to "judge Sisi indulgently if she is, perhaps, too jealous a mamma, for she is such a devoted wife and mother."

The Archduchess was furious, her anger aggravated by the fear that her son was escaping from her influence. She redoubled her attacks on her daughter-in-law and the relationship between them became absolutely unbearable. Elizabeth therefore longed to get away and forget both the insults to herself and the pain of being virtually cut off from her own babies.

Their first major tour started in November when they travelled to Trieste and then across the Adriatic to Venice. The Emperor was a man of considerable personal courage and had no fears whatever for his own safety. He was nevertheless worried about the possible danger of this visit to one of the stormy corners of his Empire so far as his wife was concerned.

Elizabeth laughed at his fears. Yet as she and Franz Joseph drove from the landing stage at Piazetta to St. Marks through crowds silent as the grave, she had to admit it was an eerie experience.

"The crowd's only feeling," wrote the English Consul-General, "was one of curiosity to see the Empress, whose reputation for marvellous beauty has naturally penetrated even to this place."

Without even the acts of mercy which changed the whole of Austrian policy in Venice, Elizabeth's beauty and charm began to have effect. The longer they stayed the warmer the attitude of the population became. Finally, when the Empress appeared alone there were cheers and applause.

It was not surprising that she was admired. She had grown almost breathtakingly beautiful since the birth of her children. Her glowing auburn hair reached below her knees and her lovely face had something spiritual and yet radiant about it which made the susceptible Venetians cry out:—

"Bellissima donna! Bellissima! Bellissima!"

The fact that his young wife had in some strange way a power over his people, which neither the presence of his troops nor the prestige of his relatives and Ministers could produce, amazed the Emperor.

"Your charm has done more to win over these people than all my soldiers with bayonets and cannon could possibly effect," he confessed to her one evening.

Elizabeth smiled with genuine pleasure at one of the first compliments about her usefulness that he had ever paid her.

"The more I learn about the Empire from all those lessons that your mother insists I have," she replied, "the more it seems to me is it necessary that we should try friendship instead of those bayonets."

Franz Joseph made no reply. The whole concept of rule in which he had been brought up was based on force. The terrible happenings which tolerance and regard for freedom could bring about were to be seen in almost every country in Europe. He himself had grown up in an atmosphere of revolution which had almost brought the great Hapsburg line to its knees.

Entirely due to Elizabeth on December 3rd, 1856, Venice awoke to the dawn of a new era. The iron grip was relaxed, the insults to the nobles were gone, so were the bullying soldiers with fixed bayonets who forced public audiences to attention when the Austrian National Anthem was played.

It was Elizabeth who had said to Franz Joseph: "The hatred of these people here can hardly bear intensifying. For God's sake do something about it."

"It is too late now!" he replied. "How can I right so many wrongs?"

Elizabeth had told him she was not concerned with politics but with a decent and humane treatment of an oppressed people. "Amnesty," she said, "must be granted, prisons opened, property restored."

The populous, warm-hearted and grateful city went wild. "*Cara Elizabetta*—beloved Elizabeth!" was the cry of all Venice.

The Countess Esterhazy wrote distraught letters to Vienna. It was all very unconventional and damaging to the future of absolutism! The Archduchess read the report with the utmost misgivings. Elizabeth must be stopped.

From Venice the Imperial couple went to Milan. Here things were as bad, if not worse, than in Venice. They were received in complete silence, in a city dressed in mourning. The Governors of the City, in the name of Austria, had committed the most flagrant crimes.

At the Castello a veritable museum of Austrian infamy had been assembled for the Emperor's inspection. He was shown garrote, rack, thumbscrew and cudgel with which the rebellious natures were brought to heel.

A few months before, on Franz Joseph's birthday, two women described in the Austrian text as *Dirnen* (trollops) but in the Italian version as *donne dell teatro* (actresses) had sung a scurrilous ballad, which cast aspersions upon the Hapsburgs, in the Milanese cabarets.

For this they had been imprisoned and sentenced to corporal punishment. Clad only in linen chemises they had been flogged (thirty blows each) after which their wounds were bathed in vinegar to prevent infection.

No wonder Milan was sullen! The authorities had ordered all aristocratic subscribers to the famous La Scala to occupy their seats under a severe fine for disobedience. The seats were full, but with the servants of the *nobili*.

Elizabeth pleaded with Franz Joseph to show mercy. He dismissed the Governors; a general pardon was granted to all political prisoners, and each morning official lists were published announcing restoration of property.

Like magic the black gloves and the other emblems of mourning disappeared. People attended the Court functions. The Royal couple was cheered in the streets, and finally, one week after their ignominious entry into Milan, the town's nobles and prominent citizens entertained them.

A gala performance took place at La Scala; the Emperor and Empress appeared in their box and the whole auditorium rose to applaud them. Once again Elizabeth had triumphed.

Countess Esterhazy was not the only person writing letters from Italy about Elizabeth. Prince Alexander of Hesse, brother of the Tzarina (wife of Alexander II) wrote to his sister: "She is glorious, and unlike anyone I have ever seen."

His young daughter Marie recalled in later life her first vision of Elizabeth:

"Of queenly beauty, her rich russet hair was braided in coils which fell below her shoulders. . . . I stared at her in a trance as though she were some marvellous apparition. When she noticed me she smiled and two dimples appeared at the corners of her mouth."

The Archduchess Sophie was, however, writing long letters and imploring her son to come home. She was desperately worried about Elizabeth's influence over him. She felt it definitely meant a diminution of her own power. As usual, Franz Joseph gave in to her demands. He and Elizabeth left for Vienna.

Elizabeth was, in fact, glad to be home. She was wild with

joy at seeing her babies again, but hurt to find they had grown used to their grandmother and half forgotten her.

The Archduchess, in the meantime, had been thinking to good effect. One day Elizabeth found on her writing table an odd-looking pamphlet. It was open and on one page certain passages were underlined. She read them.

". . . The natural destiny of a Queen is to give an heir to the throne; and the King who says to his wife, Madame, We took you to give Us sons and not advice; and thus puts the ambitious creature in her place, has taught a lesson to all Queens in the World . . . If the Queen bears no sons, she is merely a foreigner in the State, and a very dangerous foreigner too. For she can never be looked on kindly here and must always expect to be sent back whence she came."

Elizabeth felt suddenly sick. Who could have done this thing? Who wrote these words? Who underlined them? She recognised the pamphlet as one which had been printed against Marie Antoinette.

The malice behind these sentences was indeed redolent of another century. But human emotions do not change, and Elizabeth knew that hatred against herself was as virulent as that directed against the unhappy French Queen.

Wounded, but with her head held high, Elizabeth did not forget her resolve to play the rôle of Empress in the only way she knew. On her birthday that year the Hungarians sent a deputation to offer her their felicitations and to beg her to visit Hungary as soon as possible.

The gesture was diplomatically a clever one. The studied insolence of ignoring the Emperor completely in their message could not be taken by the Imperial Government as a deliberate affront because the Hungarians had selected the Empress's birthday as the reason for this message. The invitation, at the same time, made it virtually essential for a State Visit to be made by the Royal couple for it was obviously unlikely that the Empress could go alone.

Elizabeth delightedly told her husband how pleased she had been with the message over dinner at the Hofburg held in celebration of her birthday that evening. The Emperor scowled with annoyance.

"I know that you were a success with the Italians," he observed, "but they are a sunny and basically easy-going people. Unless malcontents arouse their anger they would rather laugh and cheer than use the sword of the assassin. But the Hungarians,"—he shivered visibly—"they are fiends who store hatred in their hearts for generations."

He reminded her of what she already knew: that when he had made visits to Hungary surrounded by strong detachments of troops the streets had either been deserted or, in those areas where they had been forced to make a show of loyalty, the people had stood on each side of the processional route sullen and passive, their smouldering hatred an almost tangible thing in the air.

The disturbances, which had resulted in the abdication of his uncle and his own ascendancy of the throne, had been most serious in Hungary of all the dominions of the Empire.

The trouble burst out again immediately after the Coronation, and unfortunately the young Emperor had been compelled by his Ministers to commit an unforgivable sin against the Hungarians. He made a formal appeal to Russia for military help to quell the revolt, and Czar Nicholas I sent 100,000 troops.

They were mostly Cossacks, who rampaged across Hungary and smashed all resistance with the most frightful carnage and cruelty, acting, of course, in the name of Franz Joseph.

In vain did the few moderate elements in the country point out that the shameful terms enforced on the Hungarians —they capitulated at Vilagos in May, 1849—were not imposed by a callow and ignorant boy of eighteen in Vienna but by the Czar of Russia. To every Hungarian the Hapsburg Emperor became the symbol of brutal force, the instigator of the unjust execution of thirteen Hungarian Generals, and of their national hero, Batthyany.

All over the country, when Franz Joseph had made his

subsequent visits, he had seen drawn on walls and even etched by hot iron in the wooden posts of town gates and bridges, a snake bearing the Imperial monogram.

This was the emblem of hate devised by the widow of Batthyany at her husband's graveside, when she called aloud to her people to regard their King as if he was a snake. Moreover, Franz Joseph was aware of the formal curse which, secretly printed, could be found in homes all over Hungary. It had been declaimed by the mother of one of the executed Generals and ran:

"May heaven and hell destroy Franz Joseph's happiness. May his family perish root and branch from the earth. May he himself be made to suffer through those persons whom he loves the most. May his life be dedicated to destruction and his children go down in misery to their graves."

Both the Government and the Emperor himself were in a quandary over this question of a visit to Hungary. All the attempts to placate the Hungarians by raising the country to the level of Austria through such means as abolition of tariff barriers, identity of the civil service, common laws and the same taxes, plus the privilege of remaining an autonomous state with the Emperor bearing the separate title of King of Hungary, would become empty symbols unless the Royal couple visited the sister nation.

Elizabeth, who had by this time quite a number of discreet friends among the younger Ministers and Court officials, was vigorously appraised as to the position. The information made her all the more eager to go.

Without any doubt this was a psychological reaction, for she had identified the prevalence of ill will towards Hungary in the Government and Court circles of Vienna with the dislike those same people had for herself. Moreover, as her political outlook was forming she was becoming a genuine Liberal—and not merely because this attitude was in direct opposition to the views of her hated mother-in-law.

She had known the joys of freedom and the misery which resulted when it was curtailed. She sympathised with a vast nation whose recent history was such a close parallel to her own life.

So determined was she to further her plans that as soon as the Christmas and New Year festivities were over she spent hours every day learning Hungarian. The absence of the Empress from the usual social occasions in the Hofburg was duly noted by Archduchess Sophie and she caused enquiries to be made to discover what her daughter-in-law was up to.

The news of these interminable lessons in Hungarian disturbed the old woman profoundly and although since the quarrel over the care of the children both women had avoided one another as much as was possible, the Archduchess now went to the Imperial suite and said without preamble:

"I am informed that you are studying Hungarian, presumably in pursuance of this ridiculous plan to visit Hungary."

"You forget, Madame Mère," Elizabeth said sweetly, "that I personally replied to the invitation contained in the birthday greetings to me that I would visit Hungary at no distant date. It would have been rude to have rejected their invitation and surely, as you so constantly have told me, it is my duty as Queen to carry out such a Queenly duty."

"There is no need for sarcasm," the Archduchess retorted angrily. "Please be frank enough to tell me your real reason for your interest in that nation of savages."

"The Magyars breed the finest horses in the world," Elizabeth replied smilingly. "Where there are fine horses there are fine people. I want to see both."

She had to raise her voice a little for the last few words, for Sophie had already turned to hide her fury and was walking as majestically as her temper permitted from the room.

From that moment Elizabeth developed an insatiable passion for goulash and paprika, Tokay and gypsy violins. She also went on with her lessons and Dr. Max Falk, one of her teachers, was enthusiastic over her diligence. One morning she handed him her translation and said:

"I was engaged the whole of yesterday with receptions, and in the evening there was a State concert, after which I was so tired that I went to bed. Then I suddenly remembered that I had not written my Hungarian composition, so I tore a leaf out of an almanac on the table by my bed and translated a tale. Please excuse it for being in pencil."

It was not until May, 1857, that most unwillingly the Emperor set out with Elizabeth on a State visit to Budapest.

Their departure was also delayed by yet another domestic battle. Elizabeth wanted to take her children with her as far as Budapest so that she could enjoy having them with her and without the Archduchess. Sophie, of course, opposed this, but for once Elizabeth persuaded Franz Joseph to let her have her own way.

To clear the air for their visit a general amnesty was declared for political prisoners. Although this was a cautious attempt by the Imperial Government to ease tension and make the risk of incidents less likely, it was universally believed by the Hungarian people that the gesture was a personal one from the Empress herself.

The journey from the border as far as Budapest was an incongruous sight. Police and troops had been transported to the route in their tens of thousands. In the rural areas cavalry trotted up and down on both sides of the road, and in the towns the guard stood shoulder to shoulder.

Behind these strategic and defensive forces the excited Hungarians did their best to catch a glimpse of their Queen and give her a cheer. The only missiles that were thrown were spring flowers, and the people of Budapest had even done their best to hide the burned and gutted buildings, relics of the Revolution, with garlands and flags.

It was not lost on Elizabeth that the banners which fluttered over Budapest in the gentle breezes of a lovely May afternoon were either the colours of Hungary or the blue and white emblem of Bavaria. Only on Government

Elizabeth, Empress of Austria. The famous 'stars in her hair' portrait by
Winterhalter of Elizabeth as a young Empress

Elizabeth's favourite portrait. In the background is Possenhofen Castle

buildings and the houses of Austrians sent to live in the city could there be seen the yellow and black flag of Imperial Austria.

The Royal couple stayed that night at the Konigsburg, where a few of the remaining habitable rooms out of the hundred and more which had been reduced to rubble in the Revolution had been prepared for them.

With typical tactlessness Franz Joseph wore the uniform of an Austrian Field Marshal. The nobility refused to take any part in the illumination of the town, and the great ball given at the Deutsches Theatre was filled only with officials and business men.

However, at a performance of the festival opera, "*Erzsébet*", the nobles appeared in the full splendour of their national costumes, and the ladies of the aristocracy wore their magnificent jewels.

Elizabeth felt her soul reach out towards these proud and steadfast people who combined loyalty with character. She felt how different in personality they were to the aristocrats at the Austrian Court whose deference to the power of the throne had become the subservience of lackeys.

After ten days in Budapest Franz Joseph agreed to extend the tour so that virtually the whole country could be visited. Unfortunately on the day they were to start, Gisela suddenly fell sick. She recovered rapidly but six days later the same symptoms appeared in little Sophie.

The elder of Elizabeth's daughters had continued to be a weakly child. It was now obvious that she was desperately ill with a fever and was wasting away.

"The little thing cries and screams incessantly in the most heartrending way," Franz Joseph wrote to his mother.

There were signs of improvement and Elizabeth felt she must start the postponed tour. The whole country was in a state of expectation and large sums of money had already been expended. The people must not be disappointed.

They started for the interior. Elizabeth would have thoroughly enjoyed the sight of such magnificent horses and handsome people if she had not been so anxious about her sick child.

When they reached Debreczin, after a journey of five days, they received a telegram from Dr. Seeburgher, who had been appointed by the Archduchess, telling them to return at once. The child was worse. They broke off their tour and returned to Budapest by the shortest route.

They found Sophie was sinking. She was very weak and her eyes were already dim. For eleven hours Elizabeth did not leave the child's bedside, while the doctors stood by helplessly.

At half past nine at night, weeping bitterly, Elizabeth realised that her firstborn was no longer breathing.

"Our little one is an Angel in Heaven," Franz Joseph telegraphed the Archduchess. "We are crushed—Sisi is full of resignation to the will of the Lord."

This was untrue. Elizabeth was prostrated with misery, blaming herself bitterly for having brought the children to Hungary against the advice of the Archduchess.

Franz Joseph also felt the loss acutely, but as always he was tongue-tied in an emotional crisis of this nature and he left his wife in lonely despair. Her reaction, quite understandable in the circumstances, was that her husband did not really care that his daughter had died because he wished only for sons.

She came as near to hating Franz Joseph in those hours following her bereavement as she ever did in her whole life. In contrast, the highly emotional Hungarians forgot whatever rules of etiquette they had ever known and from menial servant to exalted official they came to her, weeping, and poured out their sympathy.

She was grateful for their unaffected and genuine desire to help her and the spontaneity of their tenderness strengthened still further her love for Hungary and its people.

Back in Vienna they were greeted by the Archduchess with an unprecedented outburst of bitterness.

"God cursed your marriage," she cried at the unhappy

pair. "You, Franz, would marry against my wishes—and you, Elizabeth, you neglect both your church and your duty as an Empress. *Der Himmel straft* (the heavens punish)."

Elizabeth did not reply.

During the funeral she stood in the private chapel of the Palace and watched the little white coffin pass to its resting place without any outward sign of emotion. She held herself like a statue and her face was as pale as alabaster.

Although she controlled her tears, her voice, and even the trembling of her lips so that none could know her misery and agony of mind, she was suffering far more than from the bereavement of her firstborn child.

She had a terrifying feeling that, after all, the hard-eyed critics who had surrounded her ever since her wedding day were right—she was unfit to be an Empress because she could not bear male children! What was more she could not even bear healthy girl children.

When the funeral was over Elizabeth withdrew entirely into herself—walking and riding alone. She was only nineteen, but she felt that her life was finished; she had no interest left in anything. This condition was aggravated by the ceaseless hatred and antagonism of the Archduchess, who plotted against her all the time.

The weeks went by with the Emperor immersed in work and deliberately avoiding any intimacy with her. The final blow came when she overheard a couple of her ladies-in-waiting talking about the wedding of the Emperor's brother Maximilian to Princess Charlotte of Belgium.

Elizabeth liked Maximilian, who, as a younger brother, had been regarded as of no importance by his mother and had suffered much of the contemptuous neglect which Elizabeth herself had come to know so well. She knew also that her brother-in-law was desperately lonely as well as miserable because of the lack of anything for him to do.

When, shortly before the visit to Hungary, she had heard of Maximilian's engagement during a visit to the Belgium Royal family in Brussels, in her innocence she had regarded it as a genuine love match. But now from the gossiping women in her dressing room, who were unaware that she was awake, she learned the truth.

The Archduchess Sophie, immediately after the birth of Elizabeth's second daughter, had taken steps to ensure the continuance of the Hapsburg dynasty and had cast around Europe for a suitable young woman through whom the Emperor's younger brother could father a son and heir to the throne.

The almost indecent haste of this measure was not lost on Elizabeth and the insinuation that she would never bear a son brought a stabbing misery to her heart. She did not often cry through despair—indeed, it was said in later years that the Empress had been born without tear ducts—but this morning she turned her face to the pillow and wept until the silk was saturated.

The marriage of Maximilian and Charlotte took place on July 27th, 1857. The couple were promptly bundled off to Miramare near Trieste and more or less instructed by the Archduchess to remain there until Charlotte had conceived. But summer turned to autumn and autumn to winter—and still there was no news of a happy reward for Sophie's careful plotting to provide an heir to the throne.

Elizabeth, who was never spiteful, could not help but feel a little glad, and she did everything she could to revive some evidence of physical affection in her husband.

He did not unbend, however, to treat her as more than an official consort until the anniversary of her birthday came round. It was then that she frankly told him when he enquired what gift she would like that there was no article of jewellery, no new horse, no piece of furniture that she wanted.

"The loveliest gift that I could imagine," she whispered, "would be a glimpse of the lover I knew at Ischl that summer's afternoon four years ago—or the husband who told me what I meant to him when he welcomed me to his capital."

The frankness and sincerity of her words disturbed Franz Joseph profoundly. For a time at least all the carping criticism of his mother was forgotten. He also felt remorse about the affair he was having with a certain Countess, and he prayed that Elizabeth knew nothing of it—which, in fact, she didn't.

The emotional reconciliation between the two, neither the first nor the last that they would have, resulted in a starry-eyed Elizabeth being able to tell her husband towards the end of January that she was again expecting a child.

Elizabeth's third pregnancy became of vast importance as the months passed, for doctors sent to examine Princess Charlotte had pronounced her infertile, a fact which her husband had suspected from the first. The Archduchess Sophie, feeling herself thwarted on every side, did her best to atone for the past. In fact, as if some kindness and care might ensure the masculinity of the coming child, she could hardly do enough for her daughter-in-law.

Unfortunately the reason for her change of attitude was only too obvious, and there were times when Elizabeth could not stand such hypocrisy, and lost her temper, upsetting herself so much that it was feared that she might have a miscarriage.

Petulantly, the now ageing Archduchess decided that she would have to be more discreet, and for the final months of the pregnancy during the summer she left Elizabeth alone. She had informants in the household, of course, and was greatly relieved to learn that on this occasion Elizabeth herself was so anxious about the baby that she made no attempt to go riding. The walking exercise she took was far more gentle than during her previous pregnancies.

Elizabeth was, in fact, desperately anxious. In the past she had always laughed at superstition. Now she began to look for signs and omens. As soon as people knew the Empress was *enceinte* advice poured in from all corners of the Empire.

Elizabeth inspected amulets, magic phials, scarabs and

lucky charms. For the sake of producing a boy she was prepared to try anything. Then her sense of humour asserted itself and she threw the whole hocus-pocus out of the window.

She might well have felt anxious about the medical attention which she was to have. Dr. Seeburgher, who was appointed by the Archduchess, was a prejudiced and ignorant man who disliked the young Empress.

Once a swelling appeared at Elizabeth's wrist and Dr. Seeburgher's remedy was to place two silver coins on it and bandage them to the wrist with a tight bandage. This, he announced cheerfully, would discourage further swelling.

Elizabeth murmured under her breath: "His idiocy is almost fascinating!"

When the hand, through lack of circulation, turned blue Elizabeth removed the bandage. Dr. Seeburgher, needless to say, disapproved of Elizabeth's whole mode of life. The fact that she loathed heavy food was in his eyes almost a crime.

Her fondness of cold milk was an eccentricity—no one drank raw milk! Once, when meeting the chief of Police, Dr. Seeburgher poured out a flood of complaints and censure about the Empress.

"She is unfit for her position both as an Empress and a wife," he raged.

Towards the end of August the doctors said that the birth was imminent, and the whole Empire waited expectantly for news. It was with reason thought that while two girls in succession might be a coincidence a third would virtually prove that Elizabeth was incapable of bearing a male child.

Elizabeth herself felt very confident that there was a son in her womb. Her mother had arrived from Possenhofen and had brought with her an old midwife who had not only helped to bring most of Ludovica's own children into the world but also those on the ducal estate. She was deeply versed in all the folk-lore about birth. On her arrival she took one look at the Empress's swollen body and pronounced

without fear of denial that the baby would be a boy. Elizabeth had implicit faith in the old woman's knowledge, and
she said happily to her mother:

"Before tonight you will have a Crown Prince in your
arms."

"If God wills," Ludovica replied nervously.

On August 21st the Archduchess, who was at Laxenburg,
received a telegram saying:

"Her Imperial Majesty is in labour."

She at once left for the Schönbrunn.

At her previous confinements Elizabeth had hardly
uttered a sound, but at 10 o'clock that night she was in such
agony that she gave a heartrending shriek. It was not until
a quarter to eleven that she was delivered.

"Is it a son?" she asked anxiously in a whisper.

"The midwife does not know yet," Franz Joseph replied,
fearing that the sudden joy might prove dangerous.

"Of course! It must be another girl," Elizabeth murmured
piteously.

"What if it were a boy?" the Emperor enquired.

Elizabeth's lovely, exhausted face lit up, but she would
not be convinced until she had seen her son for herself.

In Vienna the guns began to fire a salute. The people of
the city paused and counted the explosions. On and on they
went until one hundred and one rounds had been fired. The
Empire had its heir to the throne. The bells of the churches
in the City and in the surrounding villages were carrying on
with the good tidings when the Emperor tip-toed into the
bedroom and looked fondly at his son lying in his cradle.

His kiss for his wife was a perfunctory one on her forehead.
He hardly took time to ask her how she was feeling before
he returned to the cradle, and, motioning to his adjutant to
step forward, took from him the sash and medallion of the
Order of the Golden Fleece. He laid them on the cradle
coverlet and then with rigid formality stepped back a pace
and saluted the sleeping child.

Elizabeth could not help smiling. In her happiness and

contentment she was ready to accept that the pride and joy of her husband was in the existence of a Prince whose name would be acceptable to the Hapsburgs. His lack of interest in her was, for the moment, comparatively of little importance.

Elizabeth's little son was a beautiful child but small and delicate. On the occasion of the birth of her daughters there had been merely formal messages of congratulation, but the arrival of a son brought dozens of visitors in person to her room to offer their congratulations. All this regard made Elizabeth very happy.

"Nobody has seemed to need me until now," she confided to her old nurse, who, at Ludovica's behest, had insisted on remaining as personal attendant to the young mother.

"Not even my little Gisela who is kept away from me seems to want me," she went on. "But I will never allow my boy to leave me to grow up among strangers; he must cling to me and we will make each other happy."

It was a reasonable expectation but Elizabeth was too optimistic. The first clash came when arrangements were put in hand for the baptism of the baby. Elizabeth told her husband that it would make her very happy if the child were named Maximilian after her father. Franz Joseph looked away uneasily and eventually replied:

"I am afraid that will not be appropriate for the heir to the throne. Mother has already discussed this matter with me and I agree with her that we should mark this new era in the family's history by naming my son Rudolph."

Elizabeth noticed that he described the child as his and she must have expected the name to be chosen by her mother-in-law. Yet in a way she could make no complaint. To call their son Rudolph was indirectly a great honour for it had been the name of the Founder of the House of Hapsburg, Count Rudolph. He had lived in Brugg, Switzerland, before the family's fortunes were founded with his title of Archduke of Austria and Emperor of Germany in the year 1273.

Just as Elizabeth was thwarted in naming her baby so her

hopes that she could mother him were dashed by the action of her mother-in-law. A fortnight passed before the Archduchess Sophie got her way and in fairness to Franz Joseph it must be admitted that the time was spent in argument and some mild protests regarding his mother's plans.

"The heir apparent to the greatest Empire in the world cannot be brought up by a chit of a girl who does not even know enough to behave herself properly," was Sophie's unshakable verdict. "You know yourself the onerous nature of your duties and these in a matter of a few years will at least in part be shared by your son. For the child's own good he must be taken away from his silly young mother."

Franz Joseph argued no more. It was perhaps partly because he was intimidated by his mother but undoubtedly another reason was that he largely agreed with what she said.

The Archduchess, noting from his silence that she had won, went immediately to Elizabeth's apartments and informed her harshly that rooms had been set aside in a distant part of the palace, with a resident doctor close at hand and a staff of skilled nurses, where the Crown Prince would be taken immediately.

"The child is delicate and will require the most careful attention if he is to survive," she went on, attempting to frighten Elizabeth.

"In that case he could not have better care than that which is provided by his mother," Elizabeth retorted. "He is my child and the decisions for his upbringing must be mine."

"Rudolph is not just your child," Sophie snapped. "He is the child of the Empire and as such whatever is done for him is of public importance and is not the private concern of you, me, or indeed of any other individual."

Elizabeth also had a surfeit of milk, but it was deemed improper for Royal mothers to nurse their children. Although she longed to feed Rudolph, and even pleaded with her mother-in-law that she should do so, the Archduchess would not hear of such a revolutionary idea.

While the baby suffered complications because the wet

nurses did not suit him, and grew weaker after each change, Elizabeth lay miserable and defeated.

This told severely on her health and she lost her will to fight. So much so that she even pleaded with her mother-in-law to be allowed to see her child for at least a few hours a day.

Brutally the Archduchess suggested that she should find other interests.

"You are a good looking young woman," she said. "You have a position any other woman in the world would envy and a husband who is remarkably tolerant, no matter what you do. It is time that you got out of this morbid and sentimental mood. Why don't you try to enjoy yourself?"

The thinly veiled suggestion that Elizabeth should find amusement in some sort of amorous intrigue indicated how strongly her mother-in-law desired to destroy whatever bonds of affection still remained between Franz Joseph and his wife.

If Sophie had been frank with herself she would have admitted that one of the many things she disliked about her daughter-in-law was her purity. It contrasted invidiously with the steadily increasing number of infidelities on the part of the Emperor, and she hated to think that there was any facet of Elizabeth's character which was better than those of her son.

Two years earlier the young Empress might not have understood the innuendo, but she had learned much in the bitter school of experience since then. The suggestion that she should find herself a lover disgusted her.

In a few short years of marriage, disillusionment had almost destroyed her natural capacity for love; in any event her feminine fastidiousness made the thought of a tawdry affair simply for vanity and physical satisfaction anathema to her.

She was too unwell to make any angry retort and she let her mother-in-law go, with the latter firmly believing that she had sown the seeds of an idea which would effectively weaken the Empress's position still further.

The Archduchess was, however, annoyed when Elizabeth

was up and about again attending Court functions, to see
there was no sign whatever of her showing any interest in
the male guests discreetly placed next to her. As this scheme
had failed, the Archduchess resorted to gossip and slander
in order to arouse suspicions in the Emperor's mind.

There was a young Count, a great noble and one of the
handsomest and most dashing officers of the Emperor's
bodyguard, who genuinely and quite understandably
became infatuated with the Empress.

One night, clad in swirling lace with great emeralds, her
favourite jewels encircling her white neck and gleaming in
her scented hair, she was walking along the rose-covered
marble terrace and talking to the Count in that soft, melod-
ious voice which captivated anyone who listened to her.

They reached a shadowy corner when the Count, losing
all control of his feelings, threw himself at Elizabeth's feet
and poured out his love, his whole body shaken with the
fierce emotion from which he was suffering.

The young Count's infatuation had been carefully noted
by the Archduchess and she watched the couple like a hawk.
When she saw them going out on the terrace she got hold of
one of the cronies of the Emperor, and asked him to find
the Count immediately because she wished to discuss some
matter concerning a parade.

The courtier searched everywhere and, as Sophie hoped,
duly surprised the Count on his knees in front of an embarrassed Elizabeth. He said nothing to the Archduchess, but
the next morning reported the matter to the Emperor.
Within twenty-four hours the Count had been banished to
his estates in the South of Hungary, and for many years he
was kept there at the Emperor's command.

Franz Joseph never taxed Elizabeth with the matter, for
indeed he barely saw her in private at this time. The story
of the Emperor's suspicions however soon came back to his
wife's ears, for the tittle-tattle of the Court existed solely on
this juicy piece of gossip for days on end.

The most trivial of incidents were exploited by the

Archduchess to destroy Elizabeth's reputation in the Court and her popularity with the people. One night, after a Court ball, as she emerged from the main doors of the Rittersaal the wintry wind caught her long train and it became entangled round the feet of the Papal Nuncio who was standing there in readiness to bow to her as she passed.

Elizabeth apologised and quickly had removed the train from the Vatican dignitary's legs. The embarrassment to both had been of the slightest, but by the following morning all Vienna was hearing the Archduchess's version of the affair which was described as "a sudden clash and quicker separation between Church and State."

This witticism was far more effective than it might sound today because the Empire was rushing headlong into political crisis. On one side were the enlightened and modern politicians who had more or less adopted the young Empress as their figurehead. She really did nothing to further their viewpoint, beyond the fact that she had very little time for ostentatious religious practices and still less for the priest who indulged in political activities.

On the other side was the powerful faction around Madame Mère, who herself was almost completely in the hands of the insidiously powerful Jesuits. Sophie had a fixation about recreating the ancient Holy Roman Empire in which the Church would be predominant and the Emperor, to all intents and purposes, the High Priest.

By stressing the incident with the train on the steps as a symbol of the division in the country the Archduchess struck a powerful blow on behalf of her faction in the minds of the, for the most part, devout Catholic population of the Empire. Encouragement in the belief that the Archduchess's faction was right was all the more necessary, because the political situation was leading the country straight to war.

Franz Joseph was by now little more than the tool of his mother's clique. When, in Paris on New Year's Day 1859, Napoleon III expressed his regret to the Austrian Ambassador that the hitherto friendly relations between France and

the Austrian Empire seemed to be deteriorating, the Archduchess was within a couple of days ensconced with her son
and demanding that he declare war.

The area of dispute was Sardinia. After considerable sabre
rattling on both sides the Emperor signed the declaration of
war on April 27th, and within a few hours a hundred
thousand Austrian troops crossed the border marked by the
River Ticino.

The Sardinians, caught unawares, made a strategic retreat
in order to give their French allies time to come to their
rescue. As soon as Napoleon's troops arrived the Austrians
suffered overwhelming defeat.

Immediately on hearing the news, Franz Joseph left for
the front and assumed the command of the army. When he
told Elizabeth of his intentions she burst into tears.

"For my sake and the children's," she pleaded, "think of
yourself too, and not only of your work and war."

She took leave of him at the station, and a few days
later appeared unexpectedly at the Church of Our Lord at
Maria-Lanzendorf, where there was a famous statue of
the Virgin, and prayed that her husband's life might be
spared.

Franz Joseph wrote to her frequently, and absence from
home seemed to revive his affection.

"My dearest Angel Sisi," he wrote on arriving at Verona
on May 31st, 1859, "I am profiting by the first moments
after getting up to tell you once again how much I love you
and how I long for you and the dear children."*

Elizabeth was very melancholy and shut herself up
entirely, if only that she might see less of her mother-in-law.
She went out riding from early to late and appeared at no
social functions. She also began to practise jumping. The
Archduchess and her cronies, of course, made the most
of this and talked themselves hoarse about her strange
behaviour.

Elizabeth found some consolation in writing long letters

* This letter, and others quoted, are now at Schloss Wallsee.

to her husband, and she begged him to let her join him. But he replied:

"For the present, unfortunately, I cannot comply with your wish, though I should love to beyond words. I beseech you, my angel, if you love me, do not grieve so much."

His mother had been able to influence the Emperor to blunder into war but she could not instruct him how to fight one successfully. Failure after failure occurred. Finally in June at the Battle of Solferino the Imperial armies were smashed to a pulp. In the blazing sun two Emperors watched their legions in desperate combat. Seated on his horse Napoleon III set up a record by smoking five dozen cigarettes while he was heard mumbling:

"Those poor people—oh those poor boys! What a dreadful thing is war!"

Franz Joseph had the horror of seeing his beautiful white Lancers gallop briskly into a hail of bullets. It was a Hapsburg's first encounter with smoke and burning horseflesh instead of the glorious tradition of single combat. The polished blades of an out-of-date, pre-Metternich Austria fell to the ground unused.

"Now I know," Franz Joseph wrote pathetically, "what it feels like to be a beaten General."

Napoleon declared an Armistice and invited Franz Joseph to Villafranca. They spoke of their children.

"My son, Loulou," Napoleon said proudly of the Prince Imperial, "is three. And so clever!"

"My Rudolph," replied Franz Joseph, "is about a year old."

There was a pause—

"About the peace," Napoleon murmured, "it will cost Austria something!"

"What will it cost?" the Emperor of Austria inquired.

"La Lombardie!"

Franz Joseph was pale beneath his tan.

"That is my most beautiful province!" he said brokenly.

Lombardy was lost for ever, and the disaster of the war

caused serious economic and political damage but even more severe injury to the Empire's prestige. And it was, of course, almost entirely the fault of the Archduchess.

Sophie had to fight hard to retain her influence but her son was so completely under her domination that when a few resignations had taken place she emerged as powerful as ever.

At the time of his defeat, while he was in despair, Elizabeth had fervently hoped that Franz Joseph would allow her to go to him, but he persistently refused. For weeks he was away in Northern Italy with his armies and there was no message from him. She felt lonely and helpless, and did her best to assuage her unhappiness by visiting hospitals in Vienna, which during the spring and early summer were crammed with thousands of wounded.

She overworked herself, partly because of her feeling of pity for the men for whom medical attention was hopelessly inadequate and also to stifle, by exhausting herself physically, the unhappiness in her heart.

"Do you love me still?" she wrote to Franz Joseph. "If you do not, then whatever else happens I shall not care."

Elizabeth was almost in despair when her husband still did not return. She imagined him in a thousand dangers.

When Franz Joseph did come back to the capital after the signing of an Armistice he was appalled by the physical change in his wife. He said nothing to her about it but she had noted his start of shocked surprise and afterwards she took good care to disguise her pallor by the careful use of cosmetics.

She also remembered that in one letter in which he had cautioned her against fatigue and loss of weight, he had written: "I hate thin women."

She began to wear her lovely hair long so that it hid the bones of her shoulders, which were by now clearly to be seen. Her horse riding activities in the morning became shorter and shorter because they tired her out so quickly. Finally she had to confess to her doctors that she felt ill.

They could discover no organic reason for her loss of weight, anaemia, and general lassitude, so fell back on the usual solution of those days and hinted that she must be suffering from incipient consumption.

They could not have known in the state of medical knowledge at that time that the symptoms of her illness lay far deeper than her lungs. She was in urgent need of psychiatric treatment to dispel the awful sense of inferiority which everyone around her, led by the Archduchess, was scheming to increase by all the devilish means at their disposal.

No one thought for a moment that three confinements in four years, the anxieties of war, or the antipathy between herself and Sophie could be the cause of her illness.

Meanwhile, as the wounds of 1859 began to heal, the Archduchess was fighting a losing battle against new and revolutionary innovations. She was violently against the idea of a Central Parliament, but Franz Joseph, while forced to concede, wrote to her:

"We are going to have a little parliamentary life, it is true, but the power remains in my hands."

Sophie, having won back her old supremacy over her son, was not prepared to tolerate any independence of thought or action on the part of his wife. The clashes between her and Elizabeth over the Crown Prince and every other matter grew more and more frequent, each one taking the toll of the younger woman's nervous strength.

Elizabeth reproached Franz Joseph for not taking her part, but he was torn between his mother, to whom he owed everything, and a wife who, beautiful as he thought her, he believed to be wild and erratic. He had also resumed his love affairs with various ladies of the Court. And there was one very unpalatable adventure during a hunting expedition which any wife would have found hard to forgive.

When Elizabeth heard about this she completely lost her balance. The interminable war with her mother-in-law had worn her down; the Court functions, intrigues and stiff formalities seemed unbearable and she saw enemies on every side. That Franz Joseph should so besmirch and befoul her love for him made her long to die so that she need think of it no longer.

Like an automaton she dragged out her life until in the autumn of 1860 came a further blow. Her brother, Leopold, had announced to the world that he was renouncing all rights to the family title and all his inheritances in order to marry an actress, Henrietta Mendel.

The fact that his bride earned her living in entertainment was bad enough, but on top of that she was a Jewess. There were many people in the anti-semitic court of the Hapsburgs who moved away from their Empress after she had attained this relationship with a Jewess as if she were suffering from a contagious disease.

It was the gentle, Jewish doctor whom Elizabeth had come to respect and love after his talk with her when she was expecting her first child, to whom she confided all her troubles. He told her that he knew only too well the cruel and relentless loathing of the Hapsburgs for "the children of God", and he added:

"I have long admired you, your Imperial Majesty, for your brave and courageous fight against the injustice that you see around you. But now, because your body is weaker than your resolution, I beg you to accept that discretion is a wiser course. Retreat so that you may fight another day. I advise you to get away to the peace and sunshine."

Elizabeth accepted the idea with relief, and Franz Joseph, realising at last that she was at breaking point, suggested Meran or some other sunny place on the Adriatic.

"No! No!" Elizabeth cried, "I must go far, far away—right out of the country."

"What about Madeira?" the doctor asked.

"Yes, Madeira. I will go to Madeira!"

For the moment, the remote island seemed to Elizabeth as far away and as desirable as paradise. What was more, much to her surprise, she found she did not mind leaving Franz Joseph. She did not even mind thinking of how he would behave when she was no longer there.

He had killed her love for him.

SEVEN

1860-1862

THE departure of Elizabeth to Madeira was as secretive as it was feasible for her mother-in-law to make it. On the pretext of disturbing a sick woman as little as possible, all formalities were cut to a minimum and Elizabeth travelled from Vienna to Trieste virtually as a private person.

The persons accompanying her had been carefully selected by Court officials. Most of them were, to all intents and purposes, paid spies. There were, however, some of the personal attendants whom Elizabeth was determined to have in her party.

One of these, her secretary, Count Imri Hunyadi, a Hungarian Officer, would have been forbidden to go if Elizabeth had not been clever enough to ensure that he did not join her party before they reached Trieste.

He was tall, slender and handsome, a Magyar of noble birth. What was more important to Elizabeth, he had the deep, sensitive, poetical streak of his countrymen. She had been starved of poetry since she became Empress. The Archduchess had even scolded her because she liked reading Lord Byron.

She had never been able to talk to Franz Joseph about anything but the daily events of the Court, or the glories of the Hapsburgs. She longed for someone with whom she could discuss the yearnings stirring within her to know more of the Universe, for someone who would help her formulate her thoughts and foster the tentative awakening of her brain.

That winter was a particularly cold and bitter one in Europe. The contrast in the weather once the ship had passed through the Straits of Gibraltar helped Elizabeth to believe that she was starting a new life.

Madeira, lying nearly five hundred miles from the coast of Europe, presented a picture of almost supernatural beauty when she went on deck early one morning and saw land a few miles ahead.

Heavy morning mist shrouded the island at first. Then the golden rays of the sun warmed the air to reveal an island which for centuries has been regarded by the romantically minded as a relic of the fabled continent of Atlantis.

On the voyage Elizabeth had been reading history books about the early exploration of the Atlantic and she could understand why the Portuguese sailors who had first sighted Madeira early in the fifteenth century had refused to launch boats at their captain's order because they believed that the place was enchanted.

She was, she told herself happily, to spend an indeterminate time in this lovely place in the company of a man who understood a little of her craving for beauty, both visible and inward.

The villa which had been rented for her was a little distance outside Funchal. It had a wide verandah and spacious rooms, with windows which could be completely removed on fine days so that one could sit in the open air and look down the green hillside to the sparkling brilliance of the blue sea below.

Few people lived in Madeira. It was extremely lonely, but Elizabeth loved it. Her psychological sickness and her physical lethargy, which had brought lines to her face and made her unnaturally thin, both disappeared like magic.

Soon, in company with Imri she was taking long walks in the hills or riding on one of the light ponies provided for her down those strange, luxuriant valleys called the Curales, which eclipsed in grandeur and desolation even the mountain peaks and glens of her beloved Bavarian Alps.

Communications with the island were so scanty that Vienna became annoyed at the lack of information about the Empress's activities which was supposed to be forwarded by the agents of Archduchess Sophie. When a ship put in with mail from Europe there were pointed enquiries about Elizabeth's health which suggested a morbid interest in it rather than any sympathy.

Elizabeth was amused by the tenor of the despatches, which, incidentally, included none from her husband. She gaily told Imri that she was sorry to disappoint her mother-in-law. "But I am afraid that in this lovely land the Arch-duchess will have to wait years before she sends a coffin to take me back."

Count Imri paled at even the thought of death to the lovely creature facing him. It was to be expected that he should be wildly, ecstatically in love with Elizabeth. He and she were the same age—two impressionable young people of twenty-three, together on an enchanted island.

Between their rides they spent long hours reading and talking. Byron and Blake, Heine and Dostoevski became a part of their world. Elizabeth awakening to love was more beautiful than she had ever been before.

She had not known that love could be of the mind as well as of the body, or that it could be strong yet gentle, demanding, yet tender. She had never before been worshipped as only a very idealistic man can worship the woman he loves.

"Imri! Imri! I'm happy!" she said a thousand times because it was so astonishing after the years of almost unrelieved misery.

Elizabeth remained at Madeira until March, when the fantastically fertile soil of the volcanic island covered the whole place with exotic flowers. Then a visit from her sister, Hélène, recently married to the Prince of Thurn and Taxis, made her uneasily aware that an idealistic life could not go on for ever.

Queen Victoria of England had in her own way done her best to show a marked sympathy for the Empress for some time. Politically it was desirable that England should pay open testimony of her friendship towards Austria as a possible bulwark against the growing power of Prussia, and because the Austro-Hungarian Empire was a powerful balancing force in Central Europe.

The Queen, on the advice of her Ministers, considered that the democratic forces symbolised by the Empress Elizabeth were better than the reactionary clique of her mother-in-law. To show her sympathy Victoria put her magnificent steam yacht *Victoria and Albert* at the disposal of Elizabeth and her party for their return to Europe.

While Elizabeth was trying to make up her mind to leave Madeira something happened to destroy her feeling of having escaped to freedom if only for a little while.

The spies in her entourage had managed to send Sophie enough information for her to arouse Franz Joseph's jealousy. Stories of the deep friendship between the Empress and Count Imri lost nothing in their telling. The Emperor had always disliked Imri because he was a Hungarian and despite his own behaviour he always showed a "dog in the manger" attitude about any man who seemed likely to arouse Elizabeth's affection.

Count Hunyadi therefore received a peremptory military order to return to Austria immediately. A ship was sent for him and the officer in charge of a squad of soldiers barely gave him time to say goodbye to Elizabeth. There is every reason to think that she never saw him again.

Madeira seemed empty and unbearably lonely without Imri. Elizabeth sailed in the *Victoria and Albert*. Almost as soon as the yacht had left Funchal Harbour it ran into storms which continued without cessation until the Straits of Gibraltar were reached.

Elizabeth gloried in the weather and seemed to behave almost foolhardily, as if she wanted to do personal battle with the elements. She never suffered from sea sickness and almost all day she insisted on remaining on deck staring out across the grey rollers and letting the white foam of the waves which crashed on deck saturate her to the skin.

Her attendants were terrified that she would be swept overboard, but the Captain admired her courage and despite the pleas of her ladies-in-waiting he refused to give the order (as he was entitled to do as Master of the ship) to send her below. The only concession he made to safety when the weather was unusually bad, was to lash the Empress to the mast.

The officers of the Royal Navy on the yacht were so struck by the fantastic slimness of their Royal passenger's waist that they were curious to find out what the measurements were. They consequently hit on an ingenious plan for measuring it.

The guard rail on the upper deck of the yacht had an almost continuous series of ornamental brass rivet heads. The Empress would often lean against the rail on the starboard side, while the officers were traditionally permitted to use the port side.

The plan made in the wardroom was that one officer should fix his eye on the rivet head just in front of the Empress and another should focus his sight on the one just behind her waist. When Elizabeth finally moved away both walked over casually, without taking their eyes off the rivet heads and were able, by measuring, to get the diameter of her waist.

This process had to be done twice, first when Elizabeth leaned over the guard rail so that the watching officers could get the widest diameter of her waist, and secondly when she was leaning sideways in profile view, which gave the narrowest diameter.

By setting down these diameters on paper and drawing an ellipse round them, they were able to measure the circumference of her waist. The result has not been officially recorded, but it is known that the Empress's waist at that time was only fifteen and a half inches.

The generous and kindly gesture by Queen Victoria to the Empress had great repercussions in Vienna. Elizabeth had been allowed to depart from the Empire with a lack of ceremony that was an insult to her position. To welcome her home the Emperor had travelled to Trieste with his full suite and came out to meet her aboard the Imperial yacht, *Fantasia*.

The ships in the harbour were dressed overall, and the *Fantasia*, with several other ships on which orchestras played martial music sailed towards the *Victoria and Albert*. The Imperial yacht then led the way to the quayside.

Guns fired a salute, and after an interval to allow Franz Joseph to get ashore first, Elizabeth was welcomed by her husband with tears in his eyes and an official kiss on the forehead.

Everyone noted how much improved was Elizabeth's health and how breathtakingly lovely she looked, but everyone also remarked on her change of character. Something had happened to her in Madeira. She was deliberately cold and remote, obviously no longer sensitive to the slights and insults of those who gave the minimum of formal greeting.

She walked from the quayside beside her husband, but observers noted with amazement that she made no attempt to converse with him. She stayed that night in her brother-in-law's palace and insisted on sleeping alone. She took good care that she announced this wish in the hearing of women whom she knew full well were on her mother-in-law's espionage list.

The next day she set out with Franz Joseph and their respective suites in a Royal train for Vienna. Sixteen miles from the capital, at Baden, the train stopped for a few hours in order that Elizabeth could see her children, who were staying there.

The Archduchess Sophie, on the pretext that it was very late and undue excitement would upset them, sent a message that the children's doctors had advised against a meeting that evening.

"It would be a mistake," she said, "because of the necessity of the train keeping to its schedule for the welcoming celebrations in Vienna."

Consequently, the only glimpse that Elizabeth had of her daughter and baby son was their faces at the windows in the nursery wing when a couple of nurses held them up for a few minutes. Elizabeth controlled her anger as well as her tears. After a smile and a wave she returned to the carriage, and without awaiting any sign from the Emperor gave orders to the coachmen to proceed.

At Vienna huge crowds lined the road between the railway station and the Hofburg. Elizabeth bowed repeatedly from her open carriage. There was little cheering, but the murmuring of the crowd and their smiling faces indicated that the bulk of the population were glad to see their Empress back and happier still to see that she was restored to health.

Elizabeth made a brave show of independence on her return to her adopted country. It was an effort which she could not maintain in face of the renewed attacks of her mother-in-law.

She did not have a single day's peace. And she was more than ever conscious of the coldness and scarcely veiled hostility of the members of the Court. With hardly an exception, they were entirely on Sophie's side.

Combined with all this were the stories she was told of how the Emperor had been amusing himself while she had been away. What was more, the cruelly brief meeting she had been allowed with her children had affected her more than she knew.

The acute longing for her children began all over again and she made one more desperate effort to see them as often as she wished. The Archduchess had, however, a splendid array of arguments with which to squash this attempt. The children were well and happy; she had been away six months and they did not miss her. In fact, why should they?

Here Sophie lost her temper, and parading furiously up and down, told Elizabeth what she thought of her. All the past misdemeanours were brought out one by one, the Archduchess finally shouting so loudly that the servants in the Palace even knew the exact words that were spoken during this quarrel.

It was spring, and at Laxenburg, to which haven Elizabeth hurriedly went a few days after her arrival in Vienna, the park was beautiful. But it had none of the serenity and peace she had known in Madeira. She developed a nervous cough; she lost weight, and her physical lassitude returned.

The Court doctors once again hinted at consumption. Elizabeth told them that they were wrong and wrote to her mother, begging her to send one of the doctors who had taken care of her in her childhood ailments. This move was necessary because the Jewish doctor who had been so helpful seemed to have been spirited away.

The Bavarian physician was by this time a very old man. He made the journey at Ludovica's urgent request but was frightened about being called in to give a second opinion after the elite of Vienna's medical faculty had pronounced their diagnosis.

Elizabeth had a long and private conversation with him. The result was that he was brave enough to issue a bulletin that the Empress was suffering from a "serious internal complaint" necessitating a temporary abandonment of married life, with treatment comprising douching and sea bathing—preferably to be taken at Corfu.

Fortunately for the old man, his distinguished colleagues did not demand more precise details of the trouble. For the ordinary people the vague wording achieved what patient and physician expected. It was passed round that the Empress had a gynæcological upset of an indelicate nature which could not be discussed.

Sophie's reaction was one of near-gloating that the illness would destroy her daughter-in-law's attractions as a woman or even prove fatal. Franz Joseph heard the news with a mixture of fear and disgust. Like many men whose sexual activities brought continuous risk of infection, he had a positive terror of the slightest contact with "female complaints".

The wildest rumours were circulated. The Bavarian Minister reported that there was small hope of the Empress's recovery and spoke of a mortal illness!* But the rest of Vienna took the news with a pinch of salt and suspected something was wrong with the Imperial menage.

The British Ambassador, Lord Bloomfield, even remarked to Count Rechberg:

"Fancy choosing Corfu! I never heard of it being recommended for consumptives!"

Within a month of setting foot in Austria Elizabeth was off again—to the island of Corfu. At Miramar she met her brother-in-law, the Prince of Thurn and Taxis, who escorted her as far as Gasturi. After a day's stay at the summer residence of the British High Commissioner which had been put at the disposal of the Empress he returned to Trieste, taking a certain Dr. Skoda with him.

The Doctor had been included in Elizabeth's entourage for the sake of appearances. He returned with the astonishing report that in less than a week's time the Empress no longer had need of him.

Elizabeth was soon going for long walks, bathing every day in the sea and exhausting her companions with her energy.

She loved not merely the physical charms of the island, at that time under British control as part of the Ionian League, but revelled in the legendary mystery which appealed to her Wittelsbach romanticism. This was the island called Scheira by Homer where Odysseus met the Phaecians, and on the beach below the villa the beautiful Nausicaea had taken Odysseus by the hand and led him to the court of her father, Alcinous. There the wandering hero had recounted much of his fantastic adventures.

Behind the villa was a steep hill, on the top of which was a cypress grove, reputedly the relic of a pagan temple to Aphrodite, goddess of desire. Every morning Elizabeth was up before five o'clock so that she could reach the grove as the rising sun sent a shaft of light between the carefully orientated trees to strike the face of the person standing in the centre of the glade.

* This despatch is in the Bavarian State Archives.

This was a ceremony once performed by high priestesses a thousand years earlier. Never on that holiday, or any of the others that she spent on Corfu, did Elizabeth omit to observe this pagan custom.

The Viennese doctors, sent periodically to report on the Empress's health, could do nothing but affirm that she was in exuberant well being. Her faithful old Bavarian physician loyally followed his patient's wishes by issuing a series of cautious statements that the internal malady, which he alone seemed to be able to identify, was "responding slowly but satisfactorily to treatment."

At Possenhofen, Ludovica was worried by the gossip which reached her from Vienna. What had got into her temperamental daughter that she did not want to behave like an Empress? She wrote at once to Hélène and said that she and her husband were to visit Elizabeth and find out the truth about her health.

At Corfu, Hélène found her sister cheerful, although excessively thin. Elizabeth was dieting to have a slim figure and owing to reckless experimentation with non-fattening foods her face showed a slight puffiness about the cheeks and eyes.

Hélène descended upon the kitchen staff and demanded a change in the menu. There was not much choice on the island and Elizabeth was obliged to eat goat twice a day as long as her sister remained with her. She had her own back by walking Hélène over the hills as far as Mount Pantokrata.

"My feet are swollen," Hélène wrote to her mother, "as are Sisi's; but she won't admit it."

In Vienna Franz Joseph was having a difficult time. Gossipmongers talked openly of the rift between the Royal couple, and the Emperor was particularly embarrassed by the aspersions cast on his character. These mainly concerned the Countess Isabella Pitocka, who was a sleepy-eyed beauty with a tremendous rope of hair which she coiled like a snake around her arms and wrists to lessen the weight.

A portrait of the Countess was exhibited in a photographers gallery and sold to the highest bidder. This was a Councillor of State called Danhelowsky, but everyone was convinced that the Councillor had acted by proxy on secret instructions from the Emperor.

It was to stop the wagging tongues that Franz Joseph made up his mind to visit Corfu. Elizabeth must be forced to see the predicament in which she had put her husband. She must understand that something must be done to check the wave of ugly scandal.

At the same time, obtuse and guilt-conscious as Franz Joseph might be, he at last saw through the whole business of Elizabeth's illness. Jealousy replaced his indifference and as his ship neared Corfu he was really anxious to see her.

If the Emperor had apologised for his earlier behaviour there might have been a real reconciliation. Instead he adopted a hypocritical attitude, saying how glad he was that she had recovered so that he would no longer have to restrain himself from taking her in his arms. This, he added, was something he had done when he last saw her out of tender consideration for her health.

Elizabeth adopted the same pretence—she thanked Franz Joseph politely for his sympathy now and his restraint in the past. She assured him that he need no longer worry about her health—she felt, and was, extremely well.

That night, however, when the Emperor tip-toed to her suite he found the bedroom door locked. He then realised that a reconciliation would not be as easy as he thought. And the following day he began to plead with her to be reasonable.

Elizabeth told him firmly she would not come back, because the Archduchess made her life in Vienna impossible. Franz Joseph then begged her to meet him half way—could she not choose a spot nearer Austria where she could recuperate?

When she still hesitated he played his trump card. If she would do this he would send the children to her. Elizabeth capitulated.

"I will go to Venice," she said, "if the children can come to me there."

In November 1861 Rudolph and Gisela arrived in Venice to join their mother. Elizabeth was overjoyed—she had longed for her little ones. All the time she had been away from them she had written to them constantly. Her letters always ended pathetically; "Do not forget your Mamma" or, "Think of your Mamma often!"*

Unfortunately disagreements began almost immediately with the Countess Esterhazy, who had received special instructions from the Archduchess about the treatment the children were to have during the whole of their visit.

In the second week of April, Ludovica arrived in Venice to see for herself what was wrong.

While she was still there, the Emperor joined them. When he left, Elizabeth returned home with her mother, staying at Reichenau so as to avoid Vienna and the Archduchess.

There she was joined by Dr. Fischer who had known her since her childhood. He announced that she was suffering from acute anæmia, which accounted for the puffiness of her face. He suggested Kissingen for a cure.

The fact that Elizabeth was now roaming around the Empire like any private person really alarmed the Court. Franz Joseph wrote her letters which were not the edicts of an Emperor, but the pleading, worried words of a remorseful husband. They were unanswered.

Franz Joseph persisted and finally, with Ludovica as go-between, he learned of his wife's terms for a return to official life. They were simply that she would not have to meet her mother-in-law. The Emperor rashly promised that this would be arranged, and the estranged couple met in August, 1862 at Ischl.

Memories of their romance in the same place and in the same month nine years before erased temporarily their antipathy. There was a glimpse, but only a glimpse, of what

* These letters are in the possession of H.R.H. Prince Konrad of Bavaria.

might have been, during the few days and nights before the Emperor insisted that they must show themselves in the capital.

"Mamma is not there," he assured Elizabeth.

The reception given to her in Vienna was incredible. The Royal train arrived late in the evening. Sixteen thousand torches illuminated the route from the station to the palace. Choirs were placed at intervals to sing hymns of welcome. The only discordant note amid the general rejoicings was when the Empress made her reply to the formal welcome from Burgomaster Zelinka:

"In close harmony with my own pleasure in being once again in my second home, Vienna, is my gratitude for the magnificent welcome prepared for me," she said. "I trust that the happiness I feel in being again in your midst may continue unalloyed by any cloud."

Even the ordinary people knew that the cloud their Empress feared was the person of the Archduchess Sophie.

One of Elizabeth's ladies-in-waiting wrote to a former member of the Household:

"The Empress was received with an enthusiasm such as I have never heard before in Vienna. *His* expression, as he helped her from the carriage, I shall never forget. I find her looking blooming, but her expression is not natural; it is forced and nervous as can be . . . The fact that Prince Karl Theodor accompanied her proves how much she dreads being alone with *him* and all of us . . ."

Elizabeth settled down at the Schönbrunn and resumed her old accustomed life. She loved having her children with her and she greeted her favourite horses in the stables enthusiastically.

The Archduchess was away. There were no rows, and oblivious of the demands of etiquette Elizabeth did exactly what she wished to do. She was only twenty-five but in many ways her life was that of an old woman who had retired.

Her lady-in-waiting wrote again to her friend on September 15, 1862:

"She walks and drives out a great deal with his Majesty, but when he is not here she goes alone in the part of the garden which is closed to the people—She is very nice to him—before us at least—talkative and natural, though *alla camera* there may be differences of opinion—that is often to be seen . . . Otherwise, thank God, things are going well. . . . I believe indeed that she has moments of despair but nobody can laugh like her, or has such childlike whims."*

Franz Joseph was doing everything he could to make life at home pleasant for Elizabeth. He was kind and attentive, gave her several fine horses, tried to anticipate her every wish. But those who watched him knew that only one thing really mattered: that the Archduchess should keep away from the Empress.

*These letters are in the possession of Count Szécsen.

EIGHT

1864-1867

ELIZABETH made an effort to take part in Court life. In the middle of February, for the first time in three years, she appeared at a small Court Ball, to which only two hundred and fifty guests were invited. She was lovelier than ever—even her enemies had to admit that. Those who believed her to be ill were surprised to see she had every appearance of good health.

Whatever effort Elizabeth made, however, she could not make much impact on the icy-cold dislike which surrounded her in Vienna. Naturally she turned towards the Hungarian nobility, who not only paid her sincere compliments, but offered her a genuine adoration and homage from the depth of their warm hearts.

She went on with her studies of Magyar. She learned her first words from the nurse to the Crown Prince. She went on to repeat aloud long lists of words while her maid was dressing her and while her hair was being brushed by her hairdresser, Fanny Angerer.

Fanny, the daughter of a midwife, had served her apprenticeship as a wigmaker in theatre dressing-rooms. Her skill spread beyond the footlights and the ladies of fashion in Vienna were just beginning to vie for her services, when to everyone's astonishment, she became "Hairdresser Extraordinary to her Majesty."

Fanny was a chatterbox, and Elizabeth encouraged her to talk of her past clients. She even discussed her own interests with her as she relaxed under the brush strokes. The Countess Esterhazy was horrified that a menial should be treated as a personal friend. She complained to the Archduchess who decided that they must find a way to remove Angerer.

Elizabeth's hair was now a yard long and Fanny was

Franz Joseph, Emperor of Austria

(Courtesy: Österreichische Nationalbibliothek. Reproduced from a painting by Winterhalter)

The Archduchess Sophie, mother of Franz Joseph and the Empress's
'bête noire'

reprimanded severely if while brushing and dressing the lovely auburn tresses a single hair was pulled out.

Since it was impossible to prevent this Fanny hit on the clever device of a sticky substance in her pocket—after each stroke of the comb she would contrive to slip it into her pocket. If there were any loose hairs then the Empress never saw them.

The Archduchess was at the same time watching Elizabeth's growing sympathy for Hungary with a jaundiced eye.

On one occasion when the Emperor and Empress appeared in the Imperial box at the theatre Elizabeth was wearing a gold embroidered head-dress of the kind generally worn by the wives of Hungarian magnates.

When the Archduchess, who was in the next box, caught sight of this, she began staring at her daughter-in-law through her lorgnettes. She actually stood up to have a better view of her. Then she sank back in her seat and shook her head in amazement.

This caused a sensation in the theatre and everybody started whispering until Elizabeth, followed by Franz Joseph, rose and left before the end of the performance.

Elizabeth went to Kissingen again for the cure where a crippled Englishman, John Collett, fell madly in love with her. She had another admirer in the blind Duke of Mecklenburg, to whom she was unfailingly kind in acting as his guide.

These three became inseparable—the fascinating, beautiful Empress, the blind Duke and the English cripple. They would talk about God and the Universe, life and death, happiness and misery. John Collett also wrote Elizabeth a little poem which began—

> "May God preserve the lady fair and true
> Whose pitying heart can feel for others' pain.
> For thou, at least, kind Queen, hast not passed through
> The trying fires of suffering in vain."*

* The letters and poem are in the Archives at Schloss Wallsee.

Political events were at this time rushing towards an acute crisis. The mighty Empire of the Hapsburgs, under the ægis of an old woman and her coterie whose outlook became more and more mediaeval, suffered setback after setback in the ruthless game of European politics.

Franz Joseph's mind was itself a battlefield at this time. Fundamentally intelligent and able, he knew well enough that the policies forced on him were wrong, yet his filial piety and the restricting discipline of his upbringing made him suppress every intelligent qualm.

The result was disaster after disaster. Basically, the Imperial policy was both desirable and understandable. Vienna feared Prussia even more than Russia or France. The vaunting, ranting, new Hohenzollern ruler, William I, was devoting all his energies and his country's resources into making Prussia a first class military power.

His chief assistant was the arrogant, cunning and ruthless Otto von Bismarck, whose reactionary outlook was such that he poured contempt on the "liberalism" of Austria, regarding even the unbending policy of Archduchess Sophie as weak and decadent.

Austria might have called the young military power's bluff if Franz Joseph had been firm. Instead, the great Empire allowed herself to be dragged by the coat tails into a ridiculous and unjustified war with Denmark in 1864 over the twin duchies of Schleswig and Holstein. Both were in fee to the Danish crown, but their status was involved because Holstein was a member of the German Confederation and Schleswig enjoyed certain autonomous rights.

Prussia's ambitions to prevent their incorporation in the Danish kingdom, if unprincipled, were also understandable. The acquisition would enlarge the kingdom and increase the defensive resources. To pretend, on the other hand, that the Austrian Empire had any business to extend her territories on the borders of Denmark was ridiculous.

The war of conquest, carried out by Prussian troops with token Austrian forces, was quick and easy. Austria quickly found that to administer the conquered Holstein, which was her share of the spoils, was not merely difficult, but virtually impossible. The little duchy was an island within Prussian territories. Problems of communication, economics, and defence became wellnigh insuperable.

This was, of course, precisely what Bismarck had intended. A year after Franz Joseph had strutted in the victory procession after the signing of the Peace of Vienna in 1864, Bismarck had seen Napoleon III and arranged for France's neutrality if Prussia attacked Austria.

Similar secret arrangements with Russia and with Italy took a few more months, but in June, 1866, Bismarck was ready. He moved troops into Holstein in order to force Austria to declare war.

Indignantly Franz Joseph appealed to the members of the German Confederation to help him in this unwarranted example of international bad manners. The little German states were full of indignation too.

Comforted with the thought that tradition meant something and that 'right was might', Franz Joseph's armies first dealt with Italy and managed to get a victory at Custozza. But while Vienna was celebrating it Bismarck's military expert, Helmuth von Moltke, sent the best equipped army in Europe on a nineteenth-century blitzkrieg which smashed the Austrians at Koniggratz.

The Empire was on her knees, and Bismarck dictated peace terms entirely of his own devising. The vanquished Italians shared in Prussia's victory with the gift of Venetia. The German states moved to the protecting arms of Prussia, and Austria's influence over them was ended.

Thanks to the domination of his mother, Franz Joseph, who had clearly seen the dimensions of the Prussian menace, had, in a mismanaged diplomatic campaign of twelve months and a disgracefully organised war of seven weeks, paved the way for two world wars. One of which he was to live to see causing the final disruption of his Empire.

As always in times of trouble, Elizabeth felt a surge of pity for her husband and at the height of the war she was back in the capital, visiting hospitals and comforting the bereaved families of the war dead. She earned herself the name of "the Angel of the Wounded."

A soldier named Joseph Fecher, son of an old blind gypsy, had refused to allow his arm to be amputated, but the Empress persuaded him, wrote to his mother and sent her money and provided for both their futures.

Needless to say, the Archduchess did not approve of an Empress demeaning herself to speak to "common soldiers." She was especially angry when she heard that when Elizabeth left the wards, the wounded men would cry out with deep emotion "God bless Elizabeth."

This was not the only quarrel Elizabeth was having with her mother-in-law. The Archduchess had appointed Count Gondrecourt as governor for Rudolph. He was entirely without any understanding of a child's mentality and his methods might have been useful in dealing with coarse country recruits but were criminal in dealing with a sensitive, highly-strung child.

Elizabeth had disliked the Count from the beginning for she saw that he was not making Rudolph stronger but weaker and more nervous. "His methods," she said "will turn Rudi practically into an idiot—It is madness to frighten a child of six with water cures and to try to turn him into a hero!"

On one occasion she heard the Count had taken the boy to the Lainzer Tiergarten, a game park near Vienna— Rushing him through the gate, he then slipped out himself and shouted "Here comes a wild boar!"

Rudolph naturally began to scream, but the more he cried the more the Count tried to frighten him, until he was in such a state that it was naturally dangerous to his health.

Elizabeth went to Franz Joseph and told him that the governor appointed by his mother was altogether unsuitable. His faith in the wisdom of the Archduchess had been shaken by the loss of the war in 1859, but he was not prepared to disregard her altogether.

Elizabeth was adamant.

"Either Gondrecourt goes or I go," she said, and going to her room wrote Franz Joseph what amounted to an ultimatum which began:

"It is my wish that full and unlimited powers should be reserved to me in all things concerning the children . . ."*

The Emperor actually had his own doubts about Gondrecourt because one morning very early he had heard words of command from the courtyard below his window. Looking out he had seen to his astonishment his delicate son being drilled in the deep snow by candlelight.

Even so, he hesitated to agree with Elizabeth.

Among a horde of critics, one devoted admirer in the person of Count Julius Andrássy meant a great deal to Elizabeth. Tall, slender, with a noble face and unbelievably picturesque in his fur-trimmed magnate's uniform, Elizabeth spoke to him openly of her feelings regarding the war and her love for Hungary. In fact on one occasion she said:

"When things are not straight with Italy, I am sorry, but if misfortune were to happen in Hungary, it would kill me."

Wherever she might be Elizabeth felt herself to be the Queen of Hungary. During a stay at the watering place, Gastein, she and her lady-in-waiting made an excursion to a hill in the neighbourhood. On the summit they found a hut and in it a visitors' book. The lady-in-waiting wrote in the book "Elizabeth, Empress of Austria" but Elizabeth, taking up the pen, wrote underneath "Erzsebet, Magyar Kyralyno" (Elizabeth, Hungarian Queen.)

In July, 1866, the Prussians threatened to march on Vienna and it was decided that Elizabeth and the little Crown Prince should take refuge in Budapest.

Elizabeth was thrilled to be with the people she loved and understood. Once more her passion for riding awoke.

* From the correspondence of the Emperor and Empress now at Schloss Wallsee.

Between visits to hospitals and routine reports to Vienna she indulged in breathless gallops over the wild *puszta*.

Franz Joseph read of this and became alarmed.

"If only you had never seen a saddle," he wrote on the margin of an official despatch.

Late in August Elizabeth asked his permission to buy an abandoned estate at Godollo, twenty-nine kilometres from Budapest. She had visions of starting a stud farm of Hungary's wonderful horses there.

"How I should like to spend my life on these Hungarian plains—just tending those splendid creatures," Elizabeth had said to some Cziskos, swarthy-skinned herd tenders and the citizens of the Magyar prairies.

Franz Joseph blasted the idea. On August 8, 1866, he wrote:

"By all means visit Godollo since there is a hospital with many wounded soldiers in that neighbourhood. But don't inspect the castle with a view to buying, because I have no money at present and we ought to economise in earnest during these hard times. I am reducing our budget for next year and selling half our stables."

If Elizabeth could not have Godollo or her Hungarian horses she had compensation in the knowledge that her affection for Julius Andrássy and his overwhelming love for her deepened every day. They understood each other and they were united in their intense devotion to Hungary.

Julius Andrássy was a Magyar of the Magyars. He had a dash of the Oriental to set off an aristocratic insouciance. He was gallant, passionate, emotional and yet he could be very tender. He had the dark, flashing good looks which, it was rumoured, turned the head of every woman at whom he smiled.

After the war, he saw his chance. Through his friendship with the Empress he believed that he could obtain for Hungary more privileges than even the revolutionaries of twenty years before had imagined in their wildest dreams.

He had many secret meetings with Elizabeth and finally she wrote a long letter to Franz Joseph in which she said:

"I am convinced that if you trust Andrássy implicitly we can still save not only Hungary but also the Monarchy. You must, however, talk over the matter with him yourself and at once because each day may change events so that ultimately it might become impossible for him to negotiate."

The Emperor cursed the day that he had agreed to Elizabeth taking refuge in Budapest. There had been a terrible scene with his mother when she had received a report from one of her agents who had eavesdropped on a conversation between Elizabeth and a Hungarian historian, Michael Horrath. This well-known man had been exiled for many years because of his seditious writings.

"Believe me," Elizabeth had said to him, "if it were in the power of my husband and myself we would be the first to recall to life all those who were condemned and executed during the Hungarian fight for freedom."

Grudgingly the Emperor agreed to make a state visit to Budapest and to negotiate with the Hungarian leaders. He was given a hearty welcome by the people in the Hungarian capital, who knew full well that they were to all intents and purposes the victors saluting the vanquished. But Elizabeth fostered the people's affection into a state bordering on religious hysteria when, with her own hands, she repaired the historic cloak of St. Stephen preserved in the Benedictine Abbey of St. Martinsburg.

The Emperor wrote to his mother:

"Sisi is a great help to me with her courtesy, tact and discretion and her excellent Hungarian in which people feel more inclined to listen to an occasional admonition from such fair lips."

Franz Joseph and his Ministers acceded to almost all the Hungarian demands. By the time they left, Hungary had a constitution which was virtually the same as that proclaimed at the Revolution of 1848—a parliament of their own, recognition of the Dual State and widespread reforms on behalf of Hungarians living within the Empire but beyond the borders of their own country.

On March 5th Elizabeth left Budapest with Franz Joseph after a stay of six weeks. Her farewell words at the station were:

"I hope soon to be able to return to my dear, dear Hungary."

She pronounced the word "dear" with such charm and feeling that tears came into the eyes of all those present.

As a sop to the Emperor's dignity the Hungarians begged him to agree to his Coronation as King of Hungary at the earliest possible moment.

Throughout the long history of the country no Queen had ever been crowned at the same time as a King. Franz Joseph, who was deeply read in the history of his domains, probably thought that tradition would be followed in this case and he would thus be able to attract a little of the limelight so lavishly bestowed on his Consort to himself.

In this supposition he was mistaken. Shortly after his return to Vienna a deputation arrived from Hungary with the proposed arrangements for the ceremonies. They stated that they wished to show their devotion and regard for the Empress by crowning her Queen of Hungary at the same time as he was made King. Franz Joseph said that the matter would have to be discussed with his Ministers and the deputation thereupon went straight off to see the Empress.

She made an immediate decision and issued an announcement which was published on the following day in the Hungarian newspapers. It stated:

"I will joyfully fulfil the wish expressed by the people of Hungary. It coincides with the desire of my own heart, and I thank God who has permitted me to live to see this auspicious moment. Convey my hearty thanks and greetings to your people."

With this statement in print before the meeting between

Franz Joseph and his advisers had taken place there was, of course, nothing that could be done but to agree.

The coronation took place on June 8, 1867. Franz Joseph rode at the head of the procession on horseback. The cheers for him were merely formal and polite. As he rode down the steep hill from the castle to the Cathedral he listened poker-faced to the frenzied shouts that burst out a hundred yards behind him.

There, escorted by a squadron of Life Guards, Elizabeth sat in a coronation coach drawn by eight grey horses and with girls dancing on either side in relays, strewing flowers from baskets under the wheels of the vehicle. Two hundred of the magnates of Hungary, the aristocracy of the country, rode immediately behind her.

The morning was very hot and a ten-hour ceremony lay ahead. Because the ancient ritual of Hungary demanded that a Queen had to be annointed with the Holy oil, not on the forehead as in the case of a King, but under the right armpit, Elizabeth, looking bewitchingly lovely, was wearing a magnificent low-cut gown of white and silver brocade, scattered with jewels and patterned with lilac blossom.

It was worn with a black velvet bodice which copied the national dress. Worth of Paris had created this masterpiece at the comparatively moderate sum of five thousand francs.

On her head, over her thickly braided hair, Elizabeth wore a coronet of diamonds and pearls, and an exquisite Brussels lace veil fell from her head to the ground.

The escort of magnates behind her had done their utmost to indicate the princely wealth of Hungary and they far outshone the Austrian personalities who, Franz Joseph had insisted, should be included in the procession. One wore a complete suit of silver-plated armour. Another had jewellery on his tunic worth twelve thousand pounds, and a third rode a horse whose caparisons were valued at fifteen thousand pounds.

The crowd's enthusiasm was such that, despite the presence of sixty thousand troops to keep them under control, as soon as Elizabeth's coach approached they swarmed out into the road. The procession broke into two parts—with the result that Franz Joseph stood on the steps of the Cathedral for a full quarter of an hour before the Queen's section arrived.

During the long ceremony while Franz Joseph was crowned King, Elizabeth sat with folded hands, her eyes cast downwards. Then the Primate of Hungary beckoned to her to come forward. She knelt on the lowest step before the High Altar and the coronet of the Hapsburgs, originally made for Maria Theresa, a mass of pearls and diamonds, was removed as a symbol that for the rest of the ceremony she would be a woman without position until the Hungarian Crown made her Queen.

After the anointing with Holy oil the enormous Hungarian crown, which had already been placed briefly on the head of Franz Joseph, was held on the Queen's right shoulder while the Primate recited a prayer. It was far too large and heavy for a woman's head. She was then handed a sceptre and orb, and conducted to a throne behind her husband.

Her eyes filled with tears of joy as the *Te Deum* was played. She was stirred to the very depths of her being by the unbounded love which she saw in the eyes of the assembled company.

"I am sorry," Elizabeth had said once, "but I don't understand politics." "Your Majesty has understood how to win the heart of a nation," Jokau, a Budapest poet had replied.

Late that night at a State Banquet Julius Andrássy, who had been sentenced to death by the Hapsburgs in 1849 as a rebel, sat at Elizabeth's right hand as Prime Minister of Hungary. Franz Joseph did his best to conceal his real feeling of disquiet and only once did he visibly glower.

That was when medals struck to commemorate the event were distributed among the guests. On one side was the head of himself and on the other of Elizabeth. Around her portrait were the words: "May the star of happiness ever shine over her." Around the head of the King was no such token of Hungarian esteem.

The Archduchess's spies among Elizabeth's ladies-in-waiting missed nothing. They saw the adoration in Andrássy's eyes, the suspicion in the Emperor's. There was a spiteful sting in the letter praising Elizabeth which Hélène Furstenburg wrote home:

"The Coronation is over," she reported. "Her Majesty looked supernaturally lovely during the solemn act, and moved absorbed as a bride. I rather felt, too, as if in *one* respect, she did interpret it in this sense."

On the following day, in order to recover from the heavy ordeal of the ceremony, Franz Joseph and Elizabeth retired to the Palace at Godollo. This was a gift by the people of Hungary to their Queen. She had longed for it, and had been refused it. But Andrássy had known of her longing and now it was hers.

It was quite small but an inexpressibly attractive building, and for a week the Royal couple remained there in semi-retirement. Elizabeth was delighted and thrilled with everything. The present because it had been thought of by the man she loved and who adored her meant more to her than she could ever put into words.

But Franz Joseph turned to her for support and understanding and as usual she did not fail him—their reconciliation was complete.

In some strange way Budapest, a magnet of happiness to Elizabeth, also seemed to bring the shadow of tragedy with it. On the previous occasion of her stay in the lovely old castle high above the Danube there had been tragic news of her baby daughter's fatal illness. This time the couriers from Vienna brought terrible tidings which were already the subject of headlines in the newspapers of Budapest.

In the spring of 1863 French troops had carried out a quick campaign of conquest in Mexico, and Napoleon III had shortly after the completion of the military action invited Franz Joseph's brother, the Archduke Maximilian, to become Emperor of Mexico.

The whole business was a sorry one of political intrigue

on the part of the French, and although Franz Joseph had had the gravest doubts about it, the delight of his brother had known no bounds. He was blissful in the belief that a Hapsburg would automatically be accepted as a beloved monarch by a nation, no matter whether it was in the Old World or the New, and he ignored the hostile reaction which came from almost every other world power.

Any sense of discretion that Maximilian might have had disappeared when he had spoken to his mother. The Archduchess Sophie, due to her reactionary creed, encouraged her younger son to accept Napoleon's offer by all the means in her power.

This time Franz Joseph, whose wisdom in government was increasing considerably through years of bitter experience, for once went into the opposite camp to his mother. Before Maximilian left Europe the Emperor forced him to sign an act of secession from membership of the Imperial family of Austro-Hungary. Franz Joseph had no desire for his descendants to find themselves entangled in the problems of yet another throne.

The triumph of the gimcrack coronation in Mexico City was the preface to almost immediate unrelieved disaster. Maximilian's wife, Charlotte, began to act more and more strangely. The unfortunate woman was in reality terrified about the future after experiencing for a few brief weeks the real conditions in Mexico. Although her brain quickly began to give way, her return to Europe was motivated by the perfectly sane desire to obtain military and diplomatic help for her husband.

Finding no nation ready to dabble in the internal politics of a country under the protection of France, the by now virtually raving woman went to see the Pope. She was activated presumably with the fervent hope that he would start a Holy War.

The Pope granted her an audience, realised that Charlotte was completely insane and gently advised her to retire to the seclusion of a convent. After a brief stay there in the care of nuns, which helped her to quieten down, she was sent to Miramare where Franz Joseph hurried to meet her. She was by then a manic depressive, sitting like a statue in her chair, her eyes unaware of any visitor, and her lips sealed.

Early in 1867 Mexico was in a state of civil war, with the entire population going over to the side of General Juarez, a fugitive from the country during the war with the French. By February 13 the scattered remnants of the French troops had been driven out of the country and Maximilian, with a handful of politicians who were not so much friends of the Emperor as enemies of Juarez, were eventually cut off in the mountain city of Queretaro.

Taken prisoner a few days later and branded as a usurper, Maximilian was given the chance to leave the country instantly or appear before a court martial. Bravely but foolishly he spurned the offer of his life. Inevitably there came the court martial verdict of guilty with the punishment of execution by a firing squad.

Little in Maximilian's life had become him so much as the way in which he faced death. There was terrible pathos in that all too common statement of the failures in this world: "I meant well." And there was magnificence in his final plea: "Aim at my heart."

The news of this unheard-of end for a Hapsburg left Franz Joseph numb with horror. Elizabeth, who had felt a deep affection for her brother-in-law as well as pity for his stiff-necked arrogance and belief in his destiny to rule, was deeply upset. The most terrible effects of the news were those which it had on the Archduchess Sophie. When her elder son had left for Budapest she had made vaunting remarks about her certainty that Maximilian would prevail.

By the time Franz Joseph returned to Vienna she had aged momentously and become a muttering old woman. She was only sixty-two years of age and had until that month shown an inexhaustible energy and had the appearance of a woman at least ten years younger. Now she looked lined and withered like an old witch.

NINE

1867

BEREAVEMENT through violence, and the sudden breaking of the maternal prop on which he had always depended, left Franz Joseph bewildered and lonely. While for the moment his emotional tension was not of the sort that yet another sexual liaison could assuage.

Consequently these were happier months for Elizabeth. Her position at the Court was changed; she was able to devote all the time she wished to her children (though they remained indifferent and strange) and, above all, she could play the rôle of a real wife.

With deep joy she was able to tell Franz Joseph that she was again expecting a child. The intimacy born of reconciliation after the coronation at Budapest had not been broken by the tragedy in Mexico. It had been strengthened. This time there was the happiness of expecting a child, without the anxiety of wondering whether it would be a son.

For a while Elizabeth's fourth pregnancy remained the personal knowledge of husband and wife, and there was none of the hateful suspicion created later. Then the remnants of the Sophie coterie described the child-to-be as "the Hungarian agreement", leaving to the prurience of the listener's mind to decide whether this suggested the child had been conceived in Hungary, or whether its father was possibly Count Andrássy.

Unalloyed happiness was not in Fate's plan for Elizabeth's life. Quickly fresh trouble arose—this time affecting her own family, which the loneliness of her marriage had made far more dear to her. The leading characters in the new drama of tragi-comedy were her sister Sophia and her cousin Ludwig II of Bavaria.

Ludwig II was the son of Prince Maximilian, who at the

age of thirty-four had married his cousin, Marie, niece of King Friedrich Wilhem III of Prussia. Marie was therefore a Hohenzollern and a Protestant. Seven months after the marriage, in October 1842, the bride suffered a miscarriage and for some weeks she lay between life and death.

The tragedy was regarded by the Bavarians as evidence of the wrath of God at the infringement of the rules as regards the relationship of people marrying and even more of Prince Maximilian's sin in taking a Protestant as a wife.

It may well have been that the death of the baby was a blessing in disguise. When, three years later, Marie gave birth to a live son, Fate decided for the child a life of strange happenings, and at the end of it a terrible tragedy. It is perhaps fortunate, however, that the future of human life is hidden from us, and the birth of little Ludwig was surrounded with tremendous joy.

The child seemed to be healthy and full of vitality. The mother, who was in labour for more than ten hours, rapidly recovered from her ordeal. There were apparently no serious after-effects as might have been expected in view of her serious illness as the result of the first miscarriage. But within eight months the misfortune which was to encompass Ludwig for all of his life began.

His wet nurse caught typhoid fever. She had been feeding the child for some days before her illness was diagnosed. There was great anxiety that he might have caught the illness as well. He did in fact become sickly, but this was apparently due to the sudden cessation of his accustomed diet and due to his mother's decision that he should be immediately weaned.

Whatever the physical results of this abrupt change far too early in his development, there can be no doubt that there was a psychological trauma which affected him for the rest of his life. It gave him a sense of insecurity and a deep suspicion of all those around him.

By 1848, when he was old enough to assimilate information without understanding it, there were more grounds for emotional disturbance. Bavaria, or rather Munich, flamed into revolt as the result of the indiscretion of his grandfather, King Ludwig I, a fine if somewhat eccentric old man in his sixties.

The King fell completely under the domination of Lola Montez, probably the most notorious courtesan of the age. She had arrived in Bavaria after affairs with, according to her own story, half the crowned heads of Europe, and proceeded to become to all intents and purposes dictator of the country.

The fantastic sums of money which the ageing King lavished on his mistress, coupled with his almost complete neglect of his duties, created such a storm that he was compelled to abdicate in favour of his son, Ludwig's father, who ascended the throne as Maximilian II.

Thus the young boy suddenly became heir to the throne of Bavaria. Shortly after the new reign began, Queen Marie gave birth to a second son who was named Otto. As sometimes will happen, the older child ignored the new baby, and the encouragement he received from his parents and nurses to demonstrate his affection unfortunately had regrettable results in later life. They produced in the neurotic young man a tendency to homosexuality.

The form of education provided for the two boys, although normal for their position and in that insensitive period of history, further aggravated Ludwig's neurotic temperament.

His sentimental mother encouraged him in the gentleness which was his real nature so that he had what was almost a girlish passion for pretty baubles, collecting wild flowers, and writing little love poems.

His father, by contrast, was very worried about training his son for the duties of a Crown Prince, insisted on young Ludwig acting imperiously and almost rudely to the servants, while at the same time meekly obeying his tutors. The Count appointed as the Prince's governor was ordered to punish any laxity or fault in the boy's lessons with the utmost physical severity.

When Ludwig was ten years old he and his brother were put under the control of a military instructor, Baron Emil von Wuelffen, whose job it was "to intensify the boy's education". This description meant in effect that the Baron's task was to break Ludwig's will, to make him physically fit, and to teach him how to apply his knowledge to action.

The soldier's programme, covering seven years of Ludwig's life so that the training would be completed by the time the Prince became of age, at 18, meant that he had to get up at five-thirty in the morning and work almost without cessation until eight o'clock at night.

The brutality of his so-called betters produced temporarily a trend towards sadism. When Ludwig was twelve years of age, for no reason at all, he took his nine-year-old brother into a remote part of the family estate of Berchtesgarden, tied him from shoulders to his feet with rope, rammed a mass of dead leaves in the boy's mouth, and was discovered about to strangle the child by twisting a handkerchief tightly round his neck. He was unable to explain his motive, but his father thrashed him more unmercifully than usual for it.

Even if there had been no trait of insanity in his family it was almost inevitable that the youth, bewildered and hurt by the constant reiteration that physical force and physical self-discipline were the ruling factors in life, should take refuge in introspective thoughts in order to escape from a world that he could not and did not wish to understand.

After twelve or fourteen hours sitting on a hard, upright seat at his lessons, Ludwig would retire to his bedroom and read books on German folk lore because in those wild and beautiful stories, he would find accounts of nobility and chivalry which in some strange way eased his tortured brain.

He pursued his lessons with sullen obstinacy, except that he began to show a great aptitude for the French language. His tutors refrained from attempting to discover the reason for this but in fact, his motive was to enable him to read everything he could about the glittering period of French history during the reign of the Sun King, Louis XIV.

In his mid-teens Ludwig was a dreamer of day-dreams. He carried out his duties in the classroom like an automaton. Simultaneously his passion for beautiful things developed enormously, and for his birthday gifts he asked for specific works of art, which would have been unusually fine examples of taste in someone three times his age.

His mother naturally encouraged him in these interests, and as a birthday treat she took him to see the Passion Play at Oberammergau. The religious drama enthralled him so much that for days afterwards he was deaf to all conversations addressed to him.

He confided to his mother that at night he kept having visions of the Virgin Mary as portrayed in the play. He said that she appeared to him as the perfection of pure beauty which Woman, and only Woman, could attain.

He omitted to tell her what he was already admitting to himself, and was to affirm openly in later years, that there were two other perfect women in history. One was his ancestral relative Marie Antoinette—and the other his cousin Elizabeth.

Ludwig was eight years younger than Elizabeth. He had only seen her occasionally, but naturally, on the occasion of her marriage to Franz Joseph, when he was eight years old, there had been much talk about the event. To the small boy the stories of the bride in immaculate white, riding through garlanded streets while the bells of the churches rang out in celebration, sounded even more wonderful than his Germanic fairy tales.

Later as he grew older, he heard, even if he could hardly appreciate, the stories of Elizabeth's unhappiness due to the neglectful behaviour of her husband. All his idealistic fervour to become Knight Errant for a perfect woman was concentrated in a remote and unspoken devotion to the Empress.

Between Elizabeth and Ludwig sprang up a friendship which ended only with his death. She was the only woman he ever trusted. He called himself "The Mountain Eagle"—

and "Eagle" became her name for him, while he called her "Dove".

Just after Elizabeth shocked most of the social world by running off to Madeira, Ludwig was taken to see a performance of Lohengrin at the Court Theatre in Munich. The story and the music enabled the youth to sublimate all his emotions and almost inevitably he began to worship the man whose brain could create such beauty.

He made the utmost use of the increased personal liberty accorded to him as he approached his majority, and devoted more and more time to attending operas and concerts. There were many scandalous stories told of his highly emotional friendships with male singers, whose performances wrongly and dangerously suggested to him that they must have caught something of the beauty inherent in the music which they interpreted.

Then suddenly came an interruption to his pre-occupation with the Arts. His father, who had been at intervals a sick man ever since he contracted syphilis in his youth, died after a week's illness in March, 1861. Ludwig, at the age of eighteen and a half, was King.

Many historians have since looked at Ludwig's life with the objectivity which is only possible when many years have elapsed. They consider that Bismarck was right when he claimed the unhappy monarch of Bavaria had one of the best brains in Europe. But at the time he lived, and among his Ministers, Ludwig II's qualifications for Kingship were gravely doubted.

However, no one could deny that in physical appearance he was a fairy-story-King. Six foot three inches tall, slim but broad shouldered, with almost jet black wavy hair, blazing blue eyes, contrasting with the ivory whiteness of his aristocratic face, he was, with justification compared to a Greek God. The most appropriate description given of him when he first appeared in public as the Ruler of Bavaria was "A most beautiful youth."

This praise carried with it the insinuation of his faults

which betokened ill in an age when force backed by the big battalions was an essential factor in government.

"I will do everything in my power to make my people happy. Their welfare and their peace are the conditions of my own happiness," he said on the first day of his reign. There was no mention of power or riches, and even if the ordinary people loved him for his aims, they cut little ice with his Ministers and still less with those of Bavaria's allies.

Within a month of becoming King, Ludwig sent a courier to the little village near Vienna where Wagner was living with the daughter of a Viennese tradesman. The courier had some difficulty in locating the composer, who was hiding from his creditors, but this heaven-sent Royal interest saved the financial day. Within twenty-four hours·Wagner was in Munich.

The first meeting between King and composer lasted for an hour and a half. Afterwards, Ludwig confessed that he had fallen head over heels in love. It was a more bizarre, emotional friendship than his previous ones of a similar type. The first had been when he was seventeen, for his valet, a young man who was at least of his own generation.

This had been followed by brief interest in operatic singers and then by a romantic attachment for Prince Paul of Thurn and Taxis, two years older than Ludwig and brother of the husband of Hélène, Elizabeth's sister. Both these close friends were of a similar type to Ludwig, romantic looking, gentle, fond of beautiful things and able to glory in the simple charms of Nature.

Wagner, by contrast, was a notorious heterosexual romantic whose affairs with inumerable women were the scandal of Europe. Moreover the composer was thirty-two years older than the young King. However beautiful the music that he produced might be, Wagner was in his person somewhat careless of cleanliness. He omitted to change his clothes very often. He took snuff. He perspired profusely whenever he got excited—which was very often.

His appearance must have contrasted strangely with that

of Ludwig, always beautifully dressed, favouring white satin lining for his outer clothes and silk for his underwear, his hair carefully waved at least once a week, and his person exuding perfume, notably chypre and jasmine.

Ludwig was, however, ready to overlook anything while thinking only of the glorious music which his adored "great friend" produced.

Wagner wrote:

"The King understands me like my own soul . . . how magical is his look . . . He is, alas, so fair, so full of spirituality that I tremble lest I should behold his life dissolve like a crystal dream. . . . I believe that if he were to die, I should die the moment after."

"Dull people," Ludwig wrote to Wagner, "cannot have any idea of our love. They do not know that you are, have been, and ever will be—all in all to me until my dying day."

But Ludwig's great friendship with Wagner could not keep to the heights in which it started. In 1865, there were disagreements and quarrels, and once again he turned to Elizabeth for inspiration. The Empress was visiting her family residence at Possenhofen. Ludwig as usual made the short journey from the other side of Lake Starnberg to talk to her.

She watched him arrive in his state coach with outriders and accompanying courtiers. It was a wet day and Ludwig had put on an officer's uniform of the Austrian Army in which he had an honorary appointment. Elizabeth wrote to her son Rudolph saying:

"Yesterday the King paid me a visit and if Grandma had not come in at last he would be here now. I was very nice and he kissed my hand so often that Aunt Sophie, who was peeping through the door, asked me afterwards whether I had any hand left. He was wearing an Austrian uniform and was all scented with *chypre*."

Ludwig was overwhelmed by Elizabeth's beauty. To be near her seemed to give him perfect happiness. He identified himself with Lohengrin.

"Lohengrin seeks the woman who believes in him," he told her; "Who asks neither who he is nor whence he came, but who will love him as he is—because he is as he is. He seeks the woman to whom he will have no need to explain nor justify himself, but who will love him without reservation. What he is seeking is the one thing that can free him from his loneliness—love—to be understood through love."

Elizabeth had also sought this type of idealistic love all through her life and she felt a profound and tragic affinity with her handsome, unbalanced cousin.

One thing they both had in common was their alienation from people and their deep love of nature.

"It is strange," Elizabeth once said, "that wherever man goes, everything is destroyed. Men only do harm to things. Only where things stay by themselves do they retain their eternal beauty."

It was the Tristan motif in them both and to Ludwig Tristan was the synthesis of all his cravings. It released in him a sense of being alive that he had never known before.

When his special train returned him to Berg Castle from the fourth (and last) performance in Munich, he pulled the alarm cord, and to calm his nerves, went on a lonely walk through the dark forest. In Tristan he had climbed a peak of human experience. No wonder Ludwig signed his letters to Wagner: "Unto death your Ludwig."

But the composer had become rather bored with the whole business, and on the pretext of having work to do, had for a time left Ludwig's Court, his debts having been settled for him and his innumerable enemies quietened for the time being.

Ludwig was back in his exciting friendship with Prince Paul, who was ever ready to step into the world of fantasy which Ludwig loved so much.

On the Schwansee, the lovely private lake inside the Royal Park, the two young men alternately dressed up as Lohengrin, pretending in turn to play a harp. They sat in a boat drawn by a large imitation swan, in which a servant was

concealed so as to provide movement by operating the feet
of the bird as paddles.

By the autumn Wagner was back again conducting his
musical works which were performed in the beautiful little
private theatre of the King's in Munich. The composer took
the opportunity of his renewed contacts with Ludwig to
extract still more money from him.

The ministers were so incensed by Wagner's rapacity that
they publicised the fact by putting forty thousand florins in
a sack and sending it on an open cart through the streets of
Munich. In this way everyone saw what was going on.

Simultaneously the newspapers nicknamed the composer
"Lolus," the masculine version of the Christian name of
Lola Montez, who only a few years before had similarly
tried to bleed the country white. The uproar about the
friendship then became so great that Ludwig was compelled
to send Wagner away. He still managed, however, to visit
the composer on many occasions during the latter's exile in
Switzerland.

In 1866, more of Ludwig's emotional world came crashing
in ruins. He heard to his disgust and horror of carousals in
which Paul had been indulging in the brothels and taverns
of Munich. Wagner was far away, and Bavaria was technically involved in the war against Denmark.

The despair and lonely unhappiness of the twenty-two
year old King were well known to everyone. The Archduchess Ludovica, at Possenhofen which was only across the Lake
from Berg where the King was then staying, had an idea.
She knew of Ludwig's adoration of her daughter Elizabeth,
and this encouraged her to believe that her younger daughter
Sophie, who was physically remarkably like her sister, might
entice Ludwig into marriage.

It was perhaps a mother's natural ambition to have two
daughters as Royal Consorts. But the suggestion, carefully
put before Ludwig's relatives and Ministers, was accepted
as a splendid one. It would they thought put the young
monarch's emotional life on an even keel.

Elizabeth was worried about her sister but did not want to interfere. She spent a few days at Possenhofen and when she left, Ludwig accompanied her part of the way to Ischl.

"You can have no idea, dear cousin," he wrote to her afterwards; "how happy you made me. The hours recently passed in the railway carriage I reckon among the happiest in my life; never will their memory fade. You gave me permission to visit you at Ischl; if the time which will be so happy for me is really approaching, when my hope of seeing you will be fulfilled, I shall be of all men upon earth the most blessed. My sense of sincere love and reverence and faithful attachment to you which I cherished in my heart even as a boy makes me see heaven upon earth, and will be extinguished by death alone. I beg you with all my heart to forgive the contents of these lines, but I could not help myself."

Ludwig had for sometime previous to this been carrying on with the prima donna of the Royal Theatre, Lila von Bulyovsky. She was a pretty Hungarian and Ludwig was so moved by her portrayal of Mary Stuart in Schiller's play, that he went straight from the theatre to the Court Chapel to pray for the Soul of the wretched Mary Queen of Scots.

A malicious little ditty swept Munich which went:

"After that other music that Richard played so long
At last Miss Bulyovsky has sung the proper song."

Ludwig wanted little from Lila but an occasional tender kiss on his beautifully groomed hair, although the King once confided that in thinking of her he frequently kissed his lonely pillow.

What annoyed her was that he treated her, even when they were alone, as if she was Mary Stuart and signed his letters "Mortimer", who was of course Mary's romantic lover in the play.

Lila was disappointed in Ludwig and the King vehemently resented Lila's petty intrigues for the best rôles in the theatre.

He turned with relief and delight to Sophie, who shared his obsession for Wagner and who, for the King's sake, had studied the part of Elizabeth in *Tannhauser* and Senta in *The Flying Dutchman*. He signed his letters to her as "Heinrich".

Ludwig wrote to a friend in January 1867 and said: "Sophie is a loyal sympathetic soul, full of spirit: her fate has a certain resemblance to mine."

The official announcement of the engagement was made on New Year's Day, 1867. For a time Ludwig delighted in being seen everywhere with his fiancée, and his Bavarian subjects could not understand that the whole thing was to him an idealistic and romantic dream.

Only rarely in those months did he regard himself as a mortal king of the nineteenth century and his fiancée as a minor aristocrat of a neighbouring country. He preferred to pretend that he was Adonis and she Venus. Or that he was Heinrich and she was Elsa.

There can be little doubt that the physical aspect of his forthcoming marriage revolted him, but he submerged his qualms by concentrating on designing for his bride a beautiful little boudoir which he placed in a wing of the palace below his own study. He even built a secret passage by which the boudoir could be reached.

The love letters which have survived from Ludwig to Sophie were almost all signed with one of his operatic or legendary names. Again and again they contain protestations of his love for Wagner and suggestions that she should read his biography, hear his music and learn to admire the composer as he himself did.

Another habit of Ludwig's of turning the days and the seasons round about was more peculiar. He took his breakfast at supper-time and vice-versa. He also travelled in midsummer in a sleigh and longed for snow.

To gratify the Royal wish the flowers and shrubberies were covered with blankets of gossamer fluff, while a grotto which had been strewn with roses in the winter was now festooned with papier maché icicles.

Ludwig's resolution to go through with the marriage began to break by March, when details of the ceremonies of the wedding were placed before him. He called them terrible. But the ceremony was still distant and he continued to suppress his fears by concentrating on the romantic side of his engagement.

He used to ride to Archduke Maximilian's house in Munich, where the family had as usual come from Possenhofen for the winter months, and hurl enormous bouquets of flowers through the first floor window of Sophie's bedroom. No matter what the weather, this window had to be wide open from dawn onwards until the gift crashed on the floor.

On one occasion, when a spring gale was blowing and the servant judged it impossible to have the window open, Ludwig threw his heavy bouquet just the same. He was delighted to think that there was no barrier that could prevent his daily token of love reaching his fiancée's bedside.

This was all very dramatic, as were Ludwig's visits in the middle of the night on horseback, but whenever the date for the wedding was discussed, Ludwig had some good reason for suggesting a postponement.

In October Duke Max lost his patience. He would not stand Sophie being a laughing stock and he sent Ludwig an ultimatum: either the wedding would take place in November or the betrothal would be cancelled at once.

Ludwig blew up in regal anger. How dare a "subject" give the King an ultimatum? The portrait bust of Sophie which had adorned his desk, hit the flagstones of the inner courtyard and broke into a thousand pieces.

But after this first flare-up he realised the Duke had opened for him an avenue of escape. He scribbled a note to Sophie:

"Your cruel father tears us apart. Eternally your Heinrich."
On the same day he wrote in his diary:

"Sophie got rid of (abgeschrieben). The gloomy picture dissolves. I longed for freedom. I am athirst for freedom, now that I live again after this torturing nightmare."

On the day that the marriage was to have taken place he added:

"Thanks be to God, the fearful thing was not realised."

Ludwig found fresh joys in the company of a new friend, "Richard, beloved of my heart," a twenty-seven year old blond German who had been appointed Royal Equerry.

Sophie took it very well, although her niece, Countess Wallersee-Larisch, in her memoirs says that she never ceased to love Ludwig, even after his death.

Elizabeth wrote to her mother in great indignation:

"You can imagine how angry I am with the King . . . I am only glad that Sophie takes it as she does. With such a husband, God knows, she could never have been happy; I now redouble my wishes that she may find a good one at last, but who will that be?"

In less than a year Sophie was married to the Duc d'Alencon, grandson of King Louis Philippe of France. The wedding took place in the chapel at Possenhofen, and in due course the bride and groom paid the necessary formal visit to Ludwig in Munich.

Callously the young King said afterwards that the meeting had bored him to death.

TEN

1868-1871

ELIZABETH'S "gift to Hungary" was born on April 22nd, 1868. The Empress went to Budapest in the early spring so that she could be sure that the baby was born on Hungarian soil.

It was the first time for a hundred years and more that a Royal child had been born in the country, and Budapest went crazy with delight. The fact that the official bulletins gave the Hungarian version of the baby's name—Muszikam, infuriated Vienna as much as the fact that the mother had deliberately gone outside the Imperial capital for the birth.

The dislike of her departure went to such lengths that the Archduchess related in a letter to her sister that one aristocratic lady had remarked tartly: "The Empress deserves to have a miscarriage!"

Elizabeth dismissed the complaints with the comment that the citizens of Vienna could not be surprised if she kept away from them after this jaundiced criticism of the happy event.

Embittered by such hostility from the Court and the misery of being separated by the Archduchess from her other children, Elizabeth virtually smothered her last child with affection. She was determined to keep this baby to herself. She would not let Valerie out of her sight, and wherever they might be living the nursery always had to be adjacent to her own bedroom.

She had been convinced that she was going to have a daughter. She had even chosen the name of Valerie, while up to the last minute the Emperor had great hopes of a son. Franz Joseph was, however, delighted with his daughter once she was born and he wrote to Rudolph and Gisela at the Schönbrunn:

"The baby is charming. She is a beauty with big dark blue eyes, a nose that is still a trifle flat, a very small mouth, enormously fat cheeks, and such thick black hair that you could already comb it."

"I shall make her as little German as possible," Elizabeth promised Andrássy, and she was as good as her word. All the nurses were Hungarian. She had spent hours every day during her pregnancy learning Magyar. She was now fluent and never addressed the baby in any other language.

It was not surprising that at Court the child was sneeringly nicknamed "*die Einzige*"—"The one and only one."

The Archduchess made no claim upon the new Princess. Even if the Emperor hailed the child as his own, she had her doubts. Spies sent her frequent reports on Valerie's progress and she was always trying to discover in just how many respects the baby did *not* resemble Franz Joseph.

Valerie was delicate, as all Elizabeth's children were, and with the approach of summer she took the child to Godollo.

Here she could have the child entirely to herself, but she was terribly over-anxious. On one occasion the baby's digestion was upset, which Elizabeth ascribed to the wet nurse's milk.

"I am terribly alarmed; really horrified," she wrote to a friend; "for, believe me, I do not have a moment's peace. It is a horrible feeling when one knows that one's dearest treasure upon earth is surrounded by untrustworthy persons."

There was a battle royal with the old nurse who was dismissed because Elizabeth said; "not even the Lord God can get on with her."

The nurse could not understand such a panic if the baby was unwell for one day. She did not realise that Elizabeth agonised over this child because it was hers and hers alone.

Elizabeth's close companion in those summer months at Godollo was Ida Ferenczy, a simple, rather plain girl who adored her.

Four years earlier Elizabeth had asked that she might have a Hungarian lady in her Household with whom she could converse. A long list of names had been drawn up, but Elizabeth had picked on one Ida von Ferenczy. She learnt that she was the daughter of a Hungarian gentleman, named Kecskemét, who had four other daughters and a crippled son.

When Ida was presented to Elizabeth she recognised at once that this quiet country girl was the type for whom she was looking—someone natural, healthy, cheerful and a true Hungarian patriot.

She wanted someone who would serve her and not the Archduchess; someone she could trust and who would not be spoiled and influenced by the Court intrigues.

The difficulty was, of course, to find a place for Ida in the strictly graded Court hierarchy. Finally, someone thought of making her "Reader to Her Majesty" which gave her the right to be called "Frau".

Elizabeth immediately warned Ida to be on her guard and never to breathe a word to anyone of what they said or did together. Blushing with deep emotion, Ida promised to serve the Empress faithfully, and speaking in Magyar, Elizabeth said:

"I am greatly pleased with you; we shall be much together."

It was a good thing that Ida had been warned. She had only been in Elizabeth's employment for a few days when the Archduchess's principal lady-in-waiting sent for her and said:

"Pray consult me in everything and confide to me all that Her Majesty says."

Elizabeth, however, soon discovered that her instinct where Ida was concerned had been right. The girl was devoted to her body and soul.

The friendship developed into intimacy. Elizabeth even protested that she suffered from insomnia at night if Ida did not sit by her bedside talking and worshipping her "dewy flower", as she called her adored mistress.

As her health improved in the serenity of Godollo Elizabeth

was able to amuse herself with her accustomed vigour. Here she could indulge her love of the circus. In Vienna she often attended public performances of circuses to the delight of the management and the horror of the Court. In the Prater, where she went for a morning canter, she sometimes made her mount perform movements which were really out of place anywhere but in the sawdust ring.

There had never been until that time, or, in fact, since, an amateur rider to equal Elizabeth. Both in the field and in the riding school she was unrivalled in grace and ability. Despite her slender, dainty build she had tremendous strength and there was no horse that she could not ride once she had made up her mind to do so.

She was extremely strict in disciplining her mounts and wore special spurs which could inflict great pain although they were very light and decoratively fashioned. If a horse was lazy or stubborn she would ride it hard, spurring it relentlessly until it submitted or was exhausted. But however severe she was in the saddle, when she dismounted her feminine gentleness reasserted itself and she never forgot to pat it or give it a carrot.

Franz Gebhardt, the foremost rider of the "haute école" —the world famous Spanish school at Vienna—said of her:

"The Empress outshines any rider of her own sex. She has the knack of putting herself into immediate and almost mesmeric communication with her horse."

Elizabeth had what was really an hypnotic influence over animals and the most unmanageable horses would allow her to approach and pet them.

The Colonel in command of the Reit Lehren Institut at Vienna would be horrified when he would receive a message from the Empress saying:

"Please send to the riding school a couple of your wildest horses for me to have a little fun with them."

He would try to refuse, but Elizabeth would force him to do as she wished and his bronzed face would turn pale as he watched the graceful figure school a horse which he would not have dared to let an experienced cavalry officer ride.

One of the wealthiest magnates and horsebreeders in Hungary owned a magnificent coal-black stallion known as "The Black Devil." It possessed such a fiendish temper that for six months the grooms had been unable to enter the stable, and had fed the animal from pails with six-foot handles.

Elizabeth heard of this, and did not rest until she had driven over to see the "Black Devil" for herself. Without a moment's hesitation, and disregarding the horrified protests from the owner and her ladies-in-waiting, she drew back the bolt and entered the stable.

Everyone held their breath, expecting to see her trampled to pieces. At first the stallion snorted and laid back his ears, but as he listened to Elizabeth's voice the fiery eyes softened.

She patted him, and then said to the petrified onlookers outside:

"He is as gentle as a lamb, poor old boy, but he is badly in need of a brush-up."

With her own hands she brushed down "Black Devil" and then accepted him as a present. It took a long time before the stallion would allow a man near him, but Elizabeth obtained such mastery over him that he would follow her about the park and grounds at Godollo like a dog.

Elizabeth's fascination for circuses was, of course, partially a realisation of a childhood ambition when she had been allowed to take part in the performances her father staged at his private circus in Munich. But it was also the result of her admiration for circus people.

In Hungary a passion for spectacular exercising on horseback was not regarded as an eccentricity, but as a natural ambition for anyone with the nation's blood in his veins. The fact that the Empress had a fervid love of horseflesh made her, in her subjects' eyes, as Hungarian as the stallions she rode.

She spent a large sum of money on the Godollo circus,

Queen of Hungary. A photograph taken at the Coronation celebrations in
Budapest in June 1867, when Elizabeth was twenty-nine

Ludwig II, King of Bavaria

Katharina Schratt, the '*bonne amie*' of the ageing Emperor Franz Joseph, in stage costume

which was an exact copy of a public one in everything but size. A professional ring master was engaged to crack the whip as the Empress, dressed in a black velvet habit, put her Arab mount through his tricks of the *haute école*.

An expert horsewoman, she also longed to perform the really spectacular acrobatics of the ring and some time after the birth of Princess Valerie she formed a friendship with Ernst Jakob Renz. He was the son of a trapeze artist and had founded the most famous circus in Europe.

He had sixty trained horses representing every breed, and he also had a daughter, Elise, who was the star attraction in the performing horse acts. The girl acrobat and the Empress became close companions, with the latter a surprisingly meek and willing pupil of the more expert professional.

With one of Renz's trainers to help her Elizabeth had three circus horses on which she would perform the most professional tricks. One of these animals, "Avolo", could dance most gracefully to music, and would also kneel down with the Empress on his back.

Elizabeth could soon do more professional stunts. Dressed like a handsome boy in tights and a white silk shirt she would leap through hoops from a standing balance on the backs of galloping horses.

Stories of the circus, of course, became the talk of Vienna, and Elizabeth was nicknamed the "Circus rider." Whereupon the Hungarians retaliated by proudly acclaiming her "Queen of the Amazons."

A stiff-necked cavalry officer dared to protest to the Emperor about the Empress's behaviour, making the excuse that this sort of riding was dangerous.

"Ah, my friend," sighed the Emperor, "you don't understand women. They do what they like, without asking permission."

Franz Joseph never permitted the newspapers to print a line concerning Elizabeth's circus performances. In fact fifty years later it was almost impossible to buy a picture of the Empress on horseback. They had all been destroyed by the police.

To the great indignation of the Viennese, Elizabeth had spent exactly three quarters of the year following the conclusion of the treaty with Hungary in that country. What was more, she dismissed the last survivors of the Household chosen for her by the Archduchess and replaced them with Hungarians.

The German state newspapers complained that Elizabeth now lived in a world that was wholly Hungarian. She always spoke Magyar; all her women friends were Hungarians; and she engaged nurses for little Valerie who would sing Hungarian folk songs to the child.

She therefore had a very cold reception when she returned to Vienna. She wrote to her mother in January 1869:

"I am desperate at having to be here, and long for Buda all the time, where it is so much more beautiful and pleasanter in every respect."

Julius Andrássy was also left behind at Budapest. He missed Elizabeth desperately and wrote to her regularly. Ida Ferenczy was in their confidence and helped them to avoid the peeping and prying of the Austrian secret police. Elizabeth and Ida were very careful and always referred to Andrássy as "our friend" and not by name.

Elizabeth suffered from what she called "a terrible Hungarian home sickness". She hated nearly everyone in Vienna. "Except for you and my horses," she said to Ida; "I meet with nothing but unpleasantness wherever I go."

Elizabeth's passion for horses was a comparatively inexpensive pastime. She had others which caused deeper forebodings in the Emperor's mind for they cost the Imperial Exchequer a vast amount of money. Elizabeth herself had no idea whatever of the value of money. Her latest interest in architecture was to run away with several fortunes.

Like her cousin Ludwig, she could find sublimation in her building projects. There were within the confines of the

Empire more than fifty castles, houses and villas maintained in a state of readiness for Royal occupation, and it would not have been difficult for her to discover one sufficiently remote from her husband and the Court.

All of them, however, failed to interest her, partly because her every move and action would have been reported by the Crown servants in the official residences, and also because they offered no novelty of design or furnishing.

The lesson of Ludwig's flagrant and blatant extravagancies was not lost on her, and although her own more modest architectural activities were proportionately as extravagant she was reasonably circumspect, being ready to wait so that the expenditure would not appear over-great, in any one year.

One place she was pleased to call 'a villa,' but was big enough to house a Court, she planned during her first visit to Corfu in 1861.

No government representative was allowed to enter it, and it was only revealed as a fantastic testimony to her restless imagination after her death.

She named this dream house "Achilleon," in honour of Achilles. As a basis for the project she bought a half-ruined villa on a steep wooded hill near Gasturi. From its upper windows the coast of Albania could be seen.

She planned the grounds before tackling extensions to the house, and her whole concept was to make it a symbolic fortress protecting her from the world beyond.

The cart track from the town of Corfu was allowed to go back to the semi-tropical vegetation which lay on either side. Entrance to the grounds was therefore possible only from the sea. The jetty in the bay below the house was built of white marble, and at its base was a marble building to house generating equipment so that she, like Ludwig, could create mystic scenes at night with the help of coloured electric lamps.

More marble terraces and steps led up and up to the house, and a further flight of marble steps led to the very crown of the hill where a pseudo-Greek temple was built, consecrated to her favourite poet, Heinrich Heine.

All around were sacred cypresses in imitation of a pagan grove. And on every side there was evidence of Elizabeth's pre-occupation with classical mythology. On the villa's colonnade, frescoes depicted Apollo and Daphne, Homer reciting his poems, and Aesop reading his fables. In the gardens, the Greek Muses and the Greek heroes stood in the statuesque whiteness of valuable marble amid the dark green of laurel and cypress.

Everywhere there were flowers—twenty-five thousand rose-bushes—and pink marble for steps and columns. The stables, saddles and harness-rooms were all bought from England even down to the light oak wainscotting which lined the coach-houses. Little wonder that this retreat of Elizabeth's cost forty million florins, not including the art treasures and the picture gallery.

It was known that Elizabeth often wandered around the precipitous mountain paths in the middle of the night. Except in the depth of winter she was invariably out by five in the morning, making her way to the sacred grove in order to watch the slanting shaft of sunlight creep lower and lower until the woods and pasturage at sea level sprang to life.

No one was ever allowed to accompany her on this morning routine, and when stories about it intrigued British officials, and they went to the crest of a neighbouring hill to watch her, she had a high wall erected to cut off the view.

Her beauty and her kindness to the peasants of the village of Gasturi made them almost worship her. Whenever they saw her they would kneel in the dust and cry: "Oh Queen of Beauty, may God bless thy every step."

If Achilleon was a Greek legend come to life, the Palace of Lainz was straight from a book of fairy tales. Elizabeth planned this with the deliberate intention of having a hide-away even if she had officially to be in residence in the capital.

Built in the Tiergarten, the undulating and lovely Royal

game preserve for eight centuries, it was difficult to realise it was so near the capital. The castle was embedded in masses of blossom. There was a winter garden for tropical plants, and the decorations were all Renaissance. Floors were covered in white bearskins, and there were fountains of marble, wonderful carvings and alabaster statues to make a perfect setting for Elizabeth's fabulous beauty.

But when the Imperial family went into residence in 1887 Valerie did not like it.

"These marble reliefs, these luxurious carpets," she wrote: "these fireplaces of chased bronze, these innumerable angels and Cupids . . . this mannered rococo style! How I wish we were back at home again!"

As at Corfu, a private staircase led directly to the Empress's private apartments, which included a vast gymnasium containing every conceivable device for weight reducing and muscular development. Inevitably, of course, the stables were on a grandiose and magnificent scale.

Elizabeth's preoccupation with building was in reality merely an attempt to convince herself that in the right environment she could take root and settle down. In fact she knew that they were experiments doomed to failure. Her restless spirit drove her perpetually onward, ostensibly in search of a cure for sciatica, next on the excuse that the weather was too hot, too cold or too damp.

Not even to herself would she admit that she not merely found it more glorious to travel than to arrive, but that motiveless journeys were becoming the only form of existence she could tolerate.

When one of Elizabeth's ladies-in-waiting got married, Count Andrássy suggested another Hungarian to take her place—Countess Marie Festetics.

Although the Countess had fallen under Elizabeth's spell she had some misgivings about the post, but the Count urged her to accept it—

"It is your duty to make this sacrifice for your country," he said. "The Queen stands in need of someone faithful."

The Countess soon found out the truth of this. The Archduchess acknowledged her presence with the merest inclination of her head, while other members of the family did not even speak to her.

"One has to get used to that sort of thing," Elizabeth told her. "Anyone attached to me is naturally persecuted."

At that time all sorts of stories were being circulated about the Empress and how she and the Emperor quarrelled. The Countess noted how she avoided society and sought solitude.

"Are you not surprised," Elizabeth asked her new lady-in-waiting, "at my living like a hermit?"

"I am indeed, Your Majesty; for you are still too young."

"Yes, I am," Elizabeth replied; "but I have no choice but to live like this. I have been so persecuted, misjudged and slandered, so hurt and wounded in this great world. God looks at my soul. I have never done what was evil. . . . I have withdrawn into myself and turned to nature."

There is no doubt at all that this feeling of persecution directly affected Elizabeth's health. However well she might be during her travels, the moment she returned to Vienna she became ill again.

In the years to come there was continual grumbling and dissatisfaction in Austria that their Empress spent so much time abroad that she refused to appear at public functions, and that the social life at Court fell mainly on the Emperor's shoulders. The fault lay entirely with the Archduchess and the 'coterie' who had been against Elizabeth from the very beginning.

Their coldness and unkindness ate into her soul until like a plant without sunshine, she literally withered whenever she entered the portals of the Schönbrunn or the Hofburg.

The idea of escape was always in her mind, and the sea passage back from Madeira in Queen Victoria's yacht had in the years that followed become a memory of youth and freedom. She felt she must have a yacht which could carry her wherever she wished, and she persuaded Franz Joseph to spend a considerable amount of money in re-equipping the Imperial yacht *Miramare*.

The vessel was a paddle steamer of ancient design, almost a museum piece for that period of rapid development in navigation. More modern engines were put in in order to obtain the speed for which Elizabeth yearned, and the deck was completely re-built to enable her to walk round and round from bow to stern without interruption.

The *Miramare* was used for all Elizabeth's trips around the Adriatic and Mediterranean, but there was a secret order from the Imperial Ministry of Marine which forbade the ship's Master taking his vessel out into the Atlantic, for which, indeed, she was quite unsuitable.

Even so, there were often stormy passages and when bad weather occurred the Empress would invariably insist on putting out further to sea so that she might enjoy the storm.

"The sea is my Father Confessor," she once told the Captain. "It restores my youth while it removes from me all that is not myself. All that I know I have learned from the sea."

On deck a little forward from the bridge was a large circular glass-enclosed room in which Elizabeth had her hair dressed every morning, and afterwards read and wrote for hours on end. For bad weather the after-deck had a partition which could be closed in order that she might enjoy the storm without the crew being able to see her.

"It is like being on an island from which all worries and fretting have been banished," she said. "It is an ideal existence without desire and without the sense of time."

This was all very well for Elizabeth but a most worrying situation for the Captain whose task it was, of course, to ensure the safety of the Empress. Just at the time when there might have been danger of her being washed overboard, the partition would go up and he could not see a thing.

The rigours of her daily activities on the ship contrasted with the feminine comforts with which Elizabeth provided herself. All the furniture and hangings in the cabins were in white silk and enormous trouble had to be taken to ensure that no matter how long the journey might be, fresh flowers should appear in the vases.

The bathroom had a marble bath for which sea water had to be obtained every morning by a boat which took casks some distance from the yacht, in order that the water could not possibly be contaminated with oil or debris from the ship.

Elizabeth was happier at sea than anywhere else.

"The waves seem to draw me towards them, as if they knew I love them," she would often say.

Once, after a storm in which the waves had broken all over the yacht and the Captain had been desperately afraid for his Empress's life she said, laughing:

"How many more times must I declare my principles and ideas about the length of life which is allotted to each of us? We live just as long as God permits, and if I have been entrusted with a mission here below, Providence will protect me from every danger."

ELEVEN

1872-1880

HOWEVER hard Elizabeth strove for independence, the march of the years forced her to shoulder some of her responsibilities as a wife and mother. Franz Joseph had now lapsed into a sort of taciturn resignation about her continual travels.

He had dozens of flirtations on hand, some of a very passionate nature, but nevertheless he missed her when she was not there. He often signed his letters *"Dein einsames Manneken"*. (Your lonely little husband.) And in one letter he wrote:—

"My dear angel; here I am alone with my many worries again, and longing for you . . . I love you so infinitely that I cannot exist without you."

Another letter ended:—"I embrace you, my glorious, passionately beloved wife, together with the children, and remain, your Manneken."

Franz Joseph was, however, totally lacking in imagination and could never understand the world of dreams in which Elizabeth wished only to exist. She was hurt when he described her enthusiasm as *Wolkenkraxlerei*—"scaling the clouds".

In April, 1873, Elizabeth left for Budapest where a rapturous welcome from the enormous crowds assured her of her great popularity in Hungary. A surprise awaited her at the Royal Palace, Gisela had become engaged to Prince Leopold of Bavaria.

Gisela's prospective marriage was a real love match. She had met Prince Leopold at Ischl and they had become inseparable. She was not quite sixteen years old and her lover ten years older. It was true that she was heart-hungry and looked forward eagerly to marriage as a means of escape from the remnants of the strict supervision she had known all her life under the care of her grandmother, but Leopold was just as insistent that the wedding date should be soon.

Elizabeth protested that the girl was very young, ignoring the fact that she herself had been married at almost the same age. Of course, her enemies at Court whispered that her misgivings were not entirely disinterested; Gisela's marriage would make her a mother-in-law and possibly within a year a grandmother.

The Emperor and his ministers were, however, delighted. The marriage meant another small tie with the potential forces to keep Prussia in order, and the prospective bridegroom was in religion and by birth a perfectly appropriate addition to the Hapsburgs. As usual, they were quite unconcerned about the question of consanguinity and ignored the fact that Leopold had the taint of insanity in his Wittelsbach ancestry.

The marriage was delayed by the death of Archduchess Sophie. She had contracted a severe chill and had for some time been suffering from somnolence and a trembling in her hands and feet.

The Archduchess grew worse, but her mind remained clear and she took an affectionate farewell of every member of the Imperial Family. Elizabeth was constantly at her bedside but at eleven-thirty at night she went back to the Hofburg for a brief rest. She had barely arrived when a messenger came with news that the Archduchess was dying.

Elizabeth told the coachman to drive to the Schönbrunn as fast as he could. She was terribly afraid that she might be too late, being well aware that if she was, everyone would say her absence was intentional.

The Archduchess lived until a quarter to three the following afternoon. Elizabeth, as usual, showed herself touchingly sweet in a crisis. She never left the Archduchess's bedside although she had nothing to eat for ten hours. In the presence of death her hostility was forgotten and she was very gentle to the mother-in-law she had hated for so many years.

As soon as the funeral was over Elizabeth left for Ischl. At last she was free from the woman who had overshadowed and spoiled her life for so many years. But the scars had gone too deep, and although the Archduchess was dead the poison of her personality remained. Her friends in the Court, who had never understood or appreciated Elizabeth, now said: " 'Our Empress' is lost and buried."

But at Ischl not even her black mourning clothes could hide Elizabeth's glorious figure and enchanting face. The Countess Festetics wrote:

"It is a joy to be with her and even to follow her. It is enough to gaze upon her. She is the very incarnation of the word charm. Sometimes I think of her as a lily, then again a swan, a fairy or an elf. And then after all I think: No! She is a Queen! From the crown of her head to the soles of her feet, a queenly woman! Fine and noble in all things. And then again all the gossip comes into my head and I think there must be a great deal of envy behind it, for, to sum it all up, she is bewitchingly lovely and full of charm."

Gisela's wedding took place on April 20th, 1873. Elizabeth attended the ceremony wearing a dress of black satin embroidered all over in silver, and a diamond crown on her glorious masses of hair. She was thirty-six but looked more like a young girl than a mother.

She broke down towards the end of the service. Although Gisela had never really been her child, having been taken from her by the Archduchess, she was sad at parting with her.

The festivities which followed were as usual a torture for Elizabeth. There were receptions, a concert, enormous dinner parties and a gala performance at the theatre. She went to some of them but then retired, saying she was not well.

The year 1874 was only four days old when Elizabeth became a grandmother. Gisela gave birth to a daughter at Munich. Cholera was raging in the town and after the baptism Elizabeth insisted on visiting a cholera hospital.

"I am going alone," she said, "because I cannot take on myself the responsibility of letting anyone attend me."

The Countess Marie Festetics was aghast and begged her to change her mind. But when they reached the hospital and Elizabeth wished to leave her in the carriage she insisted in accompanying her mistress.

In the hospital they saw the most harrowing sights. Elizabeth went from bed to bed speaking words of comfort to the sick and dying. She was over-anxious where her children were concerned, but quite heedless of danger to herself.

After a visit to Ludwig's mother, Elizabeth was back in her beloved Hungary. The magnetism of that country was more than usually strong. There was a new attraction in the shape of the handsome young Count Elemer Batthyany, son of the national martyr in the Hungarian revolution.

On his mother's Bible the Count had sworn never to speak to the Emperor, and this oath he never broke. Even though there were times when, as a guest of Elizabeth at Godollo, he should have paid his respects to Franz Joseph.

A magnificent rider, single, and with a somnolent look in his eyes which suggested tremendous masculinity, Batthyany attracted a great many women, but when the Countess Marie Wallersee suggested to her Aunt that she found him charming and hinted that he might make her a good husband, Elizabeth shook her head, and said:

"My dear Marie, as a husband Elemer would be very disappointing."

"Why?" the girl asked.

"Never mind why," Elizabeth replied. "You would soon know why if you married him."

The general belief among Batthyany's cronies was that both his health and his emotional outlook made him a poor ladies' man, but at the same time Elizabeth's warning to her niece may have been motivated by jealousy. She did not like her special favourites to marry, were they men or women.

Marie was a very pretty girl, coquettish, and an amusing

companion, so that she received many proposals. Count Nicholas Esterhazy, always in attendance on the Empress when she was in Hungary and very often in Vienna as well, became infatuated with Marie and proposed to her.

Marie told her aunt, despite Esterhazy's warning that she should not do so. Elizabeth, after turning away apparently indifferent, visited the girl in her bedroom and said in cold, angry tones:

"I must tell you that Count Esterhazy has a liaison with a married woman, who loves him. After hearing this, I personally feel sure that you will not accept his proposal."

The inference was obvious and Marie could do nothing but refuse.

While fox hunting at Godollo was good because Elizabeth had inaugurated it strictly on British lines, she began to have a longing to see for herself what went on in the English Shires.

The opportunity came in August 1874 when Valerie was ill, and it was suggested that the sea-bathing at Ventnor in the Isle of Wight might be good for her. After a few weeks at Ventnor, Elizabeth visited the Duke of Rutland at Belvoir Castle and hunted for the first time on English soil. She spent the next night at Melton, visited the kennels and the idea of spending the whole hunting season there thrilled her so much that the possibility was seriously discussed.

The two day's hunting was so exhausting that even the men were dead-beat, but Elizabeth was in her element and enjoyed herself so enormously that she did not feel tired. She went back to Ventnor, determined that somehow she would return.

Queen Victoria, accompanied by John Brown, called, and was quite dazzled by Elizabeth's beauty. But in a letter to Franz Joseph, the latter reported:

"The Queen was very kind and said nothing that was not amiable, but she is not sympathetic to me."

Little Valerie was terrified of the Queen. "I've never seen such a stout lady," she exclaimed.

In March, 1876, Elizabeth realised her wish and rented Easton Neston, Towcester—a lovely country house with a big park. It was a mile from another attractive hunting box where her sister Marie, the Queen of Naples, was staying.

Besides Elizabeth's immediate attendants she was joined by a little band of horsemen who were all devoted to her. Among them Prince Rudolf Liechtenstein, who, Elizabeth called *Szépherczeg*, "the handsome prince," and who had adored her for some years.

Elizabeth hunted the day after her arrival at Easton Neston and after that hardly missed a day with the famous Bicester and Duke of Grafton's hounds.

The English had not believed the stories of her horsemanship, thinking that anyone as lovely as the Empress would only be a "park-rider". In fact when two picked horsemen, Colonel Hunt and Captain Bay Middleton, were instructed to give Elizabeth a lead they were not too pleased about it.

"What is an Empress to me?" Captain Middleton asked. "How can I look after her? I will do it, but I would rather be on my own."

He soon changed his mind. One of the best amateur riders in England, he recognised the brilliance of the Empress on a horse besides her incomparable loveliness as a woman. He fell deeply in love, as did almost every man she met. Their interest in horses was an irresistible bond between them.

There was a field of about a hundred, but Elizabeth was invariably in the lead. She was in high spirits and quite untiring.

"Other people," wrote the Countess Festetics, "ride four times a week. We ride every day!"

In a letter to Franz Joseph, Elizabeth said:

"So far I have not known a moment's fatigue . . . None of your horses are any good. They are show and spiritless: One wants quite different material here."

Elizabeth attended every steeple-chase in the neighbourhood and offered for competition a big silver cup with the inscription:

"Presented by the Countess Hohenembs."

This was her name incognito, which enabled her, she felt, to forget, at any rate in the hunting field, her Royal position. To her delight, the cup was won by Captain Middleton, for every day she admired him more and more. He was thirty— at this time, and was a tall, extremely attractive man with red-brown hair and a dark complexion. He was always called Bay after the famous horse of that name which won the Derby in 1836.

Because she was happy and with people whom she liked and trusted, Elizabeth had never been in better health. She was tanned "like a wild hare" by the March sun and winds, and her face was covered with freckles. On her return home Franz Joseph was so delighted with her well-being that he paid her expenses—106,516 gulden 93 kreuzen—without a grumble.

Bay Middleton was invited to Godollo that year for the hunting. He was rather deaf but Elizabeth said it did not matter to her as she heard what he said. Franz Joseph liked him too. Everyone teased him, laughed at his bad German, and the manner in which he confused his words.

In 1878 Elizabeth came to England again to hunt with the Pytchley, of which Earl Spencer was then the Master. She rented Cottesbrook Park in Northamptonshire for six weeks. Day after day Elizabeth was out with the hounds and there were few occasions that she did not ride three horses a day.

Bay Middleton led her skilfully and sensibly and would not allow her to take things that were too high for her. She would complain that Bay had given her "a terribly prudent day." For she was always eager to get in front and to be the first rider in at the death. In one letter to Franz Joseph she said:

"The Master, a very disagreeable man, was more behind me than in front of me. For the rest Heini tells me some of the best riders were left behind yesterday, tired out by the terribly heavy going. . . . But thanks to your good *"Bravo"*, I did not once notice it: he simply flew and was full of fire."

The Queen of Naples stayed with Elizabeth this year but English society did not find her as attractive or sympathetic as her sister. The Queen was annoyed with Bay Middleton because he had refused to pilot her in the hunting field.

In revenge she said everything she could against him and even hinted to Rudolph, when she met him in London, that the Englishman was too much in love with his mother. The Crown Prince believed this gossip and was very rude to Captain Middleton when he met him.

Elizabeth's beauty turned all men's heads so that people were all too ready to talk about her. But now she was used to it and usually it did not upset her. However, the attempt to slander her to her son made her furious, but she never found out who was at the bottom of it.

Unfortunately, it spoilt her pleasure in England and hunting, because she was well aware that Rudolph had admired her tremendously ever since he was a little boy— She was his "beau ideal" and the thought that his mind was being poisoned made her very unhappy. In the middle of February she returned home earlier than had been intended.

The following year Elizabeth planned another hunting season. But England was no longer enough for her. She had heard that the hunting in Ireland was infinitely more difficult.

Most of this season was spent in County Meath, her escort being Prince Rudolf Liechenstein and her unofficial aide, Bay Middleton, who had hunted the previous year at Godollo. In the past three years, when she had hunted in England, she had brought her entire stud from Hungary, but in Ireland she learned to appreciate Irish horseflesh.

Even the most experienced masters of hounds said she was "a wonder" and they had never seen such riding. Once after a day's hunting Elizabeth and Prince Rudolf passed a race course where one of the famous steeplechases had recently taken place.

They tried the jumps, and before the Prince could stop her, she was over them all—delighted at having got round the course without a fall.

Her brilliance as a horsewoman, coupled with her courage and bravado, made her a legend. Wherever she went the poorest villagers put on their best clothes and erected triumphal arches. She was hailed as "Queen of the Chase" and "Diana of the Moors" and poems were written about her.

Her waist was by this time a little bigger than as a young woman, but she still managed to pull it into a circumference of twenty inches. She assisted the restriction of her corsets by having her riding habit sewn into position each morning at the nearest house to the meet shortly before the hunt moved off.

Because she suffered from sciatica, she devised special undergarments made of fine chamois skin which shielded her body from sudden chills when she was riding.

Before hunting Elizabeth would have a shower bath and then a cup of soup. It was a special recipe of her own and consisted of essence of beef, chicken, roebuck or venison, and partridge. She believed that it gave her special strength and stamina.

In Ireland, glowing with health and high spirits, it was hard to recognise the Empress who in Austria crept about avoiding people who, she believed, often incorrectly, disliked her. "It is very painful, Marie," she said to Countess Festetics, "to be made the target of malignant gossip, as I have always been."

When she went for a walk in Vienna she had a perfect horror of meeting anyone and would wear a thick blue veil and carry a big sunshade or a fan.

"Let us hurry away," she would say to her lady-in-waiting, turning down the nearest path. "I can hear what they are saying, and that Bellegarde hates me so much that I break out into a perspiration when he so much as looks at me. I can feel who likes me and who does not."

Countess Festetics knew that this was often just imagination, and that Elizabeth felt suspicious of people who would have idolised her if she had given them the opportunity.

In the midst of her enjoyment in Ireland, Elizabeth received disastrous news from home. The town of Szegedin had been half destroyed by floods.

"Owing to the sad news from Szegedin," she wrote at once to Franz Joseph, "I have decided to leave here. . . . It is the greatest sacrifice I can make but in such conditions it is necessary."

Back in Vienna, Elizabeth was with Franz Joseph to celebrate their Silver Wedding in April, 1879. Elizabeth wanted to spend the whole time in Budapest, but on the violent protestations of Franz Joseph agreed to spend half the period in Vienna. In fact, she was seen in public only on the actual wedding day anniversary, and then for merely a brief time when the new Church of St. Saviour was consecrated.

To her undisguised relief the day was very wet, with rain falling ceaselessly from dawn till after nightfall and the street procession had to be cancelled.

She was, however, unaccustomedly vivacious at a reception that night at the Foreign Office, given by Count Andràssy, who was now Minister for Foreign Affairs. It was noted that she arrived alone at this function, the Emperor not appearing until 10.30 and leaving without his wife an hour later.

On the whole it was not surprising that the newspapers were critical. "Ordinary mortals," mocked the Vienna *Tageblatt*, "celebrate the twenty-fifth anniversary of *ménage* (housekeeping) which in this case will be *manège* (riding-school)!"

Elizabeth laughed, but she was deeply hurt by the coldness she received in Vienna. Still young, still beautiful and still loved passionately by so many people, she carried "a chip on her shoulder", where anything Austrian was concerned.

Next day she was off to Budapest, taking Rudolph and Gisela with her. She had said firmly that she wanted no official reception in Budapest. But as there was a week's horse-racing at the time she thoroughly enjoyed herself.

Differences between Elizabeth and Franz Joseph reached an acute stage when their son Rudolph was nineteen years of age. Rudolph adored Elizabeth. The bond which united mother and son was a very strong one. When they were apart they wrote to each other nearly every day. In a letter from Rudolph written to Elizabeth from the Istrian coast after her return from her first hunting trip to Ireland he said:

"My dearest—I never come so far south without wishing more than ever, that you were with me, you who love and appreciate this beautiful part of the world so much. . . ."

But while Elizabeth remained his ideal, a star with whom no other women could compare, Rudolph was the willing victim of any pretty woman. He was always ready to plunge into a new amorous adventure.

In 1880, Rudolph went to Elizabeth and told her that his father was making enquiries about a suitable marriage without consulting him.

"There are plenty of girls I know whom I would like to marry, but I don't intend to have some plain and dumb little princess thrust on me," Rudolph protested.

"I don't think the young ladies who interest you would be quite suitable as Consort, Rudi," his mother answered with a smile.

She was perfectly aware of the type of woman who attracted him, for most of the boy's mistresses had been ten or fifteen years older than himself. Nevertheless, she was angry to think that her husband would be so insensitive as to force their son into a loveless match for political reasons.

She had all her life, despite its sorrows and the failure of her marriage, treasured the thought that the Emperor had chosen her as his bride solely through romantic motives, and, indeed, in the face of considerable opposition from the type of person whom he was now consulting with regard to his son.

In failing to face the realities of life, she had hardly given a thought to the fact that a year after Rudolph had reached his majority the question of his marriage must inevitably be coming to the fore-front.

Elizabeth promised to see the Emperor as soon as she possibly could, find out what was happening and do everything within reason to ensure that Rudolph was not forced into a marriage he did not want.

The ensuing conversation between husband and wife proved nothing beyond the fact that both had inflexible wills. Elizabeth opened the argument by suggesting it was high time that the Crown Prince saw more of the world. Coldly the Emperor replied that Rudolph had been all over Europe.

"There is plenty for him to see and do in the Empire," he finished. "That will occupy him until his marriage."

Here, thought Elizabeth, was confirmation of her son's fears. A marriage was indeed being arranged.

"He is far too young for marriage" she pleaded.

"The stories that I hear about his amorous adventures with women certainly fail to confirm your view that he is still a boy," the Emperor retorted cynically.

"And who are you suggesting he should marry?" Elizabeth asked.

"There are singularly few Catholic princesses who merit the attentions of a Hapsburg," the Emperor replied loftily. "However, my Ministers have suggested, and I have taken steps to confirm their views, that Princess Stephanie of Belgium would make a splendid partner for our son."

He saw the anger flash through his wife's eyes and went on hurriedly.

"Belgium is becoming a country of increasing political importance. With Prussian power mounting as it is there can be no doubt that Belgium will find strong allies in Britain and France because she would be a bulwark against any absurd attempts by Prussia to expand westwards. Besides this the Royal family is tremendously rich. They have an absolute Eldorado in their African territories."

Observations on Belgium's political and military importance did not impress Elizabeth. She was only too aware that
the idea, even if it had been put forward by the Ministers of
the Imperial Crown, must have been strongly suggested as
a favourable one by the Archduchess Elizabeth.

This was the woman who first seduced Franz Joseph from
his young wife, with the result that she had naturally
incurred both Elizabeth's jealousy and hatred. The Archduchess's sister was Queen Henriette, mother of Princess
Stephanie.

Elizabeth did not express her thoughts aloud. Instead
she asked.

"Stephanie is only fifteen, isn't she? Do you think that
Rudolph should be sent to bed with a child?"

Franz Joseph winced a little at the frankness of his wife's
remark, but he replied:

"She is, as a matter of fact, fifteen and a half. Even if the
engagement was announced within a month or two she
would be the same age on her wedding day as you were
when you married me."

"That in itself is sufficient to condemn the proposition,"
Elizabeth answered. "And might I remind you that you
already have proof of the sort of disaster which can come
from any marital alliance with the Belgians?"

Elizabeth was referring to Archduke Maximilian's
marriage to Charlotte, a woman who was at the moment a
raving lunatic in the Palace of Laeken.

Franz Joseph resorted, as he had so often done during
arguments with his wife, to silence. He began his usual habit
of shuffling through papers on his desk, and Elizabeth knew
that there was no more to be said. She could only hope that
he would ponder on her words after she had left him. In
which case his instincts of a father would become stronger
than the wishes of an Emperor and the whole project would
be quietly abandoned.

There was still time for this without any risk of scandal,
for only the most discreet conversations between the Austrian

Ambassador in Brussels and the Belgian Minister of Foreign Affairs had taken place, plus, of course, some excited letters between the Archduchess Elizabeth and her sister Henriette. Unfortunately, Elizabeth made no alternative suggestion.

Franz Joseph had, somewhat to his own surprise, to admit that he had fathered an unusually brilliant son.

Rudolph could speak foreign languages with amazing facility. His tutors had no difficulty in teaching him and he had many varied tastes. He was interested in history, geography, zoology, botany, physiology, ethnography and all sciences.

True to the tradition of the Hapsburgs that all male members of the Imperial House had to learn a trade, Rudolph had chosen that of printer, but unlike his ancestors he had not regarded this as a sinecure but had actively studied it, and by the time he was eighteen was an expert compositor.

Through his apprenticeship at the Court printers and from the type of intellectual that he met while he was a student at the University of Vienna, he gradually became interested in the producers of words as well as in those who put them in print.

Editors, authors and journalists were his close friends. He, himself, learned the thrill of having his essays set up in type, and he persevered with his writing so that when he reached his majority he was an extremely skilful journalist, and not without literary abilities which could have made him a successful author.

Franz Joseph had been handed some of his son's writings by the head of the Secret Police whose duty it was to keep his Imperial master informed of everything that was going on, even in those matters which concerned his own family.

The Emperor saw, with horror, in some of these papers the independent line of thought which Rudolph was adopting. The radical and unconventional ideas came from his associates who were demagogues, liberals, Jews, and men of inflammatory theories that undermined the State.

Franz Joseph was convinced that the best antidote to all this was the joys of home life. He was sure that once the boy had a wife he would dispense with his wild bachelor friends and take more interest in the formal entertainments of the Court.

As the matter was urgent the Emperor determined to push through the marriage with Princess Stephanie at the earliest possible moment. The way he did it was characteristic of his veneration for pomp and majesty.

A Gentleman-at-Arms was sent by the Emperor to Prince Rudolph's Aide-de-camp to announce that the Emperor wished to have an interview with the Commanding Officer of the 18th Brigade of the Imperial Armies. This was one of the various military ranks which had been bestowed on Rudolph as an eighteenth birthday present. The message meant that he must appear in uniform before the Commander-in-Chief.

Consequently two officers confronted one another later that afternoon and the Emperor, as the superior, simply stated that the junior—Rudolph—was to proceed to Brussels and make formal application for the hand in marriage of her Royal Highness the Princess Stephanie of Belgium.

The Crown Prince stood stiffly at attention, one hand on the handle of his sword and the other holding his helmet, while his father gave him this order. Rudolph's face was a mask, but his brain was actively trying to work out what was going on. He was quite aware that the Emperor, if necessary, would hint at treason should he protest.

In any event, such was the prestige and disciplinary force of the Army that even in such a situation he could do no more than click his heels and snap: "At your orders, Sir."

Rudolph was bitterly angry with his mother for failing to do anything in this emergency and he did not see her before he had completed arrangements to travel to Brussels. Indeed he would have had to wait some time for advice, for quixotically Elizabeth had vanished on one of her journeys abroad. Actually she was in England, for she had heard that Bay Middleton was ill at his country house in Cheshire and she had hurried to see him.

In Brussels the Crown Prince had an interview with the Austrian Ambassador who told him that everything was arranged. As soon as it was known that the Prince was on his way, Stephanie's pigtails had been hurriedly changed into a grown-up coiffure and she had been put into her first long skirt.

The romantic moment of betrothal, which was to be whispered by various palace servants and officials to journalists so that it could be reported to the world, had been carefully rehearsed in Queen Henriette's private apartments. All that now remained was for Rudolph to learn his rôle. Briefly the Ambassador described what was to happen.

"Your Imperial Highness will meet Princess Stephanie at luncheon with the Royal Family. Afterwards everyone will move for rest and conversation into the Grand Salon. That lies at a considerable distance from the luncheon room and you will have to pass through the Blue Salon, which you will easily recognise because the hangings are of Royal blue and the furniture is upholstered in blue and gilt."

He paused to be certain the Crown Prince was following him.

"By that time you will find that the Princess will be hanging back a little," he continued. "The other guests, regardless of precedence, will leave the Salon, while you will remain by the Princess's side. Pinned to her gown will be a small spray of lilies of the valley. As soon as you are alone Her Royal Highness will unpin the flowers from her bosom and pin them to your own tunic."

He paused again, then with a side glance at Rudolph's inscrutable face, he finished:

"Eloquence and protestations of affection will be quite unnecessary. Taking the Princess's hand you will then move together into the Grand Salon. Leave the rest to their Majesties."

The Ambassador was Count Chotek, a wealthy aristocrat

from Bohemia, who privately regarded his own family connections almost as good as those of the Hapsburgs and rightly claimed that they were even older.

He knew Rudolph and liked him. The regard was returned. Consequently, he was well aware that unless he injected some cynical humour into the whole sorry business, he might have to report to his Imperial Majesty in Vienna that the Crown Prince had backed out at the last moment.

Everything went as planned. Rudolph, who found Stephanie even more stupid than he had been led to believe, felt a surge of pity as the girl stopped in the Blue Salon and looked at him with an expectant smile on her dumpy, insensitive face, while clumsily she unpinned the lilies of the valley.

The giggle she gave after he had taken the nosegay, and the way that she tugged at his hand rather like a child rushing to its mother to be patted on the head for completing a task successfully, banished the brief feelings of sympathy.

In the Grand Salon Queen Henriette looked at the young couple, spoke laughingly to all the sycophantic courtiers standing around, and then rushed across to kiss first her daughter and then Rudolph. All the latter had to do was to walk across to the King and formally ask him for the hand of Princess Stephanie in marriage.

The task completed, Rudolph left for Vienna the same night. Ahead of the train rushed the dots and dashes of the telegraph keys with long and circumstantial reports for the Viennese newspapers of the romantic scene that had "so unexpectedly but happily occurred" in the Belgian Royal Palace that afternoon.

"Well done!" was the Emperor's verdict when Rudolph reported to his Commander-in-Chief.

It had been all too rare for Franz Joseph to be able to compliment any of the officers of his army on a completely successful campaign. The Crown Prince felt that he deserved a reward and that night, with a few of his journalistic cronies he searched for sympathetic companionship in the taverns of Vienna. It was a carousal that lasted all that night and most of the next day.

When he had slept off his excesses, which took fifteen hours, another day had dawned. His valet brought him the morning newspapers. In them he read that the Emperor had been pleased to agree to the Crown Prince's earnest wish that the wedding should take place on May 10th, 1881.

The news was relayed to Elizabeth by telegram. It was early in the morning when she received it, and she turned so pale that her lady-in-waiting ventured to ask the reason. When the Empress told her, she ejaculated:

"Thank God it is not a calamity!"

"Please God that it will not become one," Elizabeth replied.

TWELVE

1886

ELIZABETH understood Ludwig as no other person could do. Apart from their blood relationship, they had uncanny similarities in physical appearance and mental outlook. If Elizabeth was the most beautiful woman in the Europe of her day, there can be little doubt that Ludwig was the most handsome Prince that Europe has known before or since.

The ordinary people of Bavaria loved their King, just as the ordinary people of Austria and Hungary loved their Empress and Queen. The eccentricities of both were forgiven. Each, through force of circumstance and by the behest of temperament, lived the life of recluses for long periods. There is little doubt that Elizabeth envied her cousin the privileges of his masculine position to create the beauty for which he yearned.

Both were romanticists, living examples of the strange but beautiful characters of European folk-lore, trying to be true to themselves in the nineteenth century world of intrigue and power politics. Elizabeth's form of escapism was to flee to remote parts of the world, or to find brief ecstacy in that strange intimacy between herself and horse, which is one of the most ancient secrets of mankind since animals were domesticated.

Ludwig was more fortunate because he had the resources and power to bring fairy-tales to life.

Neuschwanstein Castle is an enchanted palace from the world of the spirit. While anyone who has seen the Herrenchiemsee, Ludwig's castle at the foot of the Hennenkopf—a fantastic version of the Palace of Versailles, illuminated (as periodically it still is) by four thousand candles multiplied into a million by a bewildering and beautiful galaxy of mirrors—must admire his superhuman effort to capture perfection.

Yet Ludwig spent only three weeks in this superb if incredible edifice. Because there were all too few people like Elizabeth, who enjoyed his company and with whom he in his turn could enjoy himself, those three weeks were spent alone.

He had a dining table that was raised and lowered from the kitchens between courses so that he was not upset by the presence of any servants. The table was, however, always set for several guests. None saw them, for they were ghosts which Ludwig invited to be with him from the graveyards of history.

After his lonely banquet the King went to the exquisite little theatre and crouched in the inky blackness of the auditorium, alone except for the remote actors and actresses playing their parts upon the stage.

There was only one real person privileged to spend some hours in this palatial desert of loneliness—his cousin Elizabeth. She alone knew, instinctively, when to speak and when to remain quiet. She alone never betrayed the slightest amazement at the King's peculiar interests and foibles.

Yet she must have have gone through a perfect hell of forebodings every time she visited Ludwig. She knew that madness hovered around that handsome, godlike head with its carefully waved locks.

Behind every member of the House of Wittelsbach lay the shadow of insanity. Elizabeth, sane and untainted, had for a long time interested herself in the unhappy fate of the insane. Arrangements for the care of lunatics in Vienna were very bad, and she had tried to improve their conditions. Once, when Franz Joseph had asked what she would like for her birthday which was celebrated with great pomp on Christmas Day, she replied:

"What I would like best would be a fully-equipped lunatic asylum."

She was particularly interested in the possibility of alleviating or curing madness by hypnosis. So convinced was she of the possible benefits, that she arranged for one of the Viennese pupils of Mesmer to treat a distant cousin, who was an alcoholic. The treatment was completely successful.

Elizabeth, in middle-age, made a fetish of remaining slim and beautiful. Her beauty treatments were unusual. If she read in the biography of a bygone beauty some secret and wonderful method of preserving a youthful skin, or of retaining the slimness of figure, she immediately adopted it.

Often she went to bed at night with a face mask made of silk, inside which slices of raw veal were placed. Every spring she had ripe strawberries gathered while the dew was still on them and these she crushed on to her face and neck until the juice ran over her shoulders and breasts.

She was a great believer in the benefits of olive oil after she had read that Cleopatra was regularly massaged with it. She went one better and used to get in a bath full of olive oil warmed to body temperature. On one occasion the small charcoal burner underneath the bath was left there too long by a careless maid and when Elizabeth stepped into the bath the oil was so hot that it almost burned her skin away.

The famous waist, which increased but very little during the whole of her adult life, was primarily kept as tiny by the use of very carefully made corsets, while at night she often slept in long Turkish towels, wrung out in hot water and tied round her waist.

A slimming diet which she confidently believed was useful, consisted of drinking the whites of five or six eggs mixed with salt. Where she obtained this recipe is not known, but in fact it must have had the reverse effect from what she intended.

But more than any other beauty aid, Elizabeth believed in the value of milk. She travelled with a huge retinue of servants, attendants, and her favourite dogs. Besides these she was also always accompanied by her special Jersey cows.

Putsee and Daisy had been bought from a famous herd in France and Elizabeth was convinced that their milk had a special quality highly beneficial to her.

Councillor Kaula wrote in his account book. "For cows bought in Aix-les-Bains and their travelling expenses with the Empress to the account of the Foreign Office and Privy Purse; francs 1473-53 or florins 707 and kronen 57."

There were days when Elizabeth lived on nothing but milk and she used fresh cream for her face and shoulders, letting it sink deeply into the pores. After this she used a lotion of stiffly beaten whites of eggs into which was mixed olive oil. When this had made the skin taut and firm she removed the preparation with a cream made from her own recipe of Dutch lily bulbs.

Certainly the result was amazing, for Elizabeth, to the day of her death, never looked older than thirty, and was so beautiful that those who saw her exclaimed incredulously at her loveliness.

Of all her features, her long red-brown hair pleased her the most. She had it washed once a month in raw eggs mixed in brandy, and rinsed afterwards with what was known as a disinfectant. The glorious chestnut colour hardly changed and even in the last few years of her life there was hardly a grey hair.

Only Ludwig could really understand this preoccupation with remaining beautiful. He regarded it as an art comparable with that of his music and his castle-building.

He would praise Elizabeth's charms detail by detail and demand to know what she was doing to ensure that they never faded.

"You must always be beautiful," he told her. "You *will* always be beautiful."

The meeting place between Elizabeth and Ludwig was most frequently the Isle of Roses, right in the middle of the Stärnberg Lake. Some Roman officer had found security for himself and his family from the dangers of this outpost of Empire by living on the tiny outcrop of land in the lake. Towards the end of the classic period of Rome, a temple to the worship of the sun god, Mithras, was erected there, and this had been transformed into a Catholic chapel.

Ludwig's father had been the first to turn the entire island into a rose garden. His son had developed it so that by the time he became King sixteen thousand bushes were flourishing. Six gardeners worked every day on tending the flowers, and they had instructions always to be out of sight. This was not too difficult because the paths ran zig-zag between high evergreen hedges so that Ludwig could not be seen as he approached the small villa in the centre of the island, called the Hermitage.

Here Ludwig spent hours during the summer, almost in a state of trance from the overpowering scent of the roses which produced, he claimed, a hundred thousand blooms simultaneously at midsummer. He read poetry and composed his own verses. Only the most intimate of his friends were ever permitted to share these hours on the Isle of Roses; even Wagner or Prince Paul had only been asked twice.

Elizabeth was the exception; she was permitted to go there at any time, and when she was at Possenhofen was usually rowed over, to sit alone among the flowers until Ludwig joined her. He seemed to know by instinct when she was there. As the years went by she found him pathetically boring and did not often go to the island. But Ludwig would seek her out at Possenhofen and stay for hours and hours.

By 1886 Elizabeth realised, possibly better than anyone else, that her cousin was on the borderland of insanity. She had that year spent some time at Zandvoort in the Netherlands in the hopes of finding some relief at that spa for her sciatica. She loved the long and lonely sandy beaches and used to walk for hours watching the seagulls soar and swoop over the sea.

With the predilection for fantasy which was a characteristic of the Wittelsbachs, she began to identify herself with the birds, pretending that she herself was by nature a seagull rejoicing in the freedom of flight over the limitless sea.

Inevitably the image reminded her of Ludwig's own belief that he had the soul of an eagle, and she understood full well his yearning to be the king of birds soaring from some lofty mountain height free from all the troubles of earthbound man.

When she went to her family home that summer and arranged as an excursion for her daughters, Gisela and Valerie, a trip to the Isle of Roses, Ludwig hid himself from the younger women. Elizabeth wrote a little note of greeting for him as from a seagull to an eagle. She wished to have a conversation with him, and thought that by using this bird symbolism, he would understand and reply in a similar manner. At this time, however, Ludwig was consistently refusing to see anybody for days and even weeks on end.

By March the Ministers were resolved that the King should abdicate and on May 17th it was announced that Prince Luitpold, the heir presumptive, would assume the Regency, as the King was incapable of governing owing to a mental derangement.

The whole business of arresting the King was managed most irresponsibly and injudiciously. For two days previously Ludwig had been treated as a Sovereign; now he was hustled to the Castle of Berg on the Starnbergsee, which had been fitted up like a regular prison. Here he was informed that ropes and a strait jacket were kept in readiness for him.

"But I am not a madman," he protested, "so why should I be put under restraint?"

When Elizabeth heard what had happened she was deeply distressed and expressed openly her doubts that Ludwig was totally insane.

On the night before Whitsunday, Elizabeth's attendants were alarmed by an agonising scream soon after she had retired to bed. Quickly bursting into the bedroom her women found her terror-stricken.

"I have just had a dream," she said. "I saw my cousin Ludwig standing by my bedside, his clothes dripping with water. I'm sure he is drowned."

The women persuaded Elizabeth it was only a nightmare but two days later she learnt that her dream had been, in fact, a premonition of what was to occur the following day.

A cartoon of Elizabeth being piloted by Captain Bay Middleton when hunting with the Earl of Harrington's Hounds. In the foreground is the M.F.H., Lord Harrington

Two photographs taken just before the tragedy at Mayerling: Archduke Rudolph . . .

. . . and Baroness Vetsera

On Whitsunday, June 13th, Ludwig asked his Doctor and jailor, von Gudden, for permission to go for a walk. The doctor promised that he could do so after dinner, which was served at four o'clock in the afternoon. Although normally one of the keepers was also in attendance, on this occasion the doctor told the man not to come, as his presence would excite the King.

The two men set out on a dull and drizzling evening to walk alongside the lake. The doctor's dinner was ordered at eight o'clock, and it was only when the announcement was made that the meal was ready that it was realised that neither he nor the King had returned.

A police officer was sent out to look for them. When he did not come back two more police officers and one of the King's keepers were despatched. The searched for more than an hour along the labyrinth of paths and amid the dense undergrowth without avail. By this time it was dark. The whole establishment became alarmed. People were sent out in every direction to comb the area.

At half-past ten one of the servants stumbled over the King's hat, jacket and umbrella, lying on the ground at the edge of the water. He shouted continuously until other men arrived. Then two bodies were seen a little distance out into the lake. The doctor was lying face downwards in only about six inches of water. Ludwig's body, although many yards farther out, was floating in an area to which the searchers were able to wade without the water coming over their knees.

Artificial respiration was tried in vain. It ceased when one of the police officers pointed to Ludwig's watch which had stopped at 6.45 p.m., nearly four hours earlier.

The bodies were carried back to the Schlöss, where it was noted that Dr. von Gudden's face had been badly scratched and bruised. He had evidently put up considerable resistance because the nail on the middle finger of his right hand had been torn off.

Ludwig had no marks of injury on him. His face was as serene and peaceful as it had been in the days of his youth.

M

Reconstruction of what had happened after the two left the Schlöss indicated that without any doubt Ludwig had carefully contrived the walk, even so far as pretending on earlier occasions to be excited and annoyed by the presence of guards. By playing on the doctor's vanity, he had ensured that they went alone, so that he could successfully end his life.

A gentle man even in his madness, it must have been a terrible decision for him to make to murder anyone. But it was, of course, inevitable in order that he might be free to destroy himself.

Within fifteen minutes of the beginning of his walk he must have grabbed the unsuspecting doctor with his powerful hands, forced his far older and smaller adversary face downwards in the water and held him there for the two or three minutes necessary to extinguish life.

Then the unhappy King had walked slowly into the water until it was deep enough for him to lie down and become totally submerged.

His last glimpse of anything tangible on this earth must have been of his beloved Isle of Roses silhouetted against the grey sky of that Sunday evening. Beyond it was the vague outlines of Possenhofen where his idealised woman— Elizabeth was staying.

It was said afterwards that the King, in his madness, had used murder as a means of escape. He had tried, it was rumoured, to reach safety at Possenhofen, where he believed that Elizabeth, the only woman he loved, would hide him.

Elizabeth knew Ludwig better. He had, she was well aware, a practical streak which would have prevented him from attempting a swim across the treacherous lake which was more than three miles wide and, in places, dropping to a depth of three hundred feet.

"The King was no madman," she said many times later; "only an eccentric who lived in a world of ideas. They might have treated him more gently, and so, perhaps, spared him such a fearful end."

Elizabeth did not learn the news of the King's tragic

death until Whit Monday, June 14th. She was just on her
way to breakfast with Valerie, when Gisela entered the
room, and drawing her aside, said:

"I have something to tell you and must see you quite
alone."

Elizabeth accompanied her to an adjoining room. When,
pale as death, she had received the news, she insisted on
being rowed across the lake. At the castle she demanded to
see her cousin's body. Requesting everyone to leave the
chapel where he was laid, she placed a bunch of jasmine
between his folded hands and knelt in prayer by his side.

For nearly an hour her attendant waited outside, until at
length, frightened as to what was happening, the Grand
Mistress of her household entered the Chapel. She found the
Empress stretched lifeless upon the floor.

When after great difficulty they managed to restore her
to consciousness, she stared wildly around her and cried in
a shaking voice.

"For God's sake release the King from the mortuary
Chapel. He is not really dead; he is only pretending to be
so in order to be left in peace and quietness, and not to be
tormented any longer."

Her nerves were shattered by this tragedy and the terrible
proof of her cousin's madness preyed on her mind for a
long time.

Before the State funeral Ludwig's heart, as was the
tradition for rulers and princes who came from the House
of Wittelsbach, was removed and placed in a silver gilt vase.
The vase was taken to the votive Chapel at Alt-Otting and
placed among a score of others below the tender face of the
famous Black Madonna.

Elizabeth had Masses said for the repose of his soul in
every church where he or she had ever worshipped. Her
lasting memorials to her pathetic cousin were the inaugura-
tion of enlighted lunatic asylums throughout Austria and her
unremitting work from that time onwards to alleviate the
suffering of the insane.

THIRTEEN

·1881-1889

VALERIE, like Elizabeth, kept a notebook, but hers was more in the form of a diary which she had started when she was nine. She found it hard to realise that her brother, whom she had nicknamed Nazi, was engaged to be married. She wrote in red ink:

"Nazi, that boy! Nazi, who only a few years ago used to make a light luncheon off the bullfinches which he had shot himself! Nazi, who used to tease me so . . . betrothed!!"

Elizabeth, too, was upset and singularly despondent, for she knew that her son would not be happy with the plain, ungainly Stephanie. Rudolph, however, now the die was cast, appeared to be remarkably light-hearted about it.

"What is the use of making yourself miserable, Mother mine?" he asked, sitting down on a cushion at her feet and taking one of her slender hands between his own. "You know very well that as long as it's an impossibility for me to find a wife who resembles you in the very slightest degree, I may as well marry this good little Belgian girl. . . .

"So don't worry. Be satisfied that I am not madly in love with her, for in that case I know that you, jealous darling, would be a million times more unhappy still."*

Countess Festetics, who was listening, saw Elizabeth's deep blue eyes were full of sadness as she answered:

"My poor boy! My poor boy! I am afraid you do not realise what misery such a marriage as you are about to make can be."

Despite Elizabeth's fears the wedding was celebrated with magnificent pageantry. Princess Stephanie looked gauche,

* These conversations and episodes were recorded by the Countess Festetics in her diary.

insignificant and homely, while her mother-in-law, twenty-seven years older, looked overwhelmingly beautiful in pearl velvet, antique lace and a wealth of diamonds and emeralds in her red hair.

Early on the wedding morning Rudolph was in a strange mood. He met Countess Festetics in the passage and she thought he looked nervous and despondent. They talked about the bride's bouquet and then extending his hand he said:

"Goodbye, say something cheerful to me."

The Countess with tears in her eyes, said:

"God bless you, be happy, dear, good Imperial Highness."

"Thank you!"

He shook her hand and went into his own room leaving her apprehensive and afraid.

Meanwhile the King Leopold of the Belgians, whose love affairs were so notorious that Queen Victoria would have nothing to do with him, kissed his daughter, Stephanie, and said:

"My child, remember always that virtue is the highest crown."

Not having heard of Cléo de Mérode, her father's famous mistress, Stephanie meekly agreed with this lofty sentiment.

As soon as the guests had risen from the bridal supper, Elizabeth retired to her private apartments where, when Countess Festetics found her, she burst into an uncontrollable passion of tears.

"This business will bring untold misery," Elizabeth sobbed, "that girl is no more fit than a wooden doll to be Rudi's companion. She has no heart. I am not blinded by love for my boy—she will not keep him straight."

A year later Rudolph seemed to be on bad terms with his wife, and when he was discussing the risk to his life in war with his parents, remarked:

"When one has known every enjoyment, there is nothing left to interest one."

On another occasion, struck by the dark shadows under

her son's eyes and the pallor of his face, Elizabeth asked him:
"Are you ill?"

"No," he replied, "only tired and nervous."

Elizabeth and Franz Joseph were drawn together by their common worry over Rudolph. But a year after his marriage Elizabeth's antipathy to her daughter-in-law changed to one of sympathy. The unfortunate Belgian Princess was being snubbed in Court circles because, as the months went by, she still could offer no hope of producing a child. The Empress's pity was stirred by the memories of the first years of her married life.

But the girl's weeping protestations about the infidelities and neglect of her husband merely served to annoy her mother-in-law. Elizabeth, as she remembered vividly, had suffered in silence when a similar situation had made her miserable.

Elizabeth's sympathy died when in 1883, after Rudolph had been married two and a half years, Stephanie presented a child to the Hapsburgs. It was a girl and was christened Elizabeth. But the surgical measures necessary to save the life of the baby and mother had destroyed any possibility of her bearing another child.

The birth of a girl, as the only child the Crown Prince and Princess could ever have, was, of course, a dynastic disaster. The male line was broken. After Rudolph, the crown would have to go to a nephew of Franz Joseph—Franz Ferdinand, son of the Emperor's younger brother, Carl Ludwig. The latter had long since solemnly renounced all rights to the throne.

Franz Joseph did not like his nephew. He was a rather sickly and artistically minded youth who frequently announced his dislike of any idea of marriage. If anything untoward should happen to Rudolph—who was constantly risking his life in half-drunken shooting parties—the question of the succession would be acute enough to start once more all that unpleasant rumbling of discontent in Hungary and other dissident parts of the Empire.

Elizabeth took the obvious course of discussing if there was any possibility of ending a marriage which was useless to the monarchy and distasteful to the partners in it. The devout Franz Joseph literally shuddered at the very idea. He placed his faith in God to find a solution—by which he meant a convenient and early fatal illness for the very young and stockily healthy Princess.

Elizabeth mildly suggested that in such worldly matters perhaps the Pope could exert divine power to better effect. The Emperor refused point blank to submit a petition to the Vatican, asking for an investigation into the possibility of an annulment.

Elizabeth was not unreasonable or unrealistic in her idea. The web of blood relationships could be made to connect Rudolph and Stephanie in a manner that might, with suitable legalistic verbiage, indicate that the union was within the prohibited degrees.

In fact, Rudolph himself sent a petition secretly to the Vatican asking for a divorce to be authorised. The reply from the Pope came back in an open and official communiqué to the Head of State. His Holiness stated that even a discussion of the matter was out of the question.

There was a tremendous row when the infuriated Emperor confronted his son with this reply, and demanded to know why Rudolph had dared to act in this underhand manner without his father's approval.

Rudolph, forced to resign himself to a life of miserable bondage, accepted defeat despondently. He knew well enough that he would have to bow to the Emperor's order that he must effect a reconciliation with his wife and live with her under the same roof.

He went afterwards to see his mother. She was sympathetic and understanding, but copied Franz Joseph in being adamant over the question of the reconciliation.

It was difficult for Rudolph to make them understand his feelings. Stephanie was proving herself a most tiresome wife. Not only was she cold and self-centred but she resisted all efforts on her husband's part to interest her in his enthusiasms —political, intellectual or sporting.

More than this, without giving Rudolph anything herself, she was frantically jealous in a spitefully narrow-minded way, which, in an age and place where men, married or single, were expected to have their mistresses, was fatal.

Most women found Rudolph attractive. Stephanie's eldest sister described him as:—"more than handsome, he was enchanting. Behind his fragile appearance lay reserves of strength and energy. He reminded one of a racehorse, he had its temperament, breeding and caprice. His will-power was only equalled by his sensibility. . . . Like his mother, the Empress Elizabeth, he had a way of talking that held everybody and a faculty for setting all about him agog to solve the riddle of his personality."

Elizabeth took it for granted that her son would be unfaithful to his boring, barren wife. When he argued with her about the dissolution of his marriage, she answered with sound common-sense:

"After all, Rudi, you don't have to live like a peasant in a one-roomed hovel."

"Even her presence under the same roof nauseates me," grumbled Rudolph.

"When it gets too bad you can always go off to Mayerling for a little recreation," Elizabeth suggested. "No one minds a Prince enjoying some shooting once in a while, and they don't expect his wife to be with him."

If Elizabeth was understanding, Stephanie was certainly not. Rudolph confided in the Countess Festetics.

"My wife is simply unbearable," he told her, "in fact sometimes I think she cannot be altogether in her right mind. She is so jealous that if I merely look at another woman, if I dance with one, or pay any of those small compliments without which no conversation can be carried on . . . she treats me like a dog and rampages about for hours together."

The Countess tried to show him Stephanie's point of view, but he replied wildly:

"I tell you what I'll do if this goes on much longer. I will give her something serious to cry about. Until now Heaven knows I have nothing to reproach myself with . . . but when it comes to my having to give an account of every minute of my days and nights, and to finding out that my private letters are opened, my body-servant questioned and my pockets searched, I draw the line."

Elizabeth had suggested Mayerling as a retreat. This was a hunting lodge which, small and picturesque, Rudolph had decorated with all the trophies he had collected over the years. The bear he had shot at Munráco, stuffed eagles, owls, lynxes, pheasants, foxes, deer and stags, were arranged in one of the sitting-rooms.

Here he also had a wonderful collection of fire-arms— guns, carbines, pistols, matchlocks, swords, kandjars and yataghans inlaid with gold, silver and mother of pearl. Perhaps the finest item was a magnificent snow-white deer (*Edelhirsche*) which he had shot in Bohemia.

Yet even at Mayerling Rudolph could not be free of Stephanie. Once, after he had gone there for two or three days shooting, an ordinary cab drew up at the gates and a heavily veiled lady asked for admittance.

As she refused to reveal her identity to the servants, the Crown Prince's valet, Loschek, was called. When he appeared the lady threw back her veil and he saw it was the Crown Princess Stephanie. He asked her to enter and shortly afterwards the servants heard voices raised in anger. In fact, Rudolph and his wife were speaking so loudly, that what they said was repeated word for word over the countryside.

"I know that you betray me," shrieked the Princess. "You came here to receive your women friends."

"There is not a solitary woman here," Rudolph shouted in reply. "You will drive me crazy if you go on like this."

Elizabeth learnt a great deal about Rudolph's amorous

adventures through her niece, the Countess Marie Larisch. She was the daughter of the beautiful actress Henrietta Mendel, who had married Elizabeth's brother morganatically. Marie, therefore, had friends in the theatrical world as well as in Court.

Elizabeth had been captivated by her niece when she was a child and when she was eighteen invited her to stay with her at the Imperial Court in Hungary. Marie was both a liar and a schemer. She tried to make herself indispensible to the Empress and succeeded mostly because she was an excellent horsewoman.

At Elizabeth's wish she married Count George Larisch who was not in the least in love with her.

"He's harmless," the Empress is supposed to have said. "I should be dreadfully jealous of any husband who came between us and who prevented my seeing you whenever I wanted. He will be just the sort of useful husband for you."

The wedding had taken place nearly four years before Rudolph's to Stephanie, but the marriage was a failure from the start and did not change Marie's desire to keep in with the Royal family.

She had once harboured hopes of marrying Rudolph, and when she was told this was absolutely out of the question, was piqued into disliking him, although she was far too clever to show her feelings openly. Later, in her memoirs she invented many spiteful stories to discredit him.

At this time, however, she was determined to make herself useful. She fanned the flames of Rudolph's difficulties with his wife, sympathising with him and doing everything she could by sarcasm and ridicule to portray Stephanie in a bad light.

What was more, Marie became a 'go-between' for Rudolph and the girls who were either attracted to him, or by whom he was attracted.

Among these was a pretty seventeen-year-old called Mary Vetsera. Mary belonged to a wealthy family. Her maternal grandfather came from Turkey where he had amassed a fortune. The Vetsera Palace in Vienna, as ostentatious in furnishings as it was in name, was a perfect setting for the Oriental and exotic beauty of Mary, the lovelier of the two Vetsera girls. She was petite but very well developed. Her olive complexion came from her Turkish blood; her vivid blue eyes and brown hair from her European ancestry.

It was whispered that when Mary's mother, the Baroness Vetsera, made her debut in society after her marriage, the Emperor had been madly attracted by her dark Oriental beauty. The love affair had, in fact, caused a great deal of talk at the time.

The Countess Marie Larisch, knowing Mary was sensual and very impressionable, arranged the first meeting between her and the Crown Prince at the Prata, and later took her to his bachelor rooms in the Imperial Palace. She told Princess Vetsera she was taking Mary out shopping.

Mary fell madly in love with Rudolph and wrote to her former governess saying:

"I cannot live without having seen him or spoken to him. Dear Hermine, don't worry about me. I know everything you say is true, but I cannot change facts. I have two friends, you and Marie Larisch. *You* work for my soul's happiness and Marie works for my moral misfortune."

Meetings became difficult because Marie Larisch, having done her evil work, left Vienna for her house in Bohemia. Mary wrote to her governess:

"Marie Larisch had departed and I cannot see him. I wither with longing and cannot wait for the day of her return. . . . I ponder night and day how I could contrive to see him!"

Mary managed to creep out when her mother and sister were at the Opera. Rudolph was now in love with her. In a letter he wrote that he could not live without her and he would go mad if he could no longer see her.

"He is my god, my everything!" Mary cried.

In another letter to her governess Mary said:

"If only we could live together in a hut, we would be so

happy! We constantly talk of this and love doing so; but alas, it cannot be! If I could give my life to see him happy, I would gladly do it, because I do not value my own life!"

In another letter she told Hermine that they had a suicide pact should their love affair become known. They would kill themselves after a few happy hours together. "But he must not die," Mary finished, "he must live for his nation. All that surrounds him must be splendour and glory."

Rudolph contrasted Mary with his wife. One was a burden; the other an inspiration. With Mary he felt that there was nothing he could not achieve—and he began to confide in her his most secret hopes.

They were treasonable ambitions. His Liberal friends had influenced him so deeply that he dreamed of a new kind of government for the Empire which he would one day inherit. His acute and sensitive intelligence told him that, so far as the Hapsburg throne in Vienna was concerned, this was indeed a dream. His youthful impatience whispered that a way lay open for him to achieve all that he longed for and more.

This was to ascend the throne of Hungary as King while the Emperor of Austria still reigned in Vienna. Andrássy had told him that the constitution permitted this. While besides the lure of a throne was another enticement— Hungary still followed ancient customs as regards marriage. Re-marriage of divorced persons was permitted. Co-habitation for a period was accepted as proof of the existence of marriage.

Many political leaders in Hungary, survivors of the 1848 Revolution or their descendants, were actively fostering this move. Rudolph had long been in correspondence about it with them. Actually the conspiracy was well known to Franz Joseph, for the Austrian political police were examining all the correspondence to and from Rudolph. Counter-espionage agents had infiltrated into the most secret groups in Budapest. Spies watched the Crown Prince's every movement.

Rudolph had always been interested in and intrigued by

death; as a child he had a morbid interest in it. When he was older he told Moritz Szeps, with whom he discussed political affairs:

"I look for an opportunity to watch a dying person and over-hear his last breath. It is always for me a curious sight and of all the people whom I have seen dying each has died in a different way."

He talked, too, with Professor Zuckerkandl, an anatomist, and asked him if he found life among so many skulls uncanny.

"Even skulls have a certain beauty," Zuckerkandl replied. "One gets used to the idea that death is not a misfortune but a necessary, even miraculous, fulfilment of life.

Rudolph answered, "One should face the idea of death straightforwardly."

In the winter of 1888, despite the fact that he was still carrying on his intrigue with Mary Vetersa, he suddenly renewed his connections with an attractive dancer, Mizzi Kaspa. In December he proposed a suicide pact.

He had in the summer spoken of shooting himself, but he now suggested they should go together into the Vienna woods and kill themselves. Mizzi laughed, she did not take him seriously.

However Rudolph frequently asked his friends, "Are you afraid of death?" And when he heard that someone was dead he would say, "He is fortunate."

Valerie became engaged at the beginning of December to Archduke Franz Salvator. Elizabeth was unhappy at the thought of losing her most beloved child. Valerie was also afraid of telling Rudolph—he had been so strange lately.

Finally she told him and Rudolph was touched by her confession and the arms she flung around his neck.

"Never be unkind to Valerie," Elizabeth said to him, "it would bring you bad luck. I am Sunday's child and I know!"

"I promise I will be good to her," Rudolph said simply. Elizabeth made the sign of the cross on his forehead.

"God will bless you for it," she said, "and it will bring you happiness. You are my son and I do love you so."

Rudolph kissed her hand and then Valerie threw her arms round them both.

"This is how we ought to be always," she cried.

Unfortunately this was impossible because Rudolph was suffering, as Elizabeth had suffered, from frustration and being over-powered by the pomp and tradition of his position. He was followed by spies and informers, he was allowed to waste his talents year after year, without any use being made of him, except that he should look nice in his uniforms and pay the correct amount of homage to his Emperor.

Elizabeth understood this wastage so well. She knew that a young man longs to rule and must be ruled. She had said once that all through the ages the old regarded the young as an element dangerous to the State and strove to keep them ouside the political structure and away from political affairs.

"All calamities come about," she went on, "because people do not know how to use the splendid powers of youth."

Besides this feeling of stagnating mentally Rudolph had also undermined his physical state. He had drunk too much for years because when he was tired he wanted "to buck himself up." This increased his fatigue of which he often complained in his letters. In 1887 he had been given morphia for a chronic cough. He took too much and continued with it. In a letter to Stephanie he said:

"I cannot get rid of my cough. Sometimes . . . I have frightful attacks which are especially inconvenient at . . . ceremonial occasions. I am keeping the cough under with morphine, although it is an injurious thing."

Alcohol and morphine combined with frustration not only altered his personality; they gave him a frightful feeling of being weighed down. He felt driven into a dark, inescapable despondency which demanded some action on his part, however wild, however fantastic!

One Monday in January 1889, Rudolph said goodbye to Stephanie and told her he was going to Mayerling. He also said to his messenger Puchel:

"Expect me tomorrow afternoon. I shall be back by five o'clock, as I shall dine together with Her Imperial Highness and their Majesties."

He left Vienna about eleven o'clock. An hour earlier Countess Marie Larisch had called for Mary at the Vetsera Palace and taken her shopping in a *fiacre*.

They stopped in the Kohlmarkt—the central thoroughfare of Vienna—and Countess Larisch entered a shop to settle an account, while Mary remained in the *fiacre*. When she came out the girl had gone. The coachman said she had entered another *fiacre* and been driven away. She had left a brief note for the Countess which announced her intention to commit suicide!

Countess Larisch, horrified at what her scheming had brought about, and anxious to disclaim responsibility at the eleventh hour, rushed to see the President of Police.

He was well aware, from reports already received, that Rudolph was on his way to his hunting lodge.

He merely remarked to the Countess that Mayerling was outside his province.

FOURTEEN

1889

RUDOLPH arrived at Mayerling in the early afternoon of the 27th. Mary Vetsera arrived just as it was getting dark and passed in, as had been arranged, through the private entrance, which led direct to a dressing room adjoining the Crown Prince's bedroom. That evening and night the lovers were alone.

On the following morning at 8.10 Count Joseph Hoyes and Prince Philipp Coburg, Stephanie's brother-in-law, arrived for the shoot.

As they approached the lodge they saw that the blinds were drawn and the gates closed, as if no one was in residence. They went into the billiard room, where meals were usually served, and after a few minutes Rudolph appeared in his dressing gown, with a silk muffler round his neck.

He ate an excellent breakfast but told his guests that he had thought the previous night he was going to be ill. It was, however, only a cold but it would be unwise for him to go shooting.

Prince Coburg had been invited to attend the Emperor's dinner party that night, so he left his stand at 1.30 without saying goodbye to Count Hoyes and joined Rudolph for tea before going on to Vienna. The Crown Prince appeared to be in good spirits but asked the Count to make his excuses from attending the dinner.

Rudolph sent a telegram to his wife asking her also to offer his apologies to his father. He told her he had a severe cold in his head so he would stay at Mayerling with Hoyes.

When the telegram arrived at the Hofburg, Stephanie opened it and said in front of the messenger:—"Oh God, what shall I do! I feel so strange."

Count Hoyes, after his return from the shoot, arrived at

the Lodge at seven o'clock. He dined along with the Crown Prince who was very talkative and in what the Count described as "a mild and tender mood".

They talked about cooking, the intelligence of gun dogs and many other ordinary subjects. At nine o'clock Rudolph withdrew saying he must go to bed early if he was to shoot the next day, and Count Hoyes left for his lodgings which were about four or five hundred yards from the Lodge. Breakfast, he was told, was arranged for eight o'clock.

On the second night the Crown Prince ate hardly anything at dinner. Before the port was passed round he begged to be excused as he intended to get to bed immediately to throw off his cold.

Rudolph went to his bedroom, where Mary was waiting, and a cold supper and champagne were served. Bratfisch, an old coachman, was sent for because he could whistle and sing the sentimental songs they liked so much. After several hours he was told he could retire.

The servant, Loschek, had been dismissed as soon as Rudolph and Mary had finished eating.

In the light of the flickering candles Mary wrote her farewell letters. To her mother she said:

"Dear Mother, Forgive me for what I have done, I could not resist my love. In agreement with him I would like to be buried beside him at Allard. I am happier in death than in life, Yours Mary."

To her sister she said:

"We are both going blissfully into the uncertain beyond."

Rudolph had written his farewell letters in Vienna. He penned a brief note to his faithful servant, Loschek. Now they had only one thing to decide—how should they die? After some discussion they decided on the revolver rather than the use of poison.

Mary wrote on an ashtray:

"Rather revolver, a revolver is safer."

She stretched herself on the bed, she was not afraid although she cried a little. She loved Rudolph so much that it was almost an ecstacy to die at his hand. They made love to each other. Then Rudolph pulled the trigger and Mary's short life was ended.

Rudolph should have used the next bullet on himself but he hesitated. For some hours he sat alone with the dead girl. Dawn broke; at six thirty he opened the door and told Loschek to have breakfast ready in an hour's time.

Whistling softly, he went back into the bedroom locking the door behind him. He poured out a glass of brandy and placed it on the bedside table. He put a flower into Mary's hands. Then, taking up a hand mirror, he lay down on the bed beside her. Looking into the mirror, he lifted the pistol.

At seven-thirty, as he had been ordered, Loschek went to the door of his master's bedroom and knocked. There was no reply to his knocking and he became alarmed at the silence.

He sent the Lodge warden to Count Hoyes, who was up and dressed but who was waiting in his rooms before walking to the Lodge for breakfast at eight o'clock.

The Count hurried to speak with Loschek and told him to break open the door. But when the servant replied that Mary Vetsera was with the Crown Prince, he hesitated, waiting until Prince Coburg, who had returned from Vienna after the dinner, arrived.

As a relative, the Prince gave the necessary order. There was no sound from the bedroom, and it took some time to break the heavy door with an axe.

As the panel was splintered and the door was forced open, they saw the Crown Prince lying on his side with the top of his head blown off. Dark arterial blood was still dripping from the shattered cranium to the floor at the side of the bed. The hangings, the pillows and the coverlet were saturated; while the wall behind the bedhead and on the further side were bespattered with blood, which had apparently been forced there by some heavy explosion.

The three men hesitantly entered the room and the Count

almost automatically went through the useless procedure of
feeling the Prince's pulse. Both he and Hoyes noticed that the
body of the Prince, lying on top of the coverlet, was partially
hiding the bulge of another body. Fearfully they lifted the
sheet and saw the naked body of Mary Vetsera with a large
bullet wound in the side of her cheek.

Count Hoyes told Loschek to pull the body of the girl
from the bed, take it into the little dressing room and hide
it somewhere. While the servant was doing this the Count
covered the body of the Prince decently, and as best he could
removed all traces of the presence of his companion.

The door of the dressing room and the shattered one to
the corridor were then closed and given a makeshift seal.
Count Coburg was in a state of collapse so Hoyes hurried
to the station and took a special train to Vienna, in order
to acquaint the Emperor and Empress of what had happened.

It was only a little after nine o'clock in the morning when
he reached the Hofburg. He saw the Emperor's adjutant
general, Count Parr, and asked him to break the appalling
news to the Emperor.

"I cannot possibly," the Count declared. "Her Majesty is
the only person who can tell His Majesty such a thing."

Elizabeth was having her Greek lesson. When Ida Ferenczy
appeared at the door and announced that Baron Nopcsa,
Controller of the Household, wished to see her, she replied
impatiently, "Well, he must wait and come back later."

Ida, white to the lips, said urgently, "He has bad news
Your Majesty, grave news from His Imperial Highness."

Elizabeth signalled her Greek master to withdraw. The
Baron entered, but stood silent unable to begin:

"I have bad news," he managed to say at last. "His Royal
Highness the Crown Prince is——"

Elizabeth was watching him. Suddenly she knew the
truth.

"Rudolph is dead," she said for him in a voice that was
almost toneless.

When Ida entered the room a few moments later she found

Elizabeth in floods of tears. At this moment a step was heard outside, it was Franz Joseph.

"Not yet! Do not come in," Elizabeth cried.

Ida rushed to the door.

"I implore Your Majesty most earnestly to wait a moment longer."

Franz Joseph waited, talking to Baron Nopcsa, who was controlling himself by an almost superhuman effort.

Elizabeth dried her tears.

"Is anything noticeable?" she asked Ida. "No? Very well, then show him in, and may God help me!"

As soon as Franz Joseph had returned to his own apartments Elizabeth went to see Frau Katherina Schratt. She was an actress whom she had introduced to her husband. She realised he needed both a mistress and a companion when she was abroad and was anxious that he should have someone who would not influence him in the wrong way or do anything to cause a scandal.

She liked Katherina Schratt, admired her and trusted her. Fortunately the Emperor was immediately intrigued with the lovely young actress and eventually gave her a house near Vienna and a villa at Ischl.

She came nearly every day to see him at the Hofburg and luckily was in the Palace at this moment. Elizabeth sent her to Franz Joseph, while she went to break the news to Valerie, and, worst of all, to Stephanie.

While she was engaged in these tragic tasks Ida discovered Baroness Vetsera waiting for an audience.

"What do you want, Baroness?" she asked. "I cannot see you now."

"I must speak with Her Majesty the Empress," the Baroness replied.

"But, that is impossible!"

"I must, I must. I have lost my child and she alone can restore her to me."

Ida went to Elizabeth.

"Does she know all yet?" the Empress asked.

"No."

"Poor woman. Very well, I will go to her."

Although Elizabeth was absolutely calm when Baroness Vetsera came in, there must have been something in her face that betrayed the real news, for the Baroness took one look at her and then clutched her hand with the despairing cry:

"I have lost my child. Please help me to find her."

Elizabeth drew away from her and said in French: "Baroness, you must be brave. Your child is dead."

Baroness Vetsera burst into tears. "My child, my dear, beautiful child. . . ."

"My Rudolph is dead too," the Empress said.

The Baroness fell on her knees.

"My unhappy child! What has she done? She has done this!" she sobbed, then fainted away.

Elizabeth made no attempt to lift her but left her lying on the floor and walked away without another glance. Her normally sympathetic nature had died under the stress of the tragedy. She felt that the Baroness and Mary, who had infatuated her beloved Rudi, were fundamentally responsible for the tragedy.

Meantime Doctor Weiderhofer, one of the Emperor's personal physicians, had been sent post-haste to Mayerling.

The supper table in the corner of the bedroom still bore the remains of partially eaten food and there was some champagne in one of the glasses. The doctor summoned Loschek, and ordered him to clear the table and to remove the glasses and empty bottles.

He then laid the body of the Crown Prince on its back, swathed the shattered skull in bandages and as best he could washed away the blood that spread over the face and neck. A clean sheet was obtained and laid over the blood-stained coverlet.

These changes the doctor carried out on his own responsibility, for the Emperor's parting instructions had been to leave everything precisely as he found them until he arrived.

During the interval Loschek had taken the naked body of Mary from the dressing room and hidden it in a large clothes basket in an attic, which was used for storing linen. The room was lit only by a small skylight, and on the dull January day the doctor could hardly make out anything in detail. The servant had hastily thrown all the girl's clothes in the room. Her large hat, trimmed with ostrich feathers, lay grotesquely on the sheet with which Loschek had covered the body.

The doctor drew the sheet back. He said it was impossible for him to examine the injuries there. Together they carried the basket with the corpse into the nearby billiards room. There they lifted the girl out and laid her on the billiard table.

In the better light the doctor gently parted the hair, matted with blood, which partially covered the girl's face, and started back with horror. He had had no idea of the identity of the victim until that moment. Now he recognised Mary Vetsera, whom he had treated since she was a small child.

The initial shock was not quite so great as it might have been, for his first glimpse was of the left hand side of her face, which was quite unharmed. The other was badly mutilated. The force of the bullet had pushed the right eye right out of its socket.

The doctor replaced the eye, bandaged the head, washed the face and, after using the linen as a winding sheet, helped Loschek to carry the body back to the attic. His work was completed just before the Emperor arrived with the chiefs of the political police and a number of his most confidential advisers.

The Emperor insisted on going to see his son alone. He was in the bedroom by himself for fifteen minutes. When he emerged his face was ashen but he was completely in control of his emotions. Immediately he started to suggest ways in which the scandal could be hushed up.

He grew furiously angry when the doctor refused to obey

his suggestion that he should issue a death certificate stating the cause of death was apoplexy. The Emperor began muttering that there was no one in the whole of his Empire on whom he could rely for help when he needed it, and went off to have a conference with his police officers.

Despite the refusal of the doctor to co-operate, the Emperor and his men concocted the first official report, which stated that the Crown Prince had died at his hunting box at Mayerling of an apoplectic stroke. This bulletin was telegraphed to Vienna and released to the press, being simultaneously relayed to all parts of the world.

Outside Vienna it was at first accepted as the truth, but in the Imperial capital itself there were by that time too many people who had heard rumours for the bulletin to do anything but arouse curiosity. The gossip in the cafés and taverns of Vienna became so universal that the secret police reported in person to the Emperor that the prestige of the Crown was in danger if some correction was not made.

On the following day, therefore, the editor of the *Wiener Zeitung* was instructed to publish a brief paragraph admitting that the Crown Prince had taken his life with a revolver bullet. The simple truth coming after the former misleading statement was not accepted. Everyone knew the sort of orgy that had long gone on at Mayerling and most people thought that they understood the Crown Prince's character too well to admit that he could ever take his own life.

Suicide was not nearly as dramatic as murder, and it was openly stated that Rudolph had met his end at the hands of a jealous husband or even possibly, at those of a wronged mistress.

The wildest stories were passed from mouth to mouth as being the authentic version of what had happened. One said that his head had been slashed to pieces with the jagged edge of a broken champagne bottle. Another version was that he had been stabbed through the heart and his face then deliberately mutilated.

These stories were widely accepted because there was still

no sign two days after the tragedy occurred of the Crown Prince lying-in-state. By that evening, to the horror of the Court, details began to leak out about another dead body at Mayerling. The secret police—and the Emperor, who had approved of their ghoulish plan—had only themselves to blame for the emergence of the new stories.

Acting on the verbal instructions of the Emperor two trusted emissaries, Count Stockau and Alexandre Baltassi, were ordered to proceed at once to Mayerling in a large closed coach. The vehicle was to be driven by a policeman, and further police were to precede and follow the coach to ensure that no untoward interruption or delay occurred.

The two men were told to enter the attic for which Franz Joseph handed them the key. They were to dress the body of the girl in her normal outdoor clothes, and then to support it in such a way from the room, down the stairs, and across the driveway to the coach, that it would appear that she was still alive.

The emissaries could do nothing but obey an order given, as they were solemnly told, "for the sake of the security of the Crown and State". They asked for no further details. If they had done so they might well have baulked at the horror of their task.

Rigor mortis was still present in the corpse. As it had been almost doubled up in the linen basket they had to call on the assistance of a police officer to force the legs straight and to unbend the body at the waist.

Count Stockau endeavoured to pin Mary's long hair to the lacerated skin beside her temple where the bullet had entered. Baltassi washed away the pus and clotted blood which had exuded since the doctor's ministrations. Even this slight movement caused the head to roll, and to their horror the two men realised that the bullet must have splintered the bone at the back of the cranium. If they lifted the body erect the head lolled forward on the chest, suspended only by the skin and seemed as if it might fall off.

Setting aside that problem for the moment, they dressed

the body completely, the police officer insisting that all the garments that had been strewn around the dressing room must be used.

They even had to lace up Mary's corsets and tie up her long laced winter boots. In moving the body from side to side in order to get her clothes and fur coat on, the head rolled more and more and Stockau told the police officer that it would be impossible for them to carry out the body erect. The latter said that his orders were not to permit them to leave the room until the corpse stood upright between its two escorts.

He suggested that a walking stick should be rammed down the back of the clothes, laced inside the corsets and a scarf bound round the neck and stick to hold the head erect.

This was the only possible thing to do. It meant partially undressing the body once more in order to get the stick inside the rear of the corsets. When at last the dead effigy of the girl was placed upright the police officer surveyed the trio and with a nod of satisfaction opened the door and looked down the dimly lit corridor. There were no servants to be seen.

Mary Vetsera was a small girl, but even so there was a terrible physical strain for the two men in gripping her round the waist under her fur coat, to shuffle down the stairs, across the hallway, and finally down the steps to the waiting carriage.

Somehow they achieved it and placed the body on the rear seat of the coach. It was impossible to bend the knees so that the girl could appear to be sitting down and they had to leave her leaning backwards. They sat opposite her and held her in position as best they could.

They had no idea where they were going but after a comparatively short time the coach stopped before a small gateway with a door of oak strengthened by wrought iron bars. Immediately the door opened and two monks bearing lanterns came forward. The monks opened the door of the coach, took hold of the body and carried it to a stretcher just inside the door. They motioned to Count Stockau and Baltassi to follow them.

The police shut the gates and the two gentlemen found themselves in a monastery graveyard. A small chapel, open at one end, stood on the farther side. Here a plain coffin lay on two trestles. The body was put in and immediately the lid was nailed down.

Without a proper religious service the coffin was lowered into a grave, the freshly dug soil of which stood out black in the moonlight amidst the light snow which covered the other tombs. No word whatever had been spoken by the monks who quickly melted away into the darkness.

Count Stockau paused over the still unfilled grave to pray, but the police officer growled that it was time they were gone and pulled him roughly away.

The graveyard chosen for the secret burial of Mary Vetsera was in the Cistercian Monastery at Heiligenkreuz. In due course a report was made by the local police that a body of a woman with a bullet wound in the head had been found in the village. It had been identified by two witnesses, Count Stockau and Baron Baltassi, as that of Baroness Mary Vetsera and had been duly buried.

This announcement, which crept into some of the Viennese papers and dared to hint at the Royal scandal, unfortunately clashed with another pronouncement which, in a frenzied anxiety to produce circumstantial stories, one of the secret police had issued without the knowledge of his colleagues.

He had been deputed within a few hours of the Emperor's conference at Mayerling to go to the Viennese residence of Mary Vetsera's family and order her mother to leave for Venice within eight hours. The distraught woman, who had learned in her brief interview with the Empress that she could expect no sympathy in her bereavement, could do nothing but obey.

As an afterthought the policeman said that when she got to Venice she should announce in a letter to the press of

Vienna that her daughter Mary Vetsera had suddenly died in the city.

Baroness Vetsera left Vienna on the first train which departed at 5 a.m. on the morning after the tragedy. In due course, hoping that her co-operation with the authorities might produce some authentic news of how her daughter had met her end she duly sent the death notice to Vienna, where it obtained publication in some newspapers before the authorities could suppress it.

By this time everyone in Vienna, and certainly the news editors of the world's press, were perfectly aware that the two deaths were connected. But still there was the mystery as to whether it was a double murder, a double suicide, or a murder and suicide—and in the last case which was the victim and which the assailant.

Obstinately Franz Joseph refused to issue further details, but he did give way sufficiently to permit the traditional lying-in-state in the Chapel of the Hapsburgs.

Rudolph's head was swathed in bandages but his face was not distorted. He looked peaceful, the bitter smile with which his friends had been so familiar these last months, had disappeared.

The lying-in-state was authorised by Franz Joseph largely in order to gain time. The panic-stricken rush in which one misleading bulletin after another had been issued, had unfortunately resulted in the final version being that the Crown Prince had committed suicide. This meant that a funeral conducted by the Church, with interment in the vaults of the Hapsburgs, was impossible unless insanity was proved.

The Vatican, which had been privately informed of the real facts so far as they could be ascertained about the illicit, romantic orgy at Mayerling, was unwilling to gloss over the sinfulness of the matter simply because of the exalted position of the deceased.

The Papal Nuncio had to inform Franz Joseph that the Pope could not authorise the last rites unless physicians were able to state on oath that suicide had occurred during a fit of insanity.

Madness was, of course, a very delicate subject in the case of the Hapsburgs. Franz Joseph was extremely unwilling to tell the world that yet another member of his family, whose blood also included the strain of the notoriously unstable Wittelsbachs, had been mad.

However, in order to satisfy the Church, he asked a group of the most eminent physicians in Vienna to conduct an examination. The body of Rudolph was withdrawn from the Chapel and an autopsy made of the skull. The procedure was merely a lot of technical rigmarole, arranged by the doctors, so that they could in due course give the only possible verdict.

After cutting the skull in half and probing about inside, they issued a bulletin which probably neither the public nor the most expert alienist could have understood beyond the explanation at the end which said: ". . . And it therefore justifies an assumption that the act of self-destruction was committed while the balance of the mind was disturbed."

When Elizabeth heard this verdict she broke down and said to her husband:

"Franz, forgive me. I had no right to marry. Madness is in my family. I have brought it to yours."

The Emperor, with tears in his eyes, answered:

"You brought nothing but what is good and sweet with you when you married me, and I, my dear, have never been worthy of you in any way."

Despite the doctors' bulletin the College of Cardinals in Rome had the gravest doubts about the matter, still being most disturbed at the example of debauchery by the son of an anointed King. Their final announcement stressed that it was only in the practice of Christian mercy that the verdict of the doctors was accepted and that the Church in Vienna would be permitted to conduct the funeral.

Prince Rudolph was buried in the Church of the Capuchins on February 5th. His mother did not attend the funeral. Only the Emperor and Gisela followed the coffin. But when the day of the funeral was over, and just as it approached mid-night, Elizabeth came secretly from the Hofburg.

The door of the church was closed, and she had to ring the bell for a long time before she awakened a priest, who came and opened the door. She raised her veil to disclose her identity. "I am the Empress—please take me to my son."

He led her by the light of a lantern to the vaults and found a candle to illuminate the sarcophagus. The priest left her alone and ascended the steps to wait in the church above. He heard her call, "Rudi," time after time, her voice echoing spectrally round the vault, then there was silence.

Alarmed, he went down and found the Empress prostrate on the stone floor. Gently he raised her up and immediately she collected herself. He led her to the door of the church and she stumbled away into the darkness.

In the six days between the first news of the tragedy and the funeral, Elizabeth had been patiently and usually word-lessly helping her husband. She was always close at hand. He was deeply grateful for her sympathy. As if to make up for his neglect in the past, he admitted her help in his address to a deputation of condolence from Parliament, and said:

"I can find no words warm enough to express how much I owe to my dearly beloved wife, the Empress, during these sad days and what a great support she has been to me. I devoutly thank God for giving me such a help-mate.

"Repeat my words, for the more widely you make them known, the more grateful I shall be to you."

FIFTEEN

1890-1898

"THE Lady in Black", as the Empress came to be known to the inhabitants of a score of spas and resorts in Europe, seemed to attract the spectre of death. "His Dark Majesty is my constant companion," she once said in a wry attempt at humour about her lonely life.

Count Andrássy, who had loved Elizabeth with a wholehearted devotion for nearly twenty years, died of cancer of the bladder in 1890, a year after Rudolph's suicide. She had not been able to force herself to visit the husk of a once splendid man in his last weeks of life. But she went on foot to his lying-in-state and laid a wreath of lilies-of-the-valley on his breast in the open coffin.

"My last and only friend is dead," she said brokenheartedly to Valerie. "And now he is gone I realise for the first time what he was to me. Not until now have I felt utterly deserted without a single counsellor or friend."

Just before his death the Count had written to a friend and said of Elizabeth:

"I can only say that there is no other such woman on earth. The only thing that grieves me is that so few people know what she is. . . . I can only repeat that she hides her superior intelligence and great heart, in comparison with which Maria Theresa's were only those of a good housekeeper, as though it were not meet to display such talents. I am one of the few fortunate people who have had an opportunity of learning to know and admire a woman of whose true nature so many millions of her subjects have no idea."

Bay Middleton had been killed on April 9th, 1892. His horse had stumbled at a hurdle but did not fall, recovering at the last moment. In doing so it caught Bay such a blow on the chin as he was thrown forwards that his neck was broken.

Elizabeth had mourned him, knowing that with his death much of her youth died too. He and Julius' Andrássy were the only two men who had ever really mattered in her life. Both were so different in character and temperament, but both gave her inexpressible happiness when she could be with them.

Andrássy, all fire, passion and adoration, appealed also to Elizabeth's brain and the idealistic side of her which made her long to right wrongs and to reinstate Hungary after years of oppression and abuse. She loved him in a way that she could never have loved anyone else.

Bay was a charming, straightforward sportsman. He meant so much to Elizabeth because she admired him in the hunting field and because he too could give her something she could find in no other man. She treasured his love for her, and also his rare but very sincere compliments.

Once when he had been watching her at a fencing lesson he exclaimed: "God, you're lovely. I could watch you for ever!"

Imri was just a dream, though sometimes she thought of him. He had been the first person to teach her that love was not just a physical contact, but that it could be a unity of the heart and soul.

Andrássy had shown her that love was also of the mind. In him she found a combination of everything she had sought in her girlish dreams. Her disillusion and disagreements with Franz Joseph were always because she expected from him much more than he was capable of giving.

He, too, loved her in his own way. She was a thing apart from his amorous fumblings with other women and his flirtations with every pretty face which caught his fancy. He could never understand her, because he had no imagination, but nevertheless he both relied on her and loved her.

Two months after Andrássy's death, Elizabeth had more bad news. Her sister, Hélène, Princess of Thurn and Taxis, was reported to be on her death bed. She was at Ratisbon, and Elizabeth hurried to see her.

She was very fond of Hélène but she often wondered what her life would have been like if she had not participated in that childish plot to prevent her sister being forced into a loveless marriage with the Emperor. Elizabeth watched Hélène's agonising illness bring slow death.

She sat patiently at the bedside trying to comfort her.

"We have both had to bear some hard knocks in our lives," Elizabeth said.

"Yes, because we have hearts," Hélène replied.

A few days later she died in terrible agony and Elizabeth returned home shattered by what she had seen.

"I can understand now," she said, "how a man might be capable of committing suicide merely out of dread of such a lingering end."

The only happy incident of the whole year was the marriage of Valerie to the Archduke Franz Salvator on July 31st, 1890,—but that was bitter-sweet, for it meant the end of the intimacy and love which Elizabeth had enjoyed with her favourite child since her birth.

One evening at Ischl they heard one of Elizabeth's poems, which had been set to music, sung by the men's choral society. When it was finished Elizabeth put her arms around her daughter and said:

"I thank you for always having been a good child to me."

Valerie said afterwards that it was the happiest moment of her life.

Elizabeth was deathly pale as she drove to the church alone with Valerie in the last carriage of the bridal procession. She wore grey instead of her accustomed black, but she wept bitterly when the bride turned from the altar a married woman.

When the young couple left for their honeymoon Elizabeth felt as though her heart was being torn from her body.

She was more conscious of her solitary existence after

Valerie's marriage than ever before. Franz Joseph seemed to have found all the comfort he needed in the company of Katherina Schratt. The actress was always lively, graceful and elegant although her figure was beginning to thicken a little for she was nearly forty. Elizabeth herself liked the woman and sometimes they all three dined together, waiting on themselves.

But as time went by, Elizabeth felt a little uneasy when she saw how well Katherina was playing the part allotted to her. She was by now an absolute necessity to the Emperor. It was, Elizabeth told herself, entirely her own fault, but once when talking to Valerie, she said:

"Why was I born? My life is useless. I am nothing more than an obstacle between the Emperor and Frau Schratt. Why, sometimes I feel almost ridiculous in front of them."

But always there was the desire to escape from the realities of existence. Her longing for freedom drove her on a wayward Odyssey of travel, motiveless and exhausting, her itinerary crossing and recrossing earlier routes. Portugal, Gibraltar, Tangiers, Algiers, Corsica, Marseilles, the Hyeres Islands, Florence and Pompeii.

The Controller of her Household, Baron Nopcsa, shook his head.

"This mania for movement on the part of Her Majesty is on the increase," he wrote to Ida Ferenczy. "God knows what it may lead to."

It seemed as if Elizabeth could not keep still. Besides the strenuous morning gymnastics, she walked until her ladies-in-waiting literally dropped by the wayside.

"Her sole object," Countess Festetics wrote to Ida, "is to keep moving. When we got home I collapsed on my bed with weariness."

If Elizabeth sought peace of mind, her travels did not provide it. She grew more and more apathetic—to people, to politics, and to life itself.

Off again Elizabeth went to Miramar, Cairo, back to Vienna, off to Karlsbad, on to Switzerland and from there to Godollo. On again to Sicily, the Balearic Islands, Spain, Gibraltar, Majorca, Barcelona, Turin, Geneva and Territet.

In Cairo, as soon as Elizabeth was relieved of her sciatica by the hot sun, she began her endless walks.

"Her Majesty's pedestrian feats are so marvellous," the Austrian representative reported, "that the secret police said it was intolerable to have to follow the all-highest lady except in carriages."

In 1894, Elizabeth, now a great grandmother, was in her fifty-sixth year. Dieting and exercise had kept her incredibly supple, yet she was always worrying about her weight which varied between seven stone four and seven stone twelve pounds. She had "milk days" and "orange days", when she would eat nothing else, and she began to suffer from digestive disorders as a result of an ill-regulated diet.

She was always trying new cures which usually did her more harm than good, until Franz Joseph remarked to Valerie:

"These incessant cures are really terrible."

In June, 1896, Elizabeth went with Franz Joseph to Budapest for the Hungarian Millenary Celebrations. At the State receptions of the Hungarian Parliament Kálmán Mikszáth described her appearance, and wrote:

"There she sat in the throne room of the Royal Palace in her Hungarian costume of black, adorned with lace. Everything about her was sombre. . . . Black were the ornaments in her hair, black her pearls, everything black, only her face was marble white and ineffably sad. . . . a *Mater Dolorosa*. . . ."

The President of the Parliament, Desider Szilágyi, began to speak and pronounced the name of the Queen.

"Suddenly a cheer broke forth such as the Royal Palace had never heard before, as though a storm of emotion burst from every heart . . . louder still rang the cheers, and for minutes they refused to be silent . . . roar after roar . . . the magnates waved their hats . . . the Queen inclined her head. Her snow-white cheek showed a faint flush. Its milky whiteness was tinged with pale rose, then a crimson wave surged up, flooding it with a living red. As though by magic a Queen appeared in all the hues of life seated at the side of the King. Her eyes dilated and flashed with their former splendour. Those eyes, whose captivating smile had once had power to console a sorrowing land, now filled with tears. The land, now happy, had succeeded in consoling its Queen, but only for a moment.

"Majestically she raised her lace handkerchief to her eyes to dry her tears. The orator resumed his speech. Slowly the flush of life faded and soon by the King's side there sat once more a woman shrouded in mourning—the *Mater Dolorosa*."

Elizabeth was overcome with emotion because she knew that this was no ordinary homage. Her realisation that every Hungarian was conscious of her sympathy and love broke through the wall of gloom and melancholy which she had set up between herself and the rest of the world.

But it was all too much for her. She immediately withdrew to the seclusion of the villa at Lainz, and the public heard nothing more of her for months.

"I am too old and weary to struggle," she said. "My wings have been singed. All I long for is rest."

In July, 1891, Elizabeth spent some time at Gastern with Franz Joseph. She was very sweet and tender to him and he was grateful to her for her understanding over Frau Schratt.

"My inexpressibly beloved angel," he wrote shortly after his departure. "I am in a melancholy mood with an aching heart and a feeling of home-sickness of Gastern. . . . Once again my warmest thanks for your love and goodness during my stay. It is seldom now that I pass such happy days."

The previous year "Carmen Sylva", Queen Elizabeth of Rumania, had visited Ischl, and, while there, had asked Elizabeth if she still rebelled against fate. Elizabeth had replied:

"No. I have turned to stone."

It was not true. She could still suffer intensely.

"I long for death," she said to Valerie, "and I have no fear of it, for I refuse to believe that there is a power so cruel that, not content with the sufferings of life, it would tear the soul from the body in order to go on torturing it."

Elizabeth was at Cap St. Martin in the spring of 1897 when a telegram from Paris reported that her youngest sister, the Duchess of Alençon, was feared to have died in a fire at a charity bazaar in Paris.

The news was soon proved true. A novelty at the bazaar was an exhibition of Lumière's newly invented motion picture machine. The celluloid film had caught fire, and the Duchess, quite safe in another part of the hall, had rushed in to see if she could help to rescue some of the audience, one hundred and thirteen of whom died.

Only the Duchess's teeth in a calcined skull were recognisable by her dentist—and a half molten ring which appeared to have her monogram on it.

When Elizabeth walked behind the child's coffin which contained the few ounces of powdery bones which represented her sister's remains, she was pondering on a news item in the press that morning. It was one of the rare pronouncements of the fashionable French clairvoyant, Gabriele, which stated:

"Within twelve months Europe will be shocked by the murder of a Royal personage whose heart is broken and tired."

She felt certain that the prophecy referred to herself, and told many people so. She challenged their denials with the question:

"Who else is so heartbroken as I?"

In the summer of 1898 Elizabeth, accompanied by her daughter Valerie, went to Ischl with the intention of remaining there until the Emperor arrived to celebrate his birthday. She was still physically restless but emotionally hovering near the immobility of deep melancholia. Her jangled nerves had set up neuralgic pains which made every movement of her limbs agonising. Her wish to remain slim had become such a fixation in her mind that she was virtually starving herself to death.

She ate no meat at all and took frequent steam baths immediately followed by a very cold plunge bath. She would weigh herself three times a day which annoyed Dr. Kerzl who had been asked by the Emperor to make a report on her condition.

"Devil take the man," he exclaimed, "who advised Her Majesty to weigh herself all the time."

Despite all this Elizabeth's weight increased, and because she was desperate, she permitted a physician to examine her.

The horrified man noted her swollen ankles and the distention of her abdomen once the restricting corsets were removed and realised that his patient was suffering from oedema, the swelling of starvation. She was terribly emaciated. Her cheeks were sunken and lined with the constant effort to stifle the cries of agony from the neuralgic spasms. The bones stood out on her wrists and fingers and the latter were constantly trembling.

The doctor succeeded in frightening Elizabeth a little and for a time she followed his advice and ceased her exhausting walks. Her spirits immediately showed an improvement, but she could not face meeting Franz Joseph and decided without warning to go to Nanheim.

In order to prevent gossip of yet another rift in the Imperial family, her doctors authorised the Austrian and Hungarian newspapers to publish a formal bulletin about the Empress's health:

"Her Majesty has been suffering for some long time past from anaemia, which became worse in consequence of severe neuralgia in the course of last winter, following on insomnia of many months' standing. In addition, there is an enlargement of the heart. Under conditions of absolute rest Her Majesty's illness need not give rise to serious apprehension but her physicians have earnestly advised Her Majesty to submit to treatments at the Spa of Nanheim in order to restore her strength."

Franz Joseph was very disappointed not to see his wife. He wrote to her—"I miss you here unspeakably, my thoughts are with you and I think sorrowfully of the endless time for which we are to be parted; your empty, dismantled rooms make me sad."

Elizabeth took the baths at Nanheim, and even attempted to tackle the normal meals which her doctors insisted that she should have. But she disliked the place and on August 29th, without warning, she left for Monte de Caux in Switzerland. Here her health improved considerably and she was able to take long walks around the countryside.

On the day that Elizabeth arrived in Switzerland a young man named Luigi Lucheni read in a Budapest newspaper a brief news item about the Empress's visit. There was also a paragraph that stated that among the distinguished personages staying in the vicinity was the Duke of Orleans. Lucheni took a train the same day to Geneva.

He was an Italian born in Paris. He had been abandoned by his mother a week after his birth and the French authorities, having traced the mother and discovered that she was Italian, sent the child to a religious orphanage at Parma.

At the age of twelve he had been expelled from the orphanage and had wandered around Italy finding jobs as an unskilled labourer until the age of twenty, when he was called up for military service. By means of an employment organisation which the army ran he was, on completion of his military service, sent to the residence of the Prince of Aragon, where eventually he became a valet. His political views, which he soon made known to his employer, resulted in his being dismissed after three months.

Without a reference and quite unable to obtain any form of work, Lucheni joined an anarchist organisation. In the usual manner he was made to pledge his life to the destruction of the ruling classes and existing governments in every way possible.

For some reason which was never explained, Lucheni was sent to Budapest where, possibly, even by the year 1894 he was planning to assassinate the Empress, the Emperor, or their children. In any event, on a number of occasions he took care to get a good view of Elizabeth so that he could easily identify her.

On arrival at Geneva he bought a file at a secondhand shop and spent that night sharpening it until it became a thin stiletto, barely $4\frac{1}{2}$ins. long below the handle.

Lucheni later insisted that his intended victim was the Duke of Orleans, but there is no evidence that he made any attempt to locate this noble man, or indeed if he had, that he could have identified him.

Armed with his home-made stiletto Lucheni spent the next few days wandering around Geneva. There was a considerable Italian working population in the town and they gave him an occasional meal and could usually find him shelter for the night.

Meantime, at Caux the Empress was becoming more and more annoyed at the hovering police which the Swiss authorities had insisted on sending to guard her. She protested so violently that unwillingly the local police chief agreed to withdraw them. Elizabeth doubted whether he really intended to do so, and in search of peace and quiet she went to the Castle of Pregny, where an old friend, Baroness Adolf von Rothschild, was living. There she asked her hostess to send someone into Geneva to book her a suite of rooms at the Hotel Beau Rivage.

The reservation was duly made in the name of the Countess of Hohenembs, which the proprietor was perfectly aware meant that he would soon have a Royal guest. Unfortunately the man respected his guest's wishes for privacy and did not inform the Geneva police of the real identity of the Countess. Elizabeth arrived there on the evening of September 9th. She took no notice of the young man who was strolling in Fabris Street, where the hotel was situated.

Lucheni stared at the thin, beautiful woman dressed in deep black, carrying a large white sunshade and a black and yellow fan which she held close to her face. He memorised every detail and watched her disappear through the doors of the hotel. He then strolled down the street, turned the corner and reached the edge of the lake where he was joined by an older bearded man—the brains of the anarchist organisation in the town.

That evening Elizabeth went for a stroll with her reader of English novels whom she had in recent years come to like very much—Frederick Barker. He took with him Marion Crawford's exciting and horrific story "Corleone".

After they had walked about half a mile and left the town behind, the Empress sat down on a grassy bank dipping to the lakeside, where a boulder provided a rest for her back. She asked Barker to commence reading and while he did so she began to peel a peach that she had brought with her. She cut the fruit in half with a small pen-knife and held out one portion to her companion.

The light was failing rapidly. Suddenly there was a rustling in the air and a large black raven swooped down and knocked the fruit out of her hands with its beak. The supernatural flavour of the novel that Barker was reading made him acutely sensitive to this strange incident, and he recalled to Elizabeth that there was a tradition among the Hapsburgs that the raven's appearance always preceded bad news.

"My dear friend," she replied, "I fear nothing, what is to be will be. I am a fatalist."

Nevertheless she was visibly upset and began pacing up and down with all the agitation that her brief stay in Switzerland seemed to have eradicated. Back in the hotel she mentioned the incident of the raven to a lady-in-waiting, the Countess Sztáray, but added as if trying to re-assure herself:

"I love Geneva. I am safe here among all these cosmopolitans."

They talked together of religion and death. The Countess was deeply religious.

"I am a believer," Elizabeth told her, "though perhaps I have not so much faith as you. . . . You do not fear death, but I do, though I often long for it. It is the moment of passing and the uncertainty which makes me tremble."

"But in the world beyond are peace and bliss," Countess Sztáray assured her.

"How do you know that?" Elizabeth asked. "No traveller ever returned to tell us."

Next day, a Saturday, dawned as serene and warm as early September can so often be in Geneva. Elizabeth said that she thought it would be pleasant to go on a trip by a lake steamer to Montreux, and sent a servant to buy the tickets for the boat that left shortly after midday.

The landing stage was only a few hundred yards from the hotel, and she walked there, attended by her lady-in-waiting, and, some distance behind, by a footman.

The Empress pointed to the trees.

"Look, Irma, the chestnuts are in flower. There are chestnuts at the Schönbrunn that flower twice a year. . . . The Emperor writes that they are covered in bloom."

It was already twelve o'clock and they were late.

"Listen Your Majesty," Countess Sztáray exclaimed, "there is the siren."

The Empress walked more quickly and Countess Sztáray, ran on ahead to ensure that the gangway was not removed. Just as Elizabeth was a couple of yards from the edge of the quay, Lucheni, who had been sitting on a bench at the edge of the lake, stood up, started to walk at right angles towards her, and then turned as if he too was going to go up the gang plank.

He appeared to stumble and fall against her. While doing so he raised his arm and plunged his stiletto into her breast. Silently, without uttering a sound, Elizabeth fell backwards on to the ground.

The incident had taken place so quickly that it was difficult for anyone to know what had happened. The Countess, with the aid of a cab driver who had hurried up, tried to raise the Empress to her feet, while the assassin made off. The Countess thought the man had struck at Elizabeth with his fist.

"Is Your Majesty hurt?" she asked.

"No, No! thank you," replied the Empress, "it is nothing!"

The hotel porter, who had arrived on the scene, asked the Empress to return to the hotel.

"But no," she answered. "I am not hurt."

Elizabeth straightened her hat, the dust was shaken from her dress and the two ladies walked quickly towards the steamer. Suddenly all the colour was drained from Elizabeth's face and was followed by a deadly pallor. She turned quickly to the Countess who put her arm round her, thinking she was suffering from shock.

"Have I turned pale?" Elizabeth asked.

"Yes, Your Majesty, very. Your Majesty feels no pain?"

"I think my breast pains me a little."

At this moment they heard the porter shouting, "The criminal is caught."

Elizabeth walked as far as the narrow gangway. Here the Countess was forced to take her arm away from the Empress's waist as there wasn't room to walk two abreast. Elizabeth crossed the gangway, but as she set foot on deck she turned to the Countess and said agitatedly:

"Give me your arm—quickly."

The Countess threw her arm around her and the footman hurried to her other side, but they could not hold the Empress upright. She sank slowly to the ground, her head drooping against the Countess's shoulder as she knelt beside her.

"Water! Get some water," the Countess cried, "and a doctor."

There was no doctor on board, and the Captain hearing that a lady had fainted and not knowing who she was, advised the Countess to have her taken ashore.

"It's only a fainting fit from shock," the Countess answered. "She will be quite all right."

The Captain, reassured, gave orders for the steamer to move, while Elizabeth was carried on to the upper deck. Water was sprinkled on her face. The Countess undid her dress, cut her stay lace and pressed a piece of sugar soaked in cognac into her mouth.

After a few moments Elizabeth opened her eyes and tried to sit up.

"Does Your Majesty feel better?" the Countess enquired.

"Yes, thank you."

Elizabeth sat up and looked around her.

"Why, what has happened?"

"Your Majesty has not been very well, but you are better now, are you not?"

There was no answer. Elizabeth sank back unconscious.

"Rub her breast!" someone suggested.

Her dress was undone and suddenly to her horror the Countess saw a brownish stain about the size of a two-shilling piece on the violet batiste undergarment. She moved it and saw a tiny wound in the Empress's breast with some blood clotting round it.

"For Heaven's sake," she exclaimed, "the Empress has been murdered." She sent for the Captain.

"I beg you," she cried, "to return to the shore at once. The lady whom you see here is the Empress of Austria. She has been wounded in the breast!"

The Captain decided to return to Geneva. There was no proper stretcher on board and they improvised one out of two oars and some deck chairs. The Countess knelt beside Elizabeth desperately afraid, for the drops of sweat were dripping from her white face and her breathing was growing more and more difficult.

Elizabeth was carried to the hotel where she had spent the previous night. A doctor named Golay examined her. Anxiously the Countess asked: "Is there any hope?"

"No, Madame, none!" was the reply.

"Oh perhaps there may be," the Countess cried in desperation. "Try everything, do anything to bring her back to life."

A priest was fetched and pronounced the Absolution. All those present fell on their knees and prayed, but this was the end. Another doctor arrived but could do no more than confirm that the Empress was dead. A slight incision was made in the artery of her right arm, but not a drop of blood appeared.

Elizabeth lay there, looking surprisingly youthful. There was in death a faint flush of her cheeks and the suspicion of a smile on her lips. Her beauty was as overwhelming and entrancing as it had been all her life. Ludwig was right, she had been beautiful to the end.

Long before the doctors arrived and pronounced Elizabeth dead, Lucheni was in custody. Foolishly he had not been able to withstand the temptation of running from the scene of the crime and a couple of cab drivers, waiting beside their horses, had called out to a patrolling policeman, who took the man in for questioning.

At the local police station Lucheni refused to say anything. Later that afternoon, when the murder of the Empress became known, he was taken to police headquarters in Geneva where records existed indicating that he was a known anarchist. Taxed with the crime, he confessed and laughed with pleasure when told that his assassination had succeeded.

"I had nothing against her as a woman," he said. "But as an Empress she had to die. She was the first crowned head that I could recognise. I am glad I had the opportunity to kill her and I am glad that I did not fail."

At his trial he boasted of his guilt and was condemned to life imprisonment. On October 10th, 1910, he was found dead in his cell, having hanged himself with a leather strap.

The body of the Empress was sent on Monday morning by train to Vienna. For reasons of legal identification of the corpse, the coffin was fitted with two glass windows which could be slid back to permit a sight of the head. Everyone who saw it was overcome at Elizabeth's loveliness and serenity.

The funeral train was stopped at every important town between Geneva and Vienna so that it did not arrive in the capital until late at night on September 15th. There it was met by the Emperor and Elizabeth's two daughters. The body lay in state for two days in the Imperial Chapel at the Hofburg.

The funeral took place on Saturday, September 17th, the ceremony beginning precisely to the minute of Elizabeth's death a week before. The coffin was placed on the hearse, which had within the space of one hundred years carried three Emperors and six Empresses of the Hapsburgs to the Church of the Capuchins. It was drawn slowly through the streets by eight black horses.

The people of Vienna, who had in their time cheered the lovely young Empress and grumbled and scowled at her when she was older, now showed by their absolute silence that in death they could forgive her everything.

The Emperor, a lonely ageing and bent figure, was left alone in the plain and whitewash-walled church when the funeral was over. He managed with tremendous self-control to disguise his grief and his horror at the terrible end of the woman he had, despite his infidelities, always loved. In the majestic ceremonial of Elizabeth's death he had forced her to do her Imperial duty as he had never been able to make her do it in her lifetime.

He was aware, as everyone in the Court was aware, that for years Elizabeth had expressed wishes to be buried anywhere but in the church where the Hapsburgs lay.

Sometimes she had desired a grave in unconsecrated ground under a big tree in the grounds of Godollo where she had so often sat and dreamed. In that way she thought she could sleep in the Hungarian land which she loved more than anywhere else in the world. And then there had been the even more fervent wish which she had expressed in the words:

"I will be buried at Corfu near the shore of the sea where its waves can dash over my grave. That's where I desire to be unless I die at sea. The stars will shine over me and the moaning of the cypresses will be deeper than that of my fellow-creatures, for I shall live longer in the sighing of the trees than in the memory of my subjects."

So strong had been her desire to be buried in Corfu that she had actually written it in her Will. This, like all her deepest wishes in life, had been ignored.

Her task in death was to contribute something to the outdated and remorselessly declining glory of the Hapsburgs. In the opinion of Franz Joseph, this she could do best by resting in her plain Swiss coffin between her brother-in-law, the executed Emperor of Mexico, and Rudolph, her suicide-son.

Elizabeth's beloved Hungarians, who had always understood her, made amends the only way they could when their Government obtained permission for the women of the country to subscribe for a monument to be erected near the tomb.

It represents a *Mater Dolorosa*. On the head is a Crown of Thorns.

BIBLIOGRAPHY

Austria in 1868. Eugene Oswald.
British Officer in the Balkans, A. P. E. Henderson.
Caged Bird, The. Maureen Fleming.
Compromis Austro-hongris de 1867, Le. Louis Eisenmann.
Diplomacy of Imperialism, The. William L. Langer.
Dissolution of the Hapsburg Monarchy. O. Jaszi.
Doom of the Hapsburgs, The. H. W. Steed.
Elizabeth, Empress of Austria. Count Corti.
Elizabeth, Empress of Austria. A. de Burgh.
Elizabeth, Empress of Austria. Karl Tschuppik.
Emperor Francis Joseph and His Times. Albert Mangatti.
Emperor Franz Joseph of Austria. Joseph Redlich.
Francis Joseph and Bismarck. C. W. Clark.
Francis Joseph as Revealed by his Letters. Otto Ernst.
Golden Fleece, The. Dertita Harding.
Graf Julius Andrassy. E. von Wertheimer.
Habsburg Monarchy (1809–1918). A. J. P. Taylor.
Hapsburg Monarchy, The. Arthur J. May.
Hapsburg Monarchy, The. H. W. Steed.
Hongrie Contemporaire, La. L. Eisenmann.
Isle of Wight, The. Adams W. H. Davenport.
Italian Problem in European Diplomacy (1847–9). A. J. P. Taylor.
Jews in Vienna. Max Grunwald.
Letters of the Empress Frederick. Sir Frederick Ponsonby.
Life of the Emperor Francis Joseph. Francis Gribble.
Ludwig of Bavaria. Count Corti.
Ludwigs of Bavaria, The. Henry Channon.
Mad Monarch, The. Werner Richter.
Martyrdom of an Empress, The. Margaret Cunliffe Owen.
Mayerling. Claude Anet.
Memoirs of the Empress Elizabeth. Count Maurice Fleury.
Modern Hungary (1660–1920). Eugene Horvath.
My Early Life. William II, ex-Emperor of Germany.
My Past. Countess Marie Larisch.
Osterrich von 1848 bis 1860. Heinrich Friedjung.

Political Evolution of the Hungarian Nation, The. C. M. Knatchbull-Hugesson.

Queen Victoria. E. F. Benson.

Racial Problems in Hungary. R. W. Seton-Watson.

Road to Mayerling, The. Richard Barkeley.

Rudolph—The Tragedy of Mayerling. Count Carl Longay.

Russia and the Balkans. J. H. Sumner.

Second Empire, The. Philip Guedella.

Some Personal Impressions. Take Jonescu.

Southern Slav Question and the Habsburg Monarchy, The. R. W. Seton-Watson.

Tragic Empress. Maurice Paléologue.

INDEX